Uninvited

Jillian MacGregor

Spicy Biscuits
Press

Copyright © 2022 Jillian MacGregor
All rights reserved.

The characters and events portrayed in this book are fictitious. Any similarity to real persons, living or dead, is coincidental and not intended by the author.

No part of this book may be reproduced, or stored in a retrieval system, or transmitted in any form or by any means, electronic, mechanical, photocopying, recording, or otherwise, without express written permission of the publisher.

ASIN B0BHZC93FX
ISBN 979-8-9870942-2-8

Cover design by: Benjamin Richard
Typography by: Kristy Lynae Moore
Font created by: Mila Garret

Printed in the United States of America.

Content and Trigger Warnings:
This book contains explicit sex scenes that may not be your cup of tea. Subjects such as death of a family member, cancer, grief, controlling parental relationships, and drug/alcohol abuse/addiction are also present in this story. If these topics are triggering for you, please be advised and proceed in the manner best for you.

Uninvited

Jillian MacGregor

To That Guy I Married:
I'm sorry I spent our retirement money publishing books.

*(Okay, I'm not actually sorry,
but thank you for putting up with me anyway.)*

One

January

I woke up in Mason's apartment with a brutal hangover. My brain throbbed in my skull as I slowly let my eyes wander the room. *It's so damn bright in here.* My stomach was churning and my mouth felt like I had been licking a towel. *Why did I drink so much?* He left a glass of water and some ibuprofen on the nightstand. For a fake fiancé, he could be thoughtful sometimes.

Sometimes.

I swallowed the pills and grabbed my phone to check the time. Among a sea of notifications on my phone, I picked out the one text message I knew I shouldn't avoid.

> **Mason:** *Call me when you wake up.*

I cringed and texted my best friend, Mish, instead. I was out with her the night before to see her boyfriend's band play. The rules of our friendship dictated that if I partied at her level, she was to ensure nothing went wrong. Since I couldn't remember getting to Mason's apartment, I assumed she arranged it.

> **Me:** Of all people on the planet you had Mason pick my drunk ass up?
> **Mish:** *It's protocol* 🙄

Me: Yes, but now I have to explain myself to my keeper.

Mish: *Good luck with that. When he picked you up around 3 he was not too happy about it. Also you said some hateful things to him.*

Me: Of course I did. I can't help but dig the hole deeper.

Mish: *FWIW I think he was more upset you did it on a sidewalk in Boston than the actual words you said.*

Well, that wasn't good. I hit Mason's name on my phone to get the lecture over with. Ninety-nine percent of the time I was the responsible one — the one who picked his drunk ass up in the middle of the night, ensuring he returned home safe and unnoticed after shenanigans. I'd been cleaning up after his random bursts of rebellious behavior since we were teenagers.

"Seriously, Elle. In Boston?" His voice was thick with annoyance.

"Thanks for the save." I didn't have the stamina to argue that the roles were more often reversed. "Any issues?" For the love of coffee, I hoped no one noticed me.

"I don't think so. Nice wig."

I touched my head; the wig was gone. "It's not the first time you've seen it. Where is it?"

"In the bathroom, probably. How long until you look like an adult in charge?"

I groaned. "Where and when am I supposed to be?" Again, usually I'm the one making sure his life was in order without the world ever knowing it was out of order. I had Mish and Mason had me. *Wow, my head hurts.*

"Well, you were supposed to be at the State House earlier, but I covered for you. If anyone, especially the governor, asks, you had a crisis with Catherine." I hated that he referred to my father as "the governor," since he's known him basically his whole life, long before he was elected.

"Got it." Good thing my father and sister haven't spoken in four years. "So, we have the thing in Springfield tonight. I'll be ready for the stage then. Is my car still where I left it?"

"Yeah. I gotta run." He hung up. No hello, no goodbye. That was Mason.

> ***Mish:*** *So, um, do you remember last night at all?*
> **Me:** It's a blur.
> **Me:** Did something happen?
> ***Mish:*** *Well, no, nothing like you are thinking.*
> ***Mish:*** *You told Connor that you'd "organize his life" so he can "focus on the magic."*
> **Me:** I don't even know what that means. Any chance he forgot?
> ***Mish:*** *Nope. He says he sent you the details via email. But you solidly convinced him that signing with a label was a bad idea and that The Ninjas needed to go places because they are too good to go to waste. You gave a powerful argument. You used your "official" voice.*
> **Me**: Christ on a bike. I have got to stop drinking when I hang out with them.

I didn't feel like searching through my crowded inbox for his email. Dragging myself out of bed caused more intense throbbing in my skull that took hours, more ibuprofen than is probably recommended, and a lot of electrolytes before becoming a dull ache at the base of my skull. Luckily I had some driving around to do that could be done in silence while I recovered. As much as I valued my independence, times like these made me wish I had a personal assistant to do the everyday errands like picking up dry cleaning and grocery orders so I could've recovered in bed.

It wasn't until after I returned from the fundraiser dinner I remembered the email from Connor existed.

Jillian MacGregor

> *From: connor@handheldninjas.com*
> *To: duchesse@gmail.com*
> *Re: Ninja Help*
>
> *Len,*
> *Glad to have you on board. I know you have a lot going on and this is last minute, but can you meet up with us in Florida before our spring tour? Probably around 3 months? You'd join us on tour and we can go over specifics then. I'm thinking a long weekend? We can talk strategy with our manager. He's looking forward to your plans to make this indie thing a reality. I will give him your phone and email details in the meantime so you can catch up.*
> *C*

It took me a full week to figure out what I had agreed to: running social media pages, making sure Connor knew what city he was in, and apparently managing his everyday life. I effectively became his virtual assistant who had to show up in person once in a while. Connor had a small network of fans he was planning to utilize for local marketing via social media that was easier to coordinate in person. Putting in the face time with as many of them as I could would also help reinforce the relationships needed for an all-independent release.

It wasn't a bad gig for someone with limited obligations, but that just wasn't me. My day job as a political strategist included endless fundraising events I attended as either the daughter of the Governor or the girlfriend of a Senatorial candidate who was also the son of the sitting Vice President. I considered backing down — I was sure he'd understand — but there was this rebellious part of me that just wanted to do what was least expected of me before I succumbed to life as a politician's wife.

Uninvited

March

From: sbrowning@handheldninjas.com
To: len@handheldninjas.com; duchesse@gmail.com
Re: Florida

> *I just want to confirm you will join us in Florida in two weeks. I don't see anything here or in Connor's stuff that indicates you even got the login for the HN email address, so I copied the one he sent me just in case. This shitshow is clearly why we need your expertise. Let me know.*
>
> *-S*

I remembered in his email Connor said something about a spring tour, a long weekend, and in a few months, but this trip to Florida in two weeks was a shock. I glanced at my calendar; I'd have to juggle a bit, but I could get Mason to back me up if I said I needed a girls' weekend.

From: duchesse@gmail.com
To: sbrowning@handheldninjas.com
Re: Florida

> *Hey,*
> *I totally forgot, to be honest. I haven't heard from Connor in a while. And the HN email address is foreign to me, so maybe the details are in the account I have no idea how to access? Can you just let me know the exact dates so I can make the arrangements?*
>
> *-Len*

Jillian MacGregor

I received a reply with the dates, locations, and instructions on how to access my email address. I added it to my phone so I could have quick access and checked flights for the weekend in question. I had a fundraising event on Saturday that I texted Mason I would miss, as well as work on Monday. He wasn't pleased, but once I told him that Mish and I would stay on the beach in Florida for a few days, he seemed fine with it. It wasn't an outright lie, but it was a stretch. I wasn't sure how long we'd be in Florida and I had to travel to Atlanta for my return flight, but Mish and the band would, technically, be there.

Two

I was driving ever-so-slightly over the speed limit on the Massachusetts Turnpike toward Logan Airport when the blue lights flashed behind me. Okay, perhaps it was more than slightly too fast — eighty miles per hour in a construction zone labeled as forty-five. *Shit.* That's downright arrestable. I was already getting too close to my flight time and I still had to change. *Why on earth am I even going on this trip?*

I pulled into the breakdown lane and prayed this officer recognized me or my name and wanted to be nice today. Don't get me wrong, I believe in traffic violations, but being arrested on my way to my first meeting with my quasi-new boss was not the kind of thing I wanted to explain as a reason for missing my flight. The thought of explaining this to my father also made me shudder.

Getting arrested is "bad for the family's brand".

I put the window down to speak with the officer, shivering from the gust of cold New England wind. "Evening, Miss. Where are you headed in such a rush?" he asked as I handed him my license and registration.

"The airport. I'm so sorry. My dad's admin scheduled my flight really close to his event in Worcester today." *Lies.* I was at the event, but I booked the flight myself knowing damn well it would be a race to the airport. "It's no excuse, really. I totally deserve a ticket."

He looked at my license. "Roberts, Eleanor. You're the governor's daughter?"

"Yes, sir." I tried to look contrite.

He shook his head at me and went to his car to run my information. I tapped my foot impatiently and hoped the name drop would keep me out of jail. *I can see the headline already: 'Governor's Daughter Arrested for Reckless Driving.' Maybe if I drop the fact that my future father-in-law is the Vice President, this guy won't arrest me and just hit me with a hefty fine.* He came back to my window a few minutes later and handed me the license and registration.

"Because you've got no traffic violations in the last few years, I'm giving you a ticket for the non-construction zone speed limit of fifty-five miles per hour. Let's try to keep that speed down, eh?"

"Again, I'm so sorry. Thank you so much, I appreciate the leniency. I don't normally do this."

"Well, to be fair, this road has been under construction your entire life. The additional fine feels like a reach."

He wasn't wrong. I argued with my father on this point often, as it seemed they had labeled every road in Massachusetts a "construction zone" since the law doubling fines in construction zones went into effect. There needed to be some kind of rule, such as there physically being construction crews present for a fine to be doubled. I had suggested reforms to this law before, but they weren't sexy enough to get votes and took revenue from the state. Everything in politics is about the money, not doing what is right. "The 'Big Dig' *has* gone on much longer than expected. Thanks again. Have a great evening."

He gave me one more nod and went back to his car. It was a hefty fine, but I wasn't in the back of his car, so I'd take it. I pulled back onto the highway, careful to stay closer to the speed limit. Getting pulled over more than once on this trip to the airport would spell nothing but disaster. *Nope. Don't need that kind of drama in my life.*

I arrived at Terminal B and by some miracle could park in the terminal parking. Tucking my engagement ring in the glove box and grabbing my bag, I made a run for the security checkpoint. With a silent thanks to the creator of TSA Pre-Check, I made it through just a few minutes later, which was great because they had just started boarding my flight. *God, I hate flying commercial.*

I ducked into the first ladies' room I came across and slipped into a stall, awkwardly juggling my bags. I needed to shed what Mish and my sister, Catherine, called "Kate Middleton attire" and swap it for jeans, a tank top, and a hoodie, effectively transforming myself to my alter ego, "Len". We created Len over a year ago when Mish and I were attending a concert in the Boston area and she insisted I dress less "duchess" and more "rock goddess."

I did not know what I was going to do with the coat dress now in my hands. My other issue was that I needed to take off my heels and wool tights to switch them for jeans, socks, and sneakers without letting any of my naked body parts touch the stall or the floor. I may not qualify as a germaphobe, and maybe I'm just this side of bougie, but public bathrooms absolutely give me the creeps no matter how clean they appear. Microscopic poo particles were everywhere in here.

I flung the dress over the top of the stall and pulled my sneakers out of the bag, dropping them to the floor so I could step out of each heel onto them without my feet touching anything questionable. Thanks to the four barre classes a week I was taking, I possessed the core strength required to balance on one foo t at a time to peel the tights off and replace them with socks. I tugged on the jeans, not at all accustomed to the way the fabric felt on my legs after a lifetime of slacks and dresses. *Why do people think these are comfortable?* I balanced on one foot while attempting to put on my sneaker, nearly bumping into the wall of the stall in the process.

I was out of breath and sweaty at this point, but there wasn't time to worry about that. I finished changing and left the stall holding the dress. It was way too bulky to fit in my lone bag, so I set it on the baby changing table with no intention of ever picking it up again. Looking in the mirror I grabbed my brush and put my long brown hair in a low ponytail adjusting it under a wig cap. *Goodbye duchess.* I hastily added a black-haired bob to my head, followed by the hood of my hoodie for added stealth. *Hello, random person.* The wig was an essential, at least until I left the city. I had no intention of being recognized hopping onto that plane. Adding some extra black eyeliner, I shrugged at my efforts, knowing I was running out of time as they made the final boarding call for my flight.

Three

I rushed to the gate as they were calling my name, the dress left behind along with my other identity. I smiled apologetically at the airline attendant as she scanned my boarding pass. I was officially the last person to board the flight, but I'd made it.

I knew when I booked the last-minute ticket to Florida I would want a nap on the flight down. Sitting on the aisle and blocking my window seat was an older woman with a giant black bouffant and entirely too much bright blue eyeshadow that went all the way up to her drawn-on, pencil-thin eyebrows. "Hi. I have the window seat. Could you please let me in?" I pointed to the empty seat. She looked up at me, annoyed, but didn't budge. "Excuse me, I need to get to my seat," I tried again, even more politely.

"So sit in it," she huffed. I couldn't help but notice she had painted her red lipstick quite liberally around her lips and on her teeth.

The guy in the middle seat glanced at his feet and chuckled. *Damn, he's hot.* His amused grin was surrounded by the perfect amount of facial scruff. I wanted to run my hands through his messy, light brown hair. *Focus, Eleanor.* I was to hop over this woman, somehow sneak by the hot guy, and get to my seat. So

I, somewhat dramatically, tossed my bag over both of them and onto my seat. I straddled my way over the lap of this woman, leaving my ass to linger in front of her face longer than was strictly necessary before pulling my other leg over hers. Not wanting to be rude to the smoke-show in the middle, I profusely apologized as I tried to shuffle in front of his legs to my seat.

I was definitely in the "Len spirit" with that move. Eleanor would've been far more polite. Secretly, I loved my alter ego just for the freedom to do the shit they had bred me not to do in public.

I shoved my bag under the seat in front of me and pulled my earbuds out of the front pocket of my hoodie, preparing to have a few hours to decompress before meeting everyone in Florida.

"Having a rough day, Len?" the hottie next to me asked. I looked at him, confused. *How does this guy know me?* I mean, Len? She's fictional. "Silas Browning. I manage The Handheld Ninjas."

That still didn't solve the entire mystery. Regardless, I held out my hand to shake his. The moment we touched, my stomach did a flip. "Yes. Nice to meet you, Silas." *Why the fuck is their manager drop-dead gorgeous and sitting right next to me on my flight? Where was the old manager, Kyle?* "Sorry. .. I assumed Kyle was the manager."

Silas looked away briefly. "Kyle is my brother. I'm doing him a favor and filling in for him for a while so he can chill. All the back-to-back touring is not doing him any favors."

"I can't imagine it's very healthy. I didn't realize you were also from the Boston area."

"I'm not, really. I just had some business to wrap up here and thought I'd get a jump-start getting coordinated with you by…." He sighed. "By basically stalking you and being a weirdo who makes sure he sits next to you without mentioning it." He paused with a slight wince. "I guess I should apologize. That was creepy, and I should've mentioned it before."

I giggled. *Why did I giggle? Apparently Len is the type to giggle because Eleanor sure isn't.* "And just how did you know exactly where to find me?" I looked into his deep blue eyes and thought I'd drown there.

There was some kind of static electricity beaming between us and it made me want to back up a few minutes and *accidentally* fall into his lap while navigating to my seat. What a missed opportunity.

"You sent your flight information so we'd have it, remember?" His brow furrowed.

High-five to myself for making sure I cut my real name out of that screenshot! It may be overkill, but I was doing my damnedest to stay under the radar here. My father would lose his shit if he found out I was an assistant to a rock band. The media would love it, though. What a scandal! Eleanor Roberts, daughter of Governor Richard Roberts and long-time girlfriend to Vice President Davis's son, hanging out with a bunch of guys in a band on tour. "Sorry, it's been a rough couple of weeks. I guess I forgot I sent it." I realized not only was I staring, I had dropped my end of the conversation while daydreaming about sitting in his lap. I'd already decided that his hair had a surfer look, but he wasn't as tan as a surfer would probably be. Like me, he was wearing a hoodie and jeans. Average build, though I couldn't tell how tall he was in his seat. In another life, I'd totally hit that. *I wonder if he has tattoos?*

"I *was* told that Connor conscripted you during a drunken conversation." He smiled, revealing a dimple on his right cheek. I wanted to reach my tongue out and lick it.

What the fuck is up with me today?

"That is one-hundred percent true, I'm afraid. Mine is also a temporary gig." *Very temporary.*

"So what do you do when you aren't organizing the life of the rich and famous?"

That statement took me back a bit. I was afraid for a second that he was referring to my father, or maybe even Mason, but then I remembered Connor was rich and famous and Silas was almost certainly referring to him, given our current situation. "Media strategist," I replied, sticking as close to the truth as I could without giving away anything else .

"Makes sense for Connor to drag you into his newest conquest. Which is good because I am out of my depth here," he admitted.

"What do you do?"

"Not this. Definitely not this. I've known Connor a long time. He and Kyle have been friends since high school. Connor and Kyle always coerce me into the most insane things."

"Well, I guess we shall make the most of this adventure together, eh?"

"Adventure? I guess it is now that I have a partner in crime." *Is he flirting with me?*

Silas and I discussed some of what the long weekend held and reviewed how we would divide the tasks to make the most effective use of our skills and the limited time we had. Two shows were on Friday in different locations, followed by one show each of the following nights, at which point I would need to make another rushed trip to the airport to get back to my real life. Travel wasn't supposed to be mandatory for this gig. I was a *virtual* personal assistant, after all. Helping with some on-the-ground stuff while assessing what needed to be done remotely was a departure from my reality. This weekend I'd be meeting with "street teams," selling "merch" and such while trying to help Connor outline a growth strategy. Nothing hard with the bonus of getting to spend some time enjoying the feeling of music so loud my hair vibrates.

I lived for that feeling.

After about an hour of chatting, he told me it would be wise to get in a nap if I needed one as there would be very little sleep for the next few days, so I popped in my headphones and pulled my hoodie down over my eyes.

I woke to Silas repeating my name quietly while tapping my arm. "We landed," he explained when I opened my eyes. I was leaning on his shoulder. I prayed I didn't drool or snore. In addition to being very easy on the eyes, he smelled amazing. Like soap, strong coffee, and a cologne that conjured the image of seeing a guy about a 401k. Just mildly spicy. I resisted the urge to deeply inhale his scent.

I needed to get a grip. A hookup wasn't on the agenda for the weekend and was probably in bad form for a new job, even if it was one I didn't intend on keeping very long. But they were musicians, so maybe?

No. Stop it, Eleanor.

The plane parked at the terminal and the passengers all immediately crowded the aisle. *What the hell is wrong with people?* The door wasn't open, and no one was moving. Blue Eyeshadow Lady was no exception to the issue. She was sighing and pushing her way in the aisle as if she could get off the plane faster somehow, mumbling her annoyance the whole way. Silas and I remained seated until the line started moving a bit. I grabbed my bag from under the seat and stood, turning my phone back on. We were waiting for others to get their bags out of the overhead bins when I heard Silas say, "Hey, Len?"

I glanced up from my phone. He leaned over and kissed me. Like, full-on, put a hand behind my neck, pulled me toward him, "*I would like to fuck you now*" *kissed* me. I thought I was going to melt into the floor. *Holy shit.* Why was he such an amazing kisser? He smirked at me devilishly and said, "In case we don't get a minute alone this weekend. I thought I'd make my move."

So yes, he was probably flirting with me.

I turned back to my phone and pretended like I had an important email, like my lips weren't on fire and my heart wasn't racing. There were no words. My cheeks felt hot, and although I'd spent my entire life effortlessly hiding any emotion from my face, I was struggling to hide a shit-eating grin. Maybe a weekend hookup *could* be on the agenda. This was a temporary gig for both of us, after all.

Four

Connor picked us up at the airport and brought us back to his house on the beach. It was closing in on midnight, but he was talking a mile a minute about set lists and equipment. Honestly, I couldn't follow what he was saying. Not because it was so late, but because I was still stunned by that kiss.

"Are you listening to me, Len?" Connor looked over at me in the passenger seat. I felt my phone vibrate with a text message in my pocket.

"Uh, no, not really. Sorry. I just woke up. It was a long day."

"Right, you had that fundraising thing today."

"There's always a fundraising thing." I sighed.

"Oh, do you work for some charity?" Silas asked.

Connor and I exchanged a Look. He knew all about the drama that was my family. Mish and my sister were roommates when Connor and Mish first started dating, which gave Connor an up-close view of some of the insanity that was my life. The promise of getting away from that drama was why I agreed to do this, and Connor used that to his advantage while promising we'd attempt to keep my real life off the table. "Um, sort of. I do a lot of community work."

Silas got the hint: I didn't want to talk about it.

"Anyway," Connor continued, "like I was saying when you weren't listening," he flashed a quick grin in my direction, "the guys are all at the house and we packed everything, and we are ready to go tomorrow. So, we can have a pretty chill night."

"Is that really what you were talking about?" I asked, pulling my phone out of my pocket to check the message.

"Nope. But we've got four days to get business out of the way."

> **Kyle:** *Perhaps you found yourself distracted by me? Because I'm definitely distracted by you.* Not Kyle. Silas. *When I put the contact information for the band manager in my phone I had assumed it was Kyle. Clearly, it was Silas, so I updated the contact in my phone.*
> **Me:** Or maybe Connor just makes me dizzy with the speed of his thoughts.

I hear Silas bark a quick laugh from the back seat.

> **Silas:** *I guess that means I'll just have to try harder to get your attention.*

I resisted the urge to react visibly, but felt butterflies in my stomach. For the first time I could recall, I felt the urge to squeal with delight. *Reign it in, buddy.*

We arrived at Connor's beach house. I hadn't been before, as Connor was almost always on the road. Mish came running out the front door to greet me and grabbed my bag. "You're going to do four days with just this?" She held the bag up in disbelief.

"I'm making the most of a job that doesn't require dressing up every day," I shrugged.

"What did you tell your keepers you were doing this weekend?"

"I was vague. Which is generally code for 'sneaking off to fuck someone who isn't Mason', so there were no questions asked."

I heard Silas nearly choke behind me.

We made our way into the living room where the guys sat spread around the room, beers in hand. I sat down on an unoccupied loveseat and just absorbed the relative calm before the storm. I made sure to check my emails quickly to verify there wasn't some kind of crisis brewing at home. Then I paid for the damn speeding ticket online before I forgot it existed. *Three hundred and fifty freaking dollars for speeding! At least you aren't in jail, Eleanor.* Mish dropped a bottle of water in my lap and sat beside me with a dramatic flop. I was so tempted to tell her about the kiss on the plane, but I wasn't about to talk about it with the entire crew, including Silas, within earshot.

A few hours of chatting later, I was exhausted, so I found my way into a guest bedroom and crashed.

Since it was basically morning when I fell asleep, I was not happy to be out of bed at 7 a.m...*How do these people function with two hours of sleep?* Getting ready was easy for touring: quick shower, brush my teeth, throw on jeans and a tank top, add eyeliner and mascara. I traded the wig for a baseball hat, and I made my way to the kitchen where Mish was already sitting at the table. Her dark hair was in a messy topknot, and she had a mug of coffee cradled in her hands as if it was her most cherished possession.

As I was pouring myself coffee, Silas came in behind me and did the same. He stood just a foot away from me, and I could feel the sexual tension buzzing around us. A few times his arm brushed mine as we prepared our coffees, which I assumed was accidental but enjoyed nonetheless. I had just met this guy and yet I craved his touch. These little grazes were making me crazy. Just a few minutes later, though, the kitchen was full of people seeking their caffeine fix resulting in quite a bit of space between Silas and me. The whole group was much quieter this morning, at least until the coffee did its thing and helped us all regain consciousness.

We eventually piled into two vans. Connor, Sergio (the drummer), and Mish were in one van, and Matteo (the bassist), and Tom (the guitarist) were in the second one with Silas and me. I wasn't sure how we ended up in this configuration since it seemed to happen naturally, but being in the van with Silas gave me time to sneak covert looks in his direction. *Stop analyzing and just have fun.*

Our first stop was a music festival in Orlando. Handheld Ninja took the stage at 1 p.m. and then we packed everything back up for the second show in Daytona Beach later that night. For both shows I found myself mingling with fans and handing out things like stickers and other small items with the band's information. I liked getting to meet some of the fans that already knew of the band and followed them on social media. *I need to remember to add myself to some of these fan pages.*

Following the second show, we returned to Connor and Michelle's around 2 a.m., all wired from a successful day. Instead of heading straight to bed, we all went back to hangout with a few drinks. We didn't have to leave until late afternoon for Jacksonville.

The last thing I remembered was the sun just coming up. Connor and Mish retired a while before, but the rest of us sat around while Matteo, Sergio, and Tom told hilarious stories about Connor in high school.

I guess I fell asleep on the couch with Silas.

I only had a couple of drinks, so there was no way I was drunk, just exhausted. Matteo was out cold on the floor, an arm draped over his eyes and Tom was asleep on the loveseat across from the couch, his long legs draped over the arm on one end and his head on the other. We had perfectly good beds, yet only Sergio appeared to have made it to his. Someone had tossed a blanket over my legs, and I was using Silas's lap as a pillow, my face all but buried in his crotch. Silas laid on the end seat of the couch in the recliner, one hand behind his head, the other resting over my shoulder. I picked up my head intending to move into a less shameful position, but Silas pulled me back down. I probably should've tried harder; I wasn't even sure if he knew he had done it or that I was there. I was too tired to move and fell back asleep until I felt him trying to sneak out from under me without waking me up. I looked up at him. He flashed me a smirk, pushing some hair out of my eyes before he stood. The gesture felt *intimate*. I looked around, somewhat relieved to see we were the only two awake.

Great. Twice in twenty-four hours I'd fallen asleep on this guy. *This time in his lap.* My phone was vibrating in my pocket. A missed call from Mason's assistant, Megan, three texts from dad, and ten from Mason. *Nope. I'm off duty this weekend.*

I stumbled into the kitchen to see Mish in the same position as the day before. "Do me a solid?" I asked as I sat down across from her and Silas at the table. "Just text Mace and tell him whatever it is, it can wait until Tuesday. Tell him it's a girls' weekend and I'm not allowed to look at my phone. Anything to make the madness stop."

Mish chuckled. "Then he's just going to text me until you get home. No way, dude. He's your keeper, not mine."

"Fine, I'll just text Meg and tell her I'm out of the country until Tuesday. She will have my back." I stuck my tongue out at Mish and sent the text to Megan. She responded that she'd relay the message. *I need to get Meg a gift for dealing with my shit for me. She's not even my assistant.*

Sunday night we found ourselves in Jacksonville. We needed two sober drivers to make the overnight drive to Atlanta so that the band could make appearances at several interviews I had lined up in the morning. Those two lucky drivers ended up being Silas and me. I switched into the van with Mish, Connor, and Sergio and prepared for a five-hour drive north.

The first hour passed quickly while Mish chatted with me. Once she fell asleep, I popped in an earbud and listened to a podcast for a while. About three hours into the drive, Silas called. I answered as quietly as I could, hoping not to wake anyone.

"Hey," he said, "I need to stop for gas and supplies. Take the next exit." I agreed and hung up, following him off the next exit a few miles later.

We pulled up to the pumps and hopped out of our respective vans. After pumping both vans full of gas, I followed him into the store. "So. Tell me," he said as we grabbed some gas station coffee, "who is this 'keeper' Michelle keeps referring to?"

"My dad and his lackey," I told him. It wasn't a full-on lie; Mason was my dad's former chief of staff, which was a lot like being his lackey. He just also happened to be a guy I was engaged to in a weird relationship of convenience that meant nothing.

"Lackey? Is your dad a mob boss or something?" He laughed.

"No." I laughed with him. Though the government is kind of like the mob, so, maybe. "And as I said this morning, or I guess yesterday afternoon, I'm off duty and not talking about that." I winked and returned to preparing my coffee.

He stared at me, making my whole body erupt in goosebumps. For fuck's sake, I just wanted to strip him down and have my way with him, right here, right now. *Down girl. Control those hormones.* I didn't know this guy, but that never stopped me from a one-night stand in the past. With Silas, though, there was just this vibe that screamed 'let's fuck' and I was on board with that. So I took a page from his playbook.

I stepped closer to him and put my coffee cup back on the counter. "Hey, Silas." He lifted a brow, and I ran my hands up his chest and wrapped them around his neck to bring his mouth down to my own for a kiss. His hands went around my waist, his thumbs hooking into the belt loops of my jeans to pull me closer. The kiss continued for less than a minute, but I needed to stop before I ended up naked in a gas station convenience store. I was the epitome of hot and bothered. "Just in case I don't get you alone again, I wanted to make my move," I said breathlessly, and then left him there to walk to the counter and pay for the coffee. I couldn't explain the need to be near him. If I didn't get to fuck this guy soon, I was going to combust.

We walked out to the vans, and I tried to catch my breath from the searing kiss. I could feel his glare on my ass, and I craved to feel him closer. I stopped short, and as I hoped, he walked right up behind me, putting his hands on my hips firmly, pulling my back to his front. "Something wrong?" his breath skated over my ear. I melted back into his chest; my panties instantly damp. I was so stunned by my reaction to his contact that I couldn't answer. I wrapped a hand behind his neck to hold his cheek to mine, my body heating at the contact.

We stood there for a solid minute, his hands holding my hips tight against his. I could feel his arousal against my back and it made me want to wiggle my ass a bit to see his reaction. His mouth remained close to my ear, just barely brushing my neck, but he didn't say a word. His thumbs lightly brushed up and down against the top of my shorts as we breathed each other in. Another minute passed before he pressed a light kiss into the crook of my neck, sending shivers down my spine. "See you in Atlanta, Len," he finally whispered and let me go.

I nearly came right there in the lot.

We hopped into our separate vans and went on to Atlanta. I resisted the impulse to wake Mish to tell her about kissing Silas. Twice. I grabbed a show flier off the console and used it to fan my face, trying to stop the hormones that were flooding my body. *Why the hell didn't I get something cold?* We only touched briefly, but I could make out the faint scent of his cologne on my skin and clothes. I squeezed my thighs together as best I could while still driving in an effort to quell the ache.

This man was dangerous.

We arrived at Sergio's condo before 7 am. I was exhausted and horny as hell, but we had to be at a local radio station in an hour which left no time for sleep. We changed clothes, freshened up, and headed back out to a morning of interviews.

We spent the morning running around, finding ourselves back at Sergio's around noon. We ate a meal that could have been breakfast, lunch, or dinner because my body didn't know what was going on. I didn't think touring with a band would be any less tiring than being on the campaign trail, but at least we got a few hours sleep every night. *How? How do they do this for months at a time?*

After we ate, Connor, Silas, and I sat down at the table and went over the schedule for the next month. As we discussed the itinerary, Silas's leg brushed against mine under the table in a way that was obviously intentional and made it impossible to fully concentrate. I tried to focus on Connor, but found my eyes wandering to look at Silas instead. *If only we weren't wearing pants… Not now, Eleanor.*

I tried to pay attention to the plan Connor was outlining despite the feeling of Silas's leg moving against mine. It was becoming increasingly difficult to maintain a neutral expression. My pulse steadily grew faster every time he found a way to discreetly brush my arm or run a hand down my thigh. The guys would go on from here and make their way west playing 4-5 shows per week. Michelle and I would head back to Boston. I had planned to meet up with them in four weeks in Arizona for a few days, catching the last couple of shows and ending in California where Matteo and Tom still lived.

As I was putting show dates into my phone's calendar Connor left the room for a few minutes. "Is there something interesting here to see, Silas?" I asked quietly while maintaining eye contact with my phone.

"Yes. Stunning view from where I'm sitting." He ran his finger down my arm lightly, goosebumps trailing his finger. "Shame I'm not going to see it for the next four weeks."

I felt my cheeks heat. "I'm sure it will pass quickly. Those boys are a handful."

He groaned. "I'm in over my head."

"I think at this point just keep them alive. I can help with the logistics piece." *In the spare time you don't have already, Elle?*

"I was hoping you'd help me with something –" Connor interrupted him by sitting back down at the table, immediately talking about the importance of figuring out the laundry situation.

I was sure whatever Silas was implying he needed help with, I was absolutely willing to assist.

All the planning went on until it was time to make our way over to the venue to set up. I had officially been awake for thirty hours straight. I was honestly looking forward to the flight back to Boston so I could sleep and then spend some quality time with my vibrator to work off this sexual frustration as soon as I got home. Just six more hours.

Silas and I were sitting next to each other in the back seat of the van when I received a text message.

> **Silas:** *I've been thinking about the feeling of your body against mine all day. Being near you is making me crazy.*

He was sitting closer to me than was strictly necessary. His thigh aligned tightly to mine. *Making me crazy, too.* I had to repeatedly remind myself that I couldn't just reach out and grope him. Still, just the proximity had my body thrumming, desperate for more.

> **Me:** You do seem to have an issue keeping your body parts to yourself.

Maybe the venue has a closet or something?

Silas: *Does that bother you? Or do you like it when I'm touching you?*

He flashed me a smoldering grin as he nudged a shoulder into mine. *Oh hell no. Please touch me.*

Me: My only complaint is that it doesn't happen enough.

He quirked a brow and put his phone down. His hand made a subtle brush over the top of my thigh and I had to fight to resist the urge to touch him back. *Fuck, this guy is going to kill me with need.*
Since Mish and I had a 1 a.m. flight, we also took Sergio's car to the venue so a friend of his could drop us off immediately following the show. We got all set up, but I kept nodding off as I sat in a chair backstage. I guess someone noticed because Connor suggested I go take a nap back at Sergio's place for a couple of hours before actual show time. I wasn't about to argue; I felt like a zombie.

What I didn't expect was Silas to state that he also could use a nap before it was time for the guys to take the stage. Together we hopped into Sergio's car and made the fifteen-minute drive back to his place. I was too tired to make small talk, opting to just rest my head against the cool window. His hand rested on my thigh, unmoving. The simple touch was enough to keep me from falling asleep, afraid to miss a second of the intoxicating feeling. *I've officially hit delusionally tired if I'm this affected by a hand on my thigh.*

Silas unlocked the door and motioned for me to go in before him. I heard the door shut and lock. He grabbed my hand and pulled me back toward him, turning us both so that my back was up against the door. It happened so fast and I was so tired that it took me a minute to realize this was it. It was happening. There was no space between us. Every inch of the front of my body felt that of his. *Too many clothes.* He went in for a kiss and to be honest, I half expected to wake up to discover it was only an erotic dream. I thought for sure I was trapped somewhere between reality and fantasy but the feeling of his warm lips on mine were far better than any dream I'd ever had.

His hand traveled up under my shirt. I was still trying to process what was happening here and if it was real or a dream. It didn't matter because I had wanted him to fuck me since the second I laid eyes on him on that plane, so I wasn't squandering the opportunity — real or imagined. I tugged at his shirt, frantically trying to get it off and he graciously finished removing it, as well as my shirt. I explored the warm skin of his chest with my hands, savoring the way he tensed under them with anticipation. I traced the outline of the steampunk-style clock on his chest as he took one of my breasts in his hand, rubbing his thumb over the peaked tip of my nipple through the lacy material of my bra.

I needed more. My body felt like it was on fire and the only thing that could extinguish the flames was his touch. I wrapped a leg around his waist and he pulled the other up to join it, pressing my back harder against the wall to steady me. I could feel how hard he was through his jeans as he brought his mouth back to mine, kissing me stupid. I'd never been so consumed by a kiss that my mind calmed and focused only on how good it felt until that moment.

Once again I silently thanked barre classes for my core strength as I ground myself against his bulge. He moaned in appreciation and gripped my ass tighter, kissing me with more fervor as we rolled our hips into each other.

He carried me over to a nearby chair in the living room and sat me down on it as he trailed kisses down my shoulder and to the tops of my breasts. The warmth of his breath against my skin was intoxicating. He moved his hands to the button of my jeans and in one quick motion he relieved me of my pants and underwear and then reached behind me to unclasp my bra. I let it

fall between us. My chest was heaving, something I only thought happened in books or movies. His eyes met mine, pupils dilated with lust as his hands continued their exploration. I tried to reach for the button on his jeans but he continued his trails of kisses and nibbles down the center of my torso. He kneeled down in front of the chair and pulled my ass to the edge, trailing his mouth along my inner right thigh. Everywhere his mouth touched felt like it was alive with electric current.

He spread my legs wide and nipped my clit before licking it slowly, his tongue flat against me. As he swirled his tongue around my clit, he pushed a finger inside. A deep moan escaped my lips encouraging him to add a second. We had been in the house for less than five minutes, I'd guess, and I was damn near ready to explode. Neither of us had said a single word until I breathlessly pleaded, "Don't stop." I could feel him smile in response against my sensitive flesh, as he continued to plunge his fingers in and out of me and then he sucked hard on my clit. My toes curled and my hands grabbed at the chair around me trying to find something to hold onto. I clenched around his fingers as my orgasm took over, mumbling nonsense in between cries of pleasure.

I hadn't quite recovered when I noticed he was taking off his pants. Inhaling deeply, I could smell sweat, sex, and a hint of that spicy cologne. The sound of my heartbeat in my chest matched the thudding of my clit as I waited the few seconds it took for him to pull a condom from the pocket of his jeans and roll it on. *Son of a bitch this guy is hot.* I was still panting when he pushed inside of me, emitting a predatory noise. "Fuck," he breathed.

My body trembled with lust, all thoughts lost to the glorious feeling of him inside me. I wrapped my legs around his back and matched his rhythm as he pushed in and out. "Holy shit," I murmured, digging my fingers into his back, waves of pleasure rolling through my body.

He flashed a devilish grin, and that was it. Time seemed to stand still. I gasped as a second orgasm took over my whole body and his breath hitched as he found his release, staring into my eyes like he could see everything about me.

Hard and fast was *exactly* what this situation called for and he delivered. To be fair, this was usually my preference, but it was especially needed after days of the longest game of foreplay I'd ever experienced.

After a moment to catch his breath he took my face in his hand, gently rubbing my cheek with his thumb. "You are fucking incredible," he kissed my lips lightly before he went off to the bathroom. My whole body was spent. My limbs hung awkwardly on the chair but I couldn't bring myself to move. My arms and legs were just too heavy and the exhaustion came back in full force in my post-orgasm bliss. Silas came back into the room and laughed quietly at the sight. "C'mon. Time to get that nap." He held out a hand and helped me to my feet.

This man knew all the moves I needed today. Few words, orgasms, and a nap.

Best. Hookup. Ever.

We woke to the sound of my phone ringing. "Hello?" I croaked.

"Were you actually sleeping?" Mish yelled over the noise of the venue.

"Yes. Yes, I was. I'm up. Let me go wake up Silas and we'll be there in twenty." Silas was right next to me and had woken up to the phone as well, but she didn't need to know that. "I'm just going to shower quickly." I explained as I headed to the bathroom and turned on the shower.

I jumped in without regard to the fact the water was still freezing. I quickly soaped up my body, rinsed, and hopped out.

I dug in my bag for clean underwear and a tank top. Silas returned from the other room with our pile of clothes. I tossed the dirty clothes into my bag and pulled on the jeans and sneakers.

"So that's what you look like in normal life," he mused.

After a second or two of confusion, I realized I was without the wig or the hat, my natural hair pinned to my head in the ponytail I wore days ago. "Hardly," I replied. "I don't know that I've ever worn jeans in public in normal life." I pulled the wig back over my hair for my upcoming travel. "Hell, I rarely wear pants. Mostly dresses and skirts."

"Are you undercover or something? Why the disguise?"

"No. Yes? Not like in a law enforcement way, but I'm trying to blend. In case there are pictures on social media. Mish is a bit of a hometown hero since she started dating a famous rock star. I don't need the drama that comes with that." It was half true; Mish had been the talk of the town, but in that same town members of the media easily recognized me and started searching for a political scandal. Silas seemed to accept the answer, since he didn't follow up with any other questions.

We hopped into the car and went back to the venue in time to catch the last fifteen minutes of the set. We helped drag things back to the van without so much as looking at each other. A couple hours later, Mish and Sergio's friend hopped back into the car to head to the airport and I took off with a quick "bye" to the whole group.

Five

I arrived back in Boston with Mish at 6 am. As I drove her back to her apartment, she asked, "So, you are telling me you didn't hook up with Silas this weekend?"

"I did no such thing," I lied. "I think he said less than a hundred words to me all weekend." That, on the other hand, was probably accurate. "Why would you think that?"

"Well first, he's fucking gorgeous."

"You are literally dating a hot rock star."

"Doesn't mean I can't tell that Silas has the face of a fucking Hemsworth and an amazing ass." Silas *did* look like a Hemsworth, and his ass was a sight to behold, both with the eyes and the hands. "And second, since when was talking a prerequisite for sex? A lack of words could be hot," she mused.

She wasn't wrong. In fact, after this weekend I could absolutely confirm that it was insanely hot. I don't know if it was his panty-dropping good looks or the way he just quietly observed his surroundings, saying only what was necessary, that had me all hot and bothered, but just thinking about him gave me goosebumps. "Yes, and with that Hemsworth face I'm sure he gets plenty of ass and has no interest in me."

Mish laughed. "That guy looked at you like he wanted to eat you alive all weekend. He was constantly finding ways to touch you when he thought no one was looking. I thought for sure he made a move."

"Nope. No move," I lied again. "Anyway, I don't need any more complications."

I could see her roll her eyes at me from the passenger seat. "Complications make it even hotter. And you aren't one to shy away from a hookup. Next time, you should totally bang him."

I dropped Mish off at her place shortly after that comment and headed to Mason's apartment in Cambridge. I walked in hoping he had left for the office early, but I found myself shit out of luck on that one, noting his keys on the table by the door. I dropped my bag in the front closet. "About time," Mason called from the direction of the bedroom.

I went into the bedroom and grabbed some clean undergarments and a dress from the closet. My family certainly didn't struggle financially, but Mason's family was *old* money. While I did all my own laundry at home, someone picked up Mason's laundry, washed it, and put it away without a thought from him. This did benefit me. Whatever I left here was always clean so I never had to worry about not having clean underwear waiting for me. The prospect of not doing laundry anymore when we got married was definitely something I didn't hate.

I joined him in the bathroom where he was shaving and turned on the shower. I had pulled the ponytail out of my hair on the drive and there was no way I was getting away without washing it. Plus, I could smell the airport on my skin and it was totally grossing me out. "I see you got a speeding ticket," Mason said as I was washing my hair.

I looked through the glass door of the shower to see Mason shaking out his razor in the sink. "How would you know that?"

"Your father knows, so I know. He wanted to know what you were doing in Florida."

"Do you two stalk me? The ticket was in Boston. What the fuck?"

"No."

"So, what did you tell him about Florida?"

"I told him you were in Florida seeing a band."

"For fuck's sake, Mason." I got out of the shower and wrapped a towel around my body, tucking in the end under my arm to hold it up. "That was absolutely unnecessary."

I put my dress on, turning for assistance with the zipper. Mason met my gaze in the mirror and sighed. "That isn't going to work."

"What isn't going to work?" I asked, looking down at the dress I'd worn several times without a negative comment from him.

"The dress. You have a hickey." I looked closer in the mirror. Indeed, he was correct. My body flushed with the memory of Silas's mouth all over my body. Mason went to the closet and got a wool dress coat that had a mandarin collar. "This should work. Thought you said it was a girls' weekend."

"Can I not have sex with women?" I raised my eyebrow at him, pulling the dress over my head. He ignored the comment. "I don't ask about your sex life and I expect the same courtesy."

"I didn't ask about it. And if you don't want people to mention your sex life, don't leave evidence of it in plain sight." His tone was snippy, but he wasn't wrong.

He left me in the bathroom to finish with my hair and makeup. *Please don't let him be this grouchy all day. I'm way too tired to play nice.*

When we eventually made it to the State House, I was immediately pulled into my father's office where he lectured me about the traffic ticket.

Mish wondered why I was so paranoid about being recognized. These two were like bounty hunters. I could only imagine what would happen if the media got a glimpse of my weekend. "Eleanor, are you even listening to me? Your actions reflect upon this office," my dad raised his voice, "and on Mason's campaign." My father was a big dude who spent his life used to getting his way. I spent my life doing as I was told.

The man never raised a hand to me, but from a very young age I learned that resistance was futile. The man gets what he wants.

"Yes, I'm listening. It was a speeding ticket. I paid it immediately, thus proving I'm not looking to get special treatment. It's hardly a high crime."

"And you'll be spending more time with Mason in public?" I missed that part, and he knew it. "Eleanor!" He slammed a fist on the desk. "You two are engaged. You need to plan a wedding. You need to *look* like you are two people who are getting married. People are starting to talk."

Of course. I was away, and they saw Mason out and about without me over the weekend. I forgot being attached at the hip was part of my unofficial duties as the token woman of the equation. Mason just sat there without a word going through email on his phone. *Asshole.* He could've at least ushered my father to some call or meeting for which he was undoubtedly late. "We just got engaged last month. We have all kinds of events relating to that. We have at least six months before we have to announce a wedding date." I was stalling. I wasn't ready for marriage just yet.

"Mason, find a weekend this summer that we can get this done," my father directed. My life was his business deal to close. "You need to be married before the election."

This led Mason to speak up for the first time. "Summer is only a few months away. I don't think we can make that happen. We have to give plenty of notice, find a venue, announce things." He ran his hands through his hair. "We just got engaged. People will think she's pregnant."

"She better not be and when no baby arrives, they will know it was just speculation. You've been dating forever, it isn't exactly a surprise wedding. Make it happen." My father picked up his desk phone to signal this meeting was over.

Mason and I stood to leave. I followed him across the street to his office. It was one of those days that the wind stung your face like the dead of winter. *Are winters getting longer?* Making our way inside we made the obligatory small talk with his assistant before walking into Mason's office and closing the door calmly behind me. "What the fuck was that about?" I asked, dropping the act we put on in front of the world.

Mason ran his hand through his dark hair again. "I do not know, but I need you to handle all the arrangements. I'm swamped. Between the campaign and transitioning my former duties in his office, I have no time for this. I'll find a date that works and you can pick it up from there, okay?"

"No. Not okay. It's one thing to be told who to marry, but another thing entirely to have the wedding sprung on me years earlier than I expected. And I am *literally* with you working all the time. How do you figure I have time?"

"He made up his mind. You know he won't change it. Just hire someone if you don't care about the details."

I hated that Mason always took my dad's side. My upbringing had enforced all the qualities of being an obedient, proper lady who was fit to be the wife of a politician, but there were some lines I wanted to draw on my own. "And if he says to give him a grandchild immediately?"

Mason let out a long sigh. "Let's hope that doesn't come up for a while. If you want, we can make shit up to stall that."

"*Mason*! That is *not* the point here," I hissed, upset that he was just tossing it aside, but internally sighing with relief that he seemed to be on the same page with the subject of children.

He stood up and walked around the desk. He put his hands on my shoulders and looked down into my eyes. "I know," he said quietly before resting his chin on my head, pulling me in close. "It could be worse, he could be making you marry my brother Rob," he joked, his attempt to lighten the mood.

I wrapped my arms around him and leaned my head on his broad chest. His years in the military had filled him out with muscle that I knew he worked hard to maintain in the gym. I didn't hate Mason; we had been good friends our whole lives. He was as thrown into this as I was. In truth, there were far worse prospects for a husband. He was attractive and successful. I was confident that he'd never do anything to hurt me deliberately, either physically or emotionally. He was a solid partner. I just thought I had longer before I had to play the role of wife and eventually a mother. The expectations that followed our nuptials included children and running for various political offices until retirement at an old age. He and I had long ago decided, given the planned trajectory of our professional lives, our marriage would be mutually beneficial and we promised each other we wouldn't back out. Our parents set the plan into motion, but ultimately we realized that it made the most sense given our career aspirations.

We stood there a minute more. "I'll text you a few dates as far out as I can. Maybe I can get him to change his mind once he's calmed down." He kissed my forehead and sighed.

"It was a speeding ticket. He shouldn't be that pissed off."

"We weren't sure where you were. You didn't answer our calls. He was worried."

"Mason, I was quite clear that I was going away for the weekend."

"But you weren't where we expected you to be. Someone is supposed to know where you are."

"How the hell did you know where I was or was not?"

I felt him stiffen with discomfort. Mason was a lot of things, but he never outright lied to me. He would omit things *for my own good*, but he wouldn't lie to my face. "You don't want to know the answer to that."

I pulled away and stood there in his office, dumbfounded. "Did he have me tailed?" I asked incredulously. "We had an agreement. I've done everything he's ever asked of me, *including* letting him choose who I marry and when I do so. I attend every damn event so there will be some woman present to show support despite his marital status. I just wanted to be alone for the weekend."

"You know he's worried more since Catherine's pregnancy."

"I'm not Catherine. For fuck's sake, that was four years ago. I'm not even sure the public remembers he has a second daughter, forget the fact they have no idea that she's an unwed mother."

"You weren't alone, Elle."

I stood there silent for a few minutes. He knew who I was with? "Elaborate, Mason. I want to know why you and my father know where I was and with whom. "

Mason just stared at me. "I told him you were with a band. He tracks your location using your phone. Should I keep going?"

"No," I said, feeling violated. "For the record, that is overkill, and I don't appreciate the invasion of my privacy."

"Noted, but it's for your safety. Ever since my dad got elected, you know we get random death threats. It's only gotten worse since I started campaigning for the Senate."

We stared at each other for a minute while I absorbed the reality of death threats and being tracked. I sighed. "I understand the safety aspect, Mason, but we both know he doesn't need to actively follow me." I shook my shoulders out, trying to let go of my frustration. Mason looked away. This wasn't the first time this had come up and I knew that while he insisted there be a way to find me, he didn't agree with my father's intrusion on my life.

I debated storming back to my father's office but quickly decided that infuriating him further would not do me any favors. Instead, I made my way over to my desk outside of Mason's office and started going through the remarks for his upcoming speech.

Mason's and my employment was a bit of a balancing act at the moment. Technically, I worked on Mason's campaign coordinating his media strategy, but I still wrote all my father's speeches because I was a people pleaser and I couldn't say no to him. Since Mason was knee-deep in the campaign, he was also currently in the process of pulling himself out of his role working for the Roberts Administration, but my father was a demanding man and kept Mason lingering.

Having a job and earning my own money outside of either of them was what appealed about working for Connor. I certainly didn't need the money; I was a trust fund baby with a real job. I just wanted the illusion of control.

Desperately.

Six

Mason arranged for us to have an early September wedding. We convinced my father that a wedding announcement should wait until the last minute to keep speculation at bay. We would make it an "exclusive" event, especially since the Secret Service would have to be there. We would invite only close friends and family. The White House press pool would be the only media informed and allowed access. This wasn't at all what I think he had in mind, but he agreed and gave in to the conditions. For once, Mason's father's job benefited us.

Between planning a secret wedding, attending various political events, work, and keeping the Handheld Ninjas' lives, promotional plans, and social media pages in check, I had little time to breathe, let alone wallow in self-pity that my single days were ticking down quickly.

Mason and I made sure we had dinner together in public several times a week, playing the perfect couple. I let him know I had plans to go to Arizona, so he planned to travel the same days to make it look like we'd be together. I was pretty sure he would go to Puerto Rico. I didn't care where he was, as long as the good people of Massachusetts, but mostly my father, thought we were going somewhere together.

My communications with Silas remained in the form of mostly work-related emails, calls, and texts, with a bit of light flirting on the side. As far as I was concerned, we had a hot one-night stand and now we were just two people who worked together. Despite having a manager who had no idea what he was doing and an assistant that was increasingly further away, things were mostly on track for the band At least they seemed to be.

On Thursday, Mason and I made it to the airport for our chartered flight to New York too late for me to catch my commercial flight to Arizona, so I was stuck waiting for the next standby seat available. Because of my delays, I ended up meeting up with the band after their show that night back at the hotel. Connor had a list of topics to discuss, including the fact that the band was really blowing up quickly now that word was getting around. Shows were all sold out and Connor was considering recording a full-length album much sooner than expected.

"I know I'm not your manager, but at what point do we need to talk security and crisis plans?" I asked, seeing the sun had already risen out the window of the hotel room.

"Probably before the next road trip with the way things are going. I didn't expect this much of a reaction without a label backing us. You've done some solid work helping with the strategy. For now, we should get some sleep."

I left his room and made my way to the one I was sharing with Matteo. He was sound asleep in one of the two queen-size beds. The clock between the beds read 8:15 and I knew this meant very little sleep for me today. Maybe a couple of hours before I needed to get out and about I crawled into my bed, still fully clothed, and fell asleep.

Sleeping didn't last long. I woke to the sound of banging on the door. Matteo grumbled something incoherent and must have opened the door, because Tom suddenly bounced onto the bottom of my bed. "Wake up, sleepyhead!"

I could barely open my eyes. "What time is it," I groaned, certain it couldn't have been too long since I fell asleep.

"8:45."

"A.M.?"

"Well, that's a weird question, but yes."

"I literally just got to lay down half an hour ago," I whined.

"Oh, were you caught in a classic Connor all-night 'forced creativity' session?" Tom asked.

"I think he called it a business meeting, but yes. Does he not sleep?"

"There's no sleeping on tour, Len. C'mon. Silas is super grouchy this morning. Clearly not getting laid for his birthday took a toll."

"It was Silas' birthday?" I was positive he hadn't mentioned it before.

"Um, yeah. It would seem you may be part of the problem," Matteo chimed in with a suggestive wink.

"I'm ignoring that innuendo because I'm tired. I need to shower. Tell Silas I'll be ready in fifteen. Wait. Just to clarify, I'm not here to have sex with people on their birthday. That is not in the job description." I dragged my tired body to the bathroom and turned on the shower. I needed coffee.

True to my word, I emerged from the hotel room within fifteen minutes. I skipped the hat this time around and opted to just wear my hair in a topknot, something Eleanor would never do. I relished the opportunity to disregard my hair. While I was slightly concerned my father was having me stalked, I was confident no one else would have a clue who I, or my father, was and was in no mood to wear the hat or wig. My hair was wet and my eyes were puffy, but perfectly lined in too much black eyeliner, another 'never' for Eleanor.

Silas was standing in the hall waiting for me, face scrunched up as he looked at his phone. Matteo was right; he had a grouchy look about him, but he smiled when he saw me. "I see you've opted to ditch the hairpiece?"

"Yes. It's itchy and hot, and constantly making me crazy. I need coffee before I can function. Would you like to join me? I saw a cafe about a block from here."

"What time did he finally let you go?"

"About forty-five minutes ago."

"Coffee it is." He motioned toward the elevator.

We made our way outside in search of caffeine. There was an awkward silence I seemed to need to fill. "So, I hear yesterday was your birthday."

"It was."

"Happy birthday! How old?"

"Twenty-nine. But for real twenty-nine, not 'I'm thirty and in denial' twenty-nine," he winked. We walked in silence for another few minutes until we reached our destination. I insisted on buying him birthday coffee and we headed outside and took seats at a table.

"So, we should probably talk before we head back to the chaos," I started.

"So you know, I didn't say anything. Though, full disclosure, there is some suspicion, which I've just passed off as ridiculous."

"Okay, great. I didn't want to become the whore on tour. It was one of the more impulsive things I've ever done. Actually, it's my first one-night stand in which I knew the other person's name." *Oh my god, why the hell would I say that out loud?!* Sleep deprivation was not my friend.

Silas looked up from his coffee, shocked. "That was loaded. I'm going to break it down in order. First, I hardly think having sex with one guy makes you the 'tour whore'. Second, you need to be more impulsive because, third, I was hoping this would become something of a regular thing."

I tried to process the words coming out of his mouth. "Like, a casual fling when we're on the road?"

He took a deep breath. This was too much for my sleep-addled brain to analyze properly. "I mean, I wasn't exactly limiting our encounters to road trips, though I'm not really sure what other context we would be in the same proximity, so I guess that puts some limits on it. I get we don't know each other and this is a bit of an assumption of mutual attraction on my part. But I had hoped to be the only one on tour you're hooking up with. I'm not really into sharing. No judgment on those who do, it's just not my thing." He clutched his coffee tightly, tapping his foot nervously.

I pondered how much I needed to tell him. Was he suggesting some kind of relationship? Certainly not. We'd just met. That wasn't even remotely possible. "Well, the attraction is indeed mutual, and I had no intentions of hooking up with anyone else on tour. Hell, until it happened, I didn't think I'd be having sex with *you* on tour. I'm just —that's just — well, it's not me, for one. And outside of this work thing, I don't know what you're getting at. Like random hookups whenever?"

"No, uh, I don't know. I'm trying to say I'm not just using you to hook up. I wouldn't be opposed to hanging out or whatever. I guess?" He shifted a bit in his seat, seemingly hesitant to hear my reply.

I choked on my coffee. "So, there are some things about me you're going to need to know. The most important of which is that I kind of have obligations to someone."

"So you're already dating someone? Based solely on your actions and the comments you made to Mish I assumed that if you were in a relationship, it was some kind of former relationship with complications. You mentioned fucking, and I quote 'not Mason' who I assume is the guy you are referring to."

"Um, look, you are right about it being Mason. The whole thing is complicated and I haven't slept, so my brain isn't working and I don't know how to explain. It's just complicated. I can't even think of another word for complicated and I'm no longer sure I'm making any sense."

"Complex?"

"I'm sort of betrothed."

"What the fuck does that even mean?"

"It means —"

"I know what the word means," he held a hand up.

"So my dad decided long ago, like when I was legitimately a small child, that I would marry a specific person. Mason. Until now we've had separate dating lives, like normal people. But a few weeks ago my dad said it was time to actually get married and be adults and so as much as I'm totally into having sex with you, it has to stay casual, secret, and limited to road trips. And while Mason and I haven't had sex in years, there is an element of sharing here that I feel you should know given you mentioned it being an issue for you."

"Who fucking does that?"

"Lots of people have casual sex, Silas. Are you from 1950 or something?"

"Not that, *that* I'm behind one hundred percent. I was talking about the betrothal thing."

"Well, my dad has these outlandish ideals of passing on the family business to a son. He doesn't have one, as clearly a woman can't hold such an important place in society" I rolled my eyes. "So he signed me up to be the wife of his future son-in-law."

He was quiet for a moment. I took this as a sign to head back, so I stood and started walking, Silas following my lead. As we were walking, he slipped my hand into his, but stayed silent until we were just in front of the hotel. "Totally into having sex with me, eh?" he smirked and then kissed me on the cheek. I could feel my face getting red.

"I mean, I didn't hate it. I'd be open to a repeat." I said, not looking directly at him. Damn, Len was totally direct. Eleanor usually wasn't. Len was getting laid this trip, too, and she was looking forward to it.

"Good, because I'm not done with you yet." He smirked at me and I damn near swooned.

Uninvited

They canceled the gig for that evening in Arizona, which was one of the reasons for Silas' aforementioned grouchy attitude. There was an issue with the venue and they couldn't open. Connor decided we would drive to California and make use of some studio time so the band could work out some new music.

Connor and Tom rode in one van as Connor wanted to engage in one of the "forced creativity'" sessions Tom was complaining about earlier. I could see the look of total despair on Tom's face when Connor told him about the riding arrangements. It was going to be a long trip for poor Tom.

I hopped into the other van with Silas, Matteo, and Sergio, all of us dodging the same fate by opting to be out of Connor's reach, at least for a while. Silas and I hopped in back, Matteo took the driver's seat, and Sergio sat shotgun. I was beyond exhausted and well aware this may be my last time to sleep for the duration of the trip. I balled up my hoodie as a makeshift pillow and shut my eyes, leaning against the back of the seat. Silas gently tugged my arm and had me shift my "pillow" to his lap. Too exhausted to care about what that looked like to our fellow travelers, I laid across the seat with my head in his lap.

Silas played with my hair in a way I found both incredibly arousing and yet also relaxing. I was in and out of sleep when I heard Sergio ask, "So, how long are we pretending that isn't happening?"

"I don't know what you're talking about," Silas responded indifferently

Sergio laughed. "Oh come on man, she's literally in your lap right now."

"She's asleep, not giving me a blow job."

I heard Sergio and Matteo laughing. "I'm sure you wouldn't mind." Sergio teased.

"Are you saying you would? Please." Silas shot back.

"Not at all, actually. And I'd own up to it."

"Well, I'm not one to kiss and tell, whereas you like to broadcast your sexual exploits to anyone who will listen."

"So you've kissed her, then."

"I didn't say that."

"I'm just saying, my girl found what I can only assume is Len's underwear under the chair in the living room. How else does that happen? By the way, she was livid."

This caused Silas' fingers to still. "Doesn't mean they are Len's, or that I was the one that left them there."

"So how hot was it?" Sergio changed tactics.

"Fucking amazing," I responded, deciding to let Silas out of the hot seat. "Now stop talking about me while I'm right fucking here trying to sleep." I didn't bother to open my eyes, but I heard Silas choke and Matteo and Sergio laugh even more.

"Wait, before you go back to sleep, can you call my girlfriend and explain? She totally thinks we're fucking," Sergio asked.

"No. Maybe later. I don't know, I'm tired. I apologize for leaving evidence. That was unintentional and uncool. Obviously. Now let's never speak of this again."

"Nice work, Silas. I'd hit that too."

"*Serge!*" I yelled. "I am still right here."

"I know. I wanted to throw it out there in case Silas isn't satisfying you." I could hear the smirk in his voice as he said it.

"Noted, but entirely unnecessary." I didn't point out that he had a girlfriend back home as, although he didn't know it, I had a fiancé, so I wasn't one to throw stones.

Finally, the topic of discussion wasn't me and I drifted off to sleep with the realization that this was probably entirely too comfortable considering our chat earlier. But the feeling of his hands in my hair and my extreme exhaustion took precedence over labeling whatever was going on here.

I awoke to my phone buzzing relentlessly in my pocket. "What do you people have against sleep?" I muttered pulling my phone out of my pocket. Texts from Mish were flying in.

> ***Mish:*** *OMG WTF!*
> ***Mish:*** *ANSWER YOUR PHONE!*
> ***Mish:*** *Why am I finding out from Serge that you hooked up with Silas?*
> ***Mish:*** *ELEANOR ROBERTS ANSWER ME!!*
> ***Mish:*** *I get it, he's fucking hot, but you told me you didn't do it.*
> ***Mish:*** *Serge says you described it as amazing.*
> ***Mish:*** *Wait. Is he just shitting me? You'd never say that.*
> ***Mish:****Elle?*
> ***Mish:*** *Len?*

"What the fuck, Serge?" I mumbled sleepily.

"You really like the word fuck, don't you?"

"Sometimes. Why the hell did you tell Mish?"

"I assumed she knew. You two are tight." The news that I hadn't told Mish seemed to catch Silas off guard.

"I don't usually kiss and tell Serge. I only told you so I could get some sleep and now I can't sleep because Mish won't leave me the fuck alone." My phone started ringing again. "Yes, it's true. I just want to sleep. Can we talk about this later?" I snapped, trying to get her off the phone as quickly as possible.

"Wait, is he, like, right there?" She asked.

"Yes. I'm using his lap as a pillow."

"Oh, stop lying. Now I know none of it is true."

"Whatever. I have —" I pulled the phone from my face to ask the group in the van, "how long until we are wherever we are supposed to be?" Matteo muttered the info. "I have fifteen minutes before I have to deal with your boyfriend."

"Just tell me the truth first. Did you at least make out with him a little?"

"Yes. Naked. In Serge's apartment. Now go away." I hung up. "I hate you all!" I muttered. Mish had a point; this differed greatly from my normal behavior. Eleanor would not have broadcast the fact she had sex with a guy she just met and then tell a group of guys that she enjoyed it. Hell, Eleanor doesn't say "fuck" and would never consider day drinking to excess, but Len apparently does. It was weird to have two totally different personalities, but when I was with the guys on tour, I just leaned into the more wild side of myself. I didn't have to look perfectly put together. I wasn't well-spoken or polite. It was very liberating.

It sucked that just as I was getting into the whole thing, I was going to have to quit doing it.

Seven

We arrived at the studio and Connor had the whole band inside and working within minutes, including Silas. Personally, I was just glad this meant I didn't have to be involved. I was sitting on a chair in a room furnished with only the chair, a coffee table, and a couch. I planned to check up on their emails and social media pages and maybe take a nap on the couch.

I spent a few hours working on 'band' things and checked my personal emails. I checked in with Mason by texting him, "still alive," to which he responded, "ditto." I briefly wondered where he was off to and with whom. It would probably be one of the last times we got away before the wedding. Would we continue to screw other people after we were married? I hadn't thought about it. I certainly wasn't opposed, though it had been at least a couple of years since the last time he and I did it with each other. Mason and I had only had sex with each other sporadically since our teen romance died, and it was more because we needed a release than an actual attraction.

"Ah, the beautiful Len. I finally get you alone again." Silas sat down on the floor across from me with his back to the couch. He handed me a bottle of Dr. Pepper and opened a giant bag of

Swedish fish, offering me some. I moved down to the floor and sat in front of the chair to be at his level.

"Thanks," I said. I took a sip of the soda and coughed at the unexpected taste. "Captain Morgan?" I asked.

"My favorite captain. I have it on good authority you also enjoy setting sail with him."

"Indeed, but you should probably warn someone they aren't drinking what they think they are." I wondered which one of these guys was the authority he cited, but it wasn't at all wrong. I drank a lot when I was with these people. It could've been any of them. But who was he talking about me with? *Let it go. It's just a drink.*

"Tour rules, 'never drink a beverage that doesn't contain alcohol'."

"A rule I can get behind, but this is alcohol with a splash of a soda."

"You can thank Sergio for that." We sat in near silence for a few minutes. I played with the cap of the bottle. He smelled amazing. *How did he smell so good? When was the last time I showered? How badly do I smell? I think it was yesterday, but where the hell was yesterday? Wait, I think that was still today.* At least that would mean I was clean, anyway.

With the guys still off in the other room doing band things, I was ready to take advantage of this alone time Silas had pointed out. A few more sips of this drink should get me more into the 'Len' spirit, and shameless enough to get at least semi-naked with this guy despite our less-than-private location.

While I was trying to chug the drink discreetly, Silas killed the silence. "So let me get this straight," he said, popping a fish in his mouth, "you are dead-ass betrothed to some dude because your dad wanted a son?"

"Well, that's not inaccurate," I replied, taking another swig from the bottle. That was a buzzkill. I wanted to get his clothes off, and he wanted to talk about my impending nuptials with another man. "It's expected that we will marry someday." In September, to be exact, but I had no intention of thinking about that right now.

"That's some medieval shit."

I let out a small chuckle. "You know, my dad, he's under the impression he's a fucking Kennedy or some shit."

"I don't even know what that means."

"Brief history lesson." I took another gulp of my drink. "Joe Kennedy Senior, JFK's father, had this way of raising his children. The boys he raised to become politicians, the girls to be married to powerful men, preferably politicians. Joe wanted a president in the family. Like Joe, my father has this vision that includes having a POTUS in his family, but with a 'legacy' spin to it. A dynasty. You know, Kennedys, Clintons, Davises, Bushes.…" *So he's marrying off his daughter to one of those families; as one does.*

"Well, why in the hell can't you be the one to be President?"

I scoffed in mock disgust. "A woman president?! Clearly, you've gone mad! Besides, I'd probably still have to get married for the whole spectacle of it all and I have no desire to be a politician. It's very important to him, though." I grabbed more fish. "We're talking about a guy who betrothed his firstborn daughter in the name of political fame."

"Okay, but it's obviously not legally binding. No one can force you to marry this guy."

"It's true, but I suppose I could do worse. Arranged marriages happen all over the place and work out just fine. Which isn't to say that some of them end horribly, or even begin that way, but that's not really the case here. It's quite common to marry for strategic reasons rather than emotional ones in my circle. For example, my parents were a strategic match. My father wanted a descendant of the Mayflower, and my mother's father wanted someone who wouldn't squander his money." This was the mantra I told myself any time I gave much thought to the whole situation. "I mean, it's not like he's an ogre or something."

"Do you live in Victorian England? Because here in modern times, that's just fucking weird."

I laughed. "I know that's what it looks like from the outside of it all. My parents have never allowed me to act on feelings, Silas. I wouldn't even know how. I had a rather sterile upbringing. They put emphasis on not having emotions to hide. I've never entertained the fantasies of happily-ever-after love stories. Marriage is just something you do to achieve the next stage in a carefully plotted life. The relationships are for show and the sex is missionary, for procreation only."

"Sounds delightful. Where is Prince Charming, anyway? You'd think he'd be keeping close tabs on his property."

"Ah yes, the royal prince is likely just as shitfaced as we are, but on some island with his flavor of the week." I toasted the air with my soda bottle. "And for the record, I refuse to be considered property, even if it looks like someone has basically given me away as such. I have far more autonomy than a Victorian woman."

Silas held his hands up in surrender. "Whoa, didn't mean to offend you. I guess I just don't understand this."

"Because you are looking at it all wrong. It's not a relationship, it's a transaction. A future transaction. Until such time it becomes appropriate for us to get married, we do our own thing behind closed doors. They have encouraged us to sow all those wild oats and all. At least I'm allowed to have wild oats. That was a strictly male thing back in the day. Feminism has made its way to my social circles." I added a smile to show he hadn't offended me. The situation was fucked up, and I knew that.

"And until then, you have nothing to do with each other?"

"No, no, no. In the public eye, we're 'engaged.' We attend events together to sell the story of true love and all that horseshit." I took another large gulp of my drink. "Have you not Googled me?" I shot him a look of disbelief, briefly forgetting that he didn't know there would be a reason to do so, or who to search for.

"I don't even know your last name. I mean, I assume 'Len'

will not yield any hits and that it isn't your real name. I opted to stop being creepy after I realized I stalked you last time. But I didn't realize there would be anything of note on Google. Good to know."

"Indeed, it will not. This is part of my secret identity. This kind of debauchery would be a PR nightmare. Certainly can't have anyone putting the pieces together. Very few people know about this whole arrangement. It's not spoken of, it is just done."

"So, clearly you come from some kind of upper class family with money and a reputation that could be ruined."

"That is fairly on point, yes."

"Okay, at the risk of sounding all girly, don't you want true love? Maybe a spouse you like?"

I laughed. "I'm not a twelve-year-old girl, Silas. I like him just fine, but love is a farce. I just don't believe in it. Not romantic love, anyway. It's some kind of marketing scam. I literally can't fathom what that looks like. I'm not a psychopath, by the way; I care deeply about my close friends and family. I love them in a very familial kind of way, but in no way do I believe in destiny or true love. Are you saying that you do?"

Silas took a breath and stared up at the ceiling, contemplating this. "Destiny, I'm undecided. And I'm not entirely sure there is 'the one' out there for everyone, but yeah, I'd like to think that someday I'll fall for someone. I'm definitely hoping for more than obligatory missionary sex."

"It's all just lust, Silas. Blinded by hormones."

"You are so cynical."

"I *have* been called an ice queen."

Silas laughed. "I can't picture it."

"Mish calls me Duchess." This was more about the way I dressed similarly to the Duchess of Cambridge, but occasionally, she used it to refer to my demeanor as well.

"Now that I can see, *Duchess*. But in the gorgeous unattainable duchess that all the dukes are hoping to hook up with."

I mumbled some lyrics to a Taylor Swift song about appearing more desirable than was reality. That Captain was hitting me hard because I was much louder than I thought and he heard it.

"You don't strike me as the Taylor Swift type," he teased.

It somewhat impressed me he got the reference. "I don't think I am, mostly. Sometimes, lyrics just stick in my head and pop out when I don't even expect it. My sister and I have this thing, we will just text lyrics or a song title for a situation instead of saying what is really on our minds. Call it a coping mechanism. Drives Mish and Mason both nuts."

"Oh, a sister. The plot thickens. Also, I doubt you're a nightmare." He cast a sexy smirk in my direction.

I laughed. Loudly. "I wouldn't be so sure of that." I was done talking. I crawled across the floor over to where he was sitting and straddled his legs. He just stared into my eyes like he was trying to see inside my mind. "This won't end well."

He traced his finger over the swell of my breasts and my breath caught. He licked his lips and then brushed them over the sensitive skin of my neck. "Maybe not, but I plan to enjoy all the parts before the end," he breathed into my ear. He crept his hands under my shirt and palmed my breast. "At the moment, it seems to be going well from where I'm sitting."

I had a steady buzz, but not to the extent of being so drunk that I didn't know that this was a terrible, but really amazing, idea. The last time we hooked up, I had been awake for days and it was still the best sex I could remember having in a very long time. Still, I needed to be sure we were on the same page. "This can't be more than a hookup. I don't do feelings and I absolutely don't cuddle," I whispered into his ear before returning to kiss his neck. I inhaled his scent deeply. Desire pooled in my core and the longer we were this close, the more I lost control.

"Stop talking." He pulled my shirt up over my head. We were in the adjoining room to where the entire band was recording. There was a window. I was pretending to be professional and not sleeping around, though that pretense had sailed earlier thanks to Sergio, so what the fuck, right? Silas worked to unclasp my bra and slowly slid the straps down my arm with his fingers, following one hand with open-mouthed kisses down my arm. When the offending undergarment was finally on the floor beside us, he wrapped his lips around my nipple and I gasped. There was too much thinking and not enough feeling. I grabbed the bottle of Captain and took a swig.

He stopped. "Do you not want to do this?" he asked, looking into my eyes.

"Just not accustomed to getting fucked where plenty of people might see. That was to make me forget about them and concentrate on this." I ground my hips into his erection. Being in the public eye my whole life, I'd never dared such a stunt.

He gave me a quizzical look. "Who are you, Len?"

"Just a girl." I unbuttoned his jeans, and he responded by unbuttoning my shorts.

"Fabulous No Doubt song."

I focused my concentration on his hands as they slid over my ass to pull the shorts down. I wriggled out of them while he pulled his pants down enough so that I had full access to his erection. Our mouths crashed together as I returned to straddle him fully. He held up a condom and I felt my pulse skyrocket.

"Ever the boy scout, Silas. So prepared," I whispered as he put it on. I lifted my hips until I felt the heat of his cock at my entrance and slowly lowered down. He let out a groan and leaned his head back onto the couch behind him for a second. I moaned and savored the feeling of him filling me.

I rose again, but he grabbed my hips and held me in place. He kissed me hard. "If you want to continue, you have to at least give me your real name," he murmured in my ear as if my name was more important than how much I desperately needed him to move inside me.

I pushed my hips forward and I could feel him tense up to hold out. "It's better if you don't know, don't you think?" He held my right hip and used his other hand to grab my breast, his mouth covering my other nipple. I ran my hands through his hair as he tugged and nipped. *Jesus, why did he smell so fucking good?* All I could think about was how amazing he felt and how intoxicating he smelled. I moved my hips, desperate for the feeling of him moving inside me. He grabbed my ass and joined in by thrusting his hips up into mine, making him reach even deeper. I moaned with thorough appreciation.

He smiled in satisfaction and stopped. "How about now?"

"Don't make me finish this alone, Silas. You're going to have to earn the answer." That must have been an acceptable deal because the next thing I knew, I was on my back and he had lost his pants completely.

He rubbed my clit with his thumb, and my hips automatically lifted. I was aching for his touch. He watched as he worked me closer and closer to the edge. Just before I was ready to explode, I gazed into his eyes. "Fuck me, Silas." He thrust back into me and while I could vaguely feel the rug burn grow, the sensation only heightened the feeling. "Just don't stop," I pleaded. I wrapped my legs around his back tightly.

"Fuck," he rasped, changing the angle slightly. I'm pretty sure I stopped breathing. I must've had more of that captain than I thought. *Why can't I breathe?* Then it hit. The orgasm rocked through my body in a way I never thought possible. It radiated from my center all the way to the tips of my fingers and toes. "Yes, Duchess, just like that." As I clenched around him, he groaned through his own release.

My arms and legs felt like lead and fell to the floor with a thud. *Damn, that was hot.*

He rolled over to the side and took off the condom.

"Eleanor. My name is Eleanor," I panted, still out of breath.

He gave me a sexy smile. "Nice to meet you, Eleanor."

"That's top secret. My real life is complicated. The less it intersects with this, the better."

"I won't sell you out to these fools." He pointed his chin to the next room while grabbing his clothes. I completely forgot we were in a room with a potential audience. "But what's your last name?"

"I think I've told enough of my secrets for one day."

He tilted my chin upward and kissed me. "Then I guess it's a good thing I have you for a couple more days." I wanted to melt into the floor at the thought of a few days with Silas. The things I would let this man do to me if given the time.

This was not what I was supposed to be doing. This job was supposed to just be a distraction from real life. Technically, sex with Silas was a very welcome, though unexpected distraction, so that was something, right? *What the hell was I thinking?* "Well, we have a packed schedule after this. I don't think we'll be finding ourselves in this position again."

"Don't worry. There are plenty of other positions, *Duchess*." He walked into the other room, leaving me stunned. *What's with this guy?* I had more baggage than Logan Airport. A casual fuck is once. Maybe twice. This was twice. I'm pretty sure it ended there. *Right?* I never had an issue with a guy being cool with a quick fuck and then business as usual without the anticipation of more. I never felt the need to go back for more, either. *Why the hell was he under my skin?* He was just too fuckable, and I knew there was no way in hell I'd reject any further advances he made. I had no control over my hormones or body with this guy.

I saw my reflection in a window. My hair, falling out of its former messy bun in tangled pieces, was a clear indication of what I had been doing this evening. I pulled it tighter into a topknot and hoped no one would notice. I pulled my clothes back on and went back to the chair, grabbing my laptop. I read through the speech I was preparing while trying desperately to catch my breath and play it cool.

Connor came in from the other room a while later. "So, Len, we have a lot to do tonight."

"Tonight? It's after midnight. I've had like four hours of sleep since...I don't even know. What day is it?"

"Isn't that what I pay you for? Knowing where and when we are?" He smirked. "Tour is disorienting; that's where you come in. In the meantime, this situation calls for a 'wake me up'."

I was slightly terrified of what that meant, but thanks to a lot of spiced rum, I was completely on board. He left the room and came back five minutes later with a cup. "Drink this," he demanded. It smelled like coffee. It was cute that he thought caffeine could help at this point. "There's no sleep on tour, Len." Then he handed me a pill. Apparently, I had no control with Connor either, because I popped the pill and swallowed it with what tasted like espresso. *Well, that would leave me twitching for a while, for sure.* "Atta girl. Let's get back to the hotel. We have things to discuss."

Eight

Me: We have to discuss this via text. I can't talk out loud.
Me: I need to inform you that yes, I have hooked up with Silas.
Me: Twice.
Mish: TWICE? Spill.
Me: Once in Atlanta, once about an hour ago.
Mish: At the studio?
Me: Yes. On the floor.
Mish: Were you drunk? That's basically public!
Me: Eh, slightly.
Mish: So… how was it?
Me: Hands down the best sex I've ever had. Man knows what he's doing. Why does he smell so good? Seriously, thinking about it gets me all hot and bothered and we just fucked. That man can wear the shit out of a pair of jeans.
Me: Holy shit, I just want to get him out of those jeans again.
Mish: Wow, you are drunk.

Me: Absolutely.
Mish: I'm glad you are letting loose.
Me: Is that a reference to me fucking a gorgeous man without thinking about the repercussions? Because I have no regrets.
Mish: Ladies and gentlemen, we have a contender.
Me: A contender for what?
Mish: Derailing you from marrying Mason, obvi.
Me: I'm still very much marrying Mason. This is just a fun side quest.
Mish: Does Silas know this?
Me: Yes. And no. He knows I'm engaged, but not that the wedding is only a few months away.
Mish: And he was fine with that?
Me: I guess. I told him this morning and this evening we were fucking on the floor, so… I don't see why he'd have an issue with it. Guys are usually very willing to have a quick fuck and move on.
Mish: Elle, you need to proceed with caution here. Connor has already asked me several times if you are interested in Silas.
Me: Why would he ask that?!
Mish: Because Silas is very obviously into you. And he thinks you two would make a cute couple.
Me: We are not a couple. I hardly know the guy.
Mish: They've already shipped you: SiLen.
Me: FFS - fucking Sergio. Why is he such a teenage girl?
Mish: Ha! Yes. That perfectly describes Serge.
Me: This is the stupidest thing I've ever done.
Mish: Nah, agreeing to marry someone in toddlerhood was.
Me: I hardly had the capacity to understand at

two. Apparently, at 30 I'm just as stupid, though.
Mish: *Elle. For real. You don't have to do this. You know that, right?*
Mish: *Elle? You can hide away with me and Connor.*
Me: I know that, but I'm good. It's all part of the bigger plan. This is just a small diversion to keep things interesting before I am a very boring woman in politics.
Mish: *You seriously fucked Silas in Sergio's apartment?*
Me: Apparently we left my underwear as evidence and his girlfriend lost her shit.
Mish: *She's a psycho, and you did him a favor.*
Me: He doesn't seem too committed to her. He offered to fuck me if Silas wasn't getting the job done.
Mish: *Of course he did. So, at the studio? On the floor? With everyone there?*
Me: It's not like they watched, Mish. They were in the other room. But yes. Pretty sure I have rug burn on my back to prove it.
Mish: *I'm shocked, but also very proud.*

A few hours later, well into another "forced creativity" session with Connor and all the guys — none of us were happy despite plenty of alcohol and being surrounded by takeout food of basically every variety. I was pacing the room talking about what had to be nonsense. Mostly, only Connor seemed to care about what I was saying, which had something to do with my latest "brilliant" idea — the third in as many minutes.

"Now that one is worth looking into," Connor commented and wrote something down in his tattered notebook.

Silas shot me a look of concern. "Len. Sit. Please, you're making the rest of us dizzy."

I giggled. Yup, I was definitely twitchy and whatever I took had me feeling the very opposite of tired. Tour with a band was definitely much better than a campaign trail. "I'm good. I think better when I move." I started doing side lunges.

"What the fuck, Connor?" Silas growled. Connor narrowed his eyes and rubbed his chin in confusion. Silas turned back to me. "Len. How often do you get high?"

"Len? Len does whatever the fuck she wants whenever the fuck she wants. But Len is quite infrequently allowed out of her cage," I answered, now twirling around the room, speaking of myself as though I were more than one person.

"Right. That makes no sense. How about right now? What the hell is even going on over there?" he gestured with a sweep of his hand over my hyperactive body.

"Um, don't know. Lots of caffeine. I had a few shots of espresso. I'm good. But I'm not high, Silas. Just really awake. But I don't think I've blinked in a few hours, now that you mention it. It's all good though, because I am in the *zone*, baby." I kicked a leg up as if I was fighting an imaginary force.

"That's not just espresso." Silas searched my face like he was checking to see if I was really that naïve, or just in some kind of denial.

"And alcohol. Per tour rules, all of my beverages contain alcohol," I added helpfully. Or at least, I thought it was helpful.

"Right." He caught my hips with his hands and held me still. "Anything else?"

"Umm. Oh, whatever Connor hooked me up with."

Silas stared daggers over my shoulder at Connor, who suddenly appeared to figure out what the issue was. "So, you just took whatever he gave you? No questions asked?" Silas's eyes never left Connor's, but his question was clearly for me.

"Yup."

"Do you always take random drugs people hand you?"

"There is a first for everything, Silas." I got the impression I needed to explain myself, so I rattled off some of the chorus of "Trust You". "Well, and Connor. He's my boss and infatuated with one of my best friends. I figured he was safe." This reasoning was sound in my less-than-sober state.

"Somehow I don't think this is what Rob Thomas had in mind when he wrote that song," Silas muttered. I clapped because he caught the reference.

"Pretty sure you're wrong on that one," I mused.

"Well, crashing now is out so what was the plan, Connor? When she crashes, it's going to be ugly. Drugs for days?"

"Yes?" Connor answered. "I mean, it's not mandatory, but will totally work out the best. She can always sleep it off once she comes down."

"She is right here and not sleeping on tour. It's against the rules, and I'm a devout rule follower in real life." I laughed hysterically at this.

And that's how I ended up taking Modafinil for the first time. I could see the appeal. I was getting shit done and sleep wasn't even remotely necessary. Silas stayed glued to my side from that point on and declared that he'd need to accompany me on my flight home to make sure I got there fine. Connor agreed but somehow, I missed the entire conversation. I was too busy planning the band's world domination.

"That will not work for me," I said when Silas and Connor brought up the plan for Silas to escort me home, just before the last show and mere hours before I would leave San Diego. "I'm meeting Mason in New York. These two lives do not cross over."

Connor and Silas exchanged a Look. "There's no way in hell I'm letting you get on a plane alone, Len," Silas said.

"Me either," Connor agreed. "You're going to crash and I need to know you made it home. Silas will get you to Mason in New York."

Now it was my turn to be pissed at Connor. "No way. Mason will lose his shit and if my father or the media get wind of this, it'll be a shit storm." I continued laying shirts on the merch table with shaking hands. At this point I didn't know if that was due to the drugs or the thought of Mason and Silas crossing paths in public.

"We will make sure your father doesn't find out. Mason isn't going to let that happen." Connor tried to assure me. They didn't have me as convinced. Nine times out of ten Mason caved to my father. "But either Silas gets you all the way home or he gets you to New York and Mason."

Returning home without Mason wasn't an option as everyone, most importantly my father, thought we were together somewhere. "Silas can fly back with me, but the second we get off the plane, we part ways like strangers." Silas looked like I just slapped him.

"Have Mason pick you up to escort you to your flight and we have a deal." Connor sighed but agreed. Silas grew more irritated.

"We chartered our flight from New York to Boston. That's going to take coordination," I countered, thinking this would deter the two men from getting me home safely.

"Give me his number and I'll coordinate, then." Silas handed me his phone to add Mason's contact information. I didn't think he'd actually follow through with contacting Mason directly, so I added the number.

Connor went off to do other things and got caught in conversation with someone he knew. I finished setting up the table and wandered off for another water while Silas stood nearby to watch everything. When I returned, I handed Silas a drink and asked Matteo if he'd monitor things for a few minutes while Silas and I got some stuff from out back. Silas looked at me quizzically, but followed when Matteo agreed.

Uninvited

I pulled him into a supply closet I saw earlier and closed the door behind us. "Why exactly would the media give a shit about where you are and who you are with?" he asked. "Charter a fucking plane?"

I did not bring him back here to talk. I brought him back here to fuck before I left. "We aren't talking right now. We have very few minutes and those minutes are better spent doing other things." I kissed him and ran my hands up his chest. He let out a frustrated groan, though it didn't stop him from pulling me closer with both hands firmly on my ass and kissing me back. He tugged my bottom lip with his teeth before licking it. *I need more.* I slid my hands down his chest to unbutton his jeans as he used his to coast under my shirt, feeling his way to my tits. Everywhere he touched felt like live wires over my skin.

"What things are those, Eleanor?" he whispered against my lips. His use of my real name made me shiver.

"You said there were other positions, Silas. I'd like to see one of those, please."

He chuckled as he nudged my head to the side to trail kisses down the side of my neck. The electric sensation now a full-blown inferno lighting up my entire body. The more he touched me, the more desperate I became. "Well, this tiny space limits those options, but I have zero issues fucking you against that door with people walking by, so you'll have to keep it down."

"I have zero issues with the whole fucking place knowing exactly what's going on in here." I whipped my pants off and kicked them to the side. There was very little chance anyone would hear anything with the music of the first band starting up, but even if they did, I was not lying about not caring. I just needed him to fuck me before I exploded. He helped liberate me from my shirt and bra. His clothes disappeared before I noticed him taking them off, and he turned to press me up against the door. I wrapped my legs around his waist and he hitched me up so he could push inside me. "Fuck, I need this." I ran my hands over his shoulders, relishing the feeling of him inside me.

He stared into my eyes without moving. "Last name."

"You are relentless. It's Fuller." I lied a bit, using my mother's maiden name. "Fuck me, Silas. Fuck me now." I kissed him roughly as he pumped into me. "Sonofabitch, that's amazing!" I moaned, my head leaning back on the door. My whole body was tingling, and I was pretty sure it wasn't due to the drugs because it only happened whenever Silas physically touched me. Okay, it probably had a bit to do with the vibration of the door from the loud music being played on the other side, but whenever Silas was this close to me my body felt alive and my brain stopped racing. The only thing I could think about was the way it felt.

I could see his phone ringing beside his pants on the floor. It was most likely someone wondering where we were. "Look at me, not the phone, Lenny." His eyes sparkled with lust and mischief. "We have got to find a way to do this more often." His mouth returned to mine, his tongue dancing wildly with mine. I wanted to stay lost in this bliss forever. "Touch yourself, duchess." I did as commanded, rubbing my clit as he pumped harder into me. Within a minute, we both came undone with moans and groans that I was certain the people on the other side of the door could hear over whatever other background noise was there.

I slid my shaking legs back on solid ground, completely out of breath and ready for a nap. I bent over to grab our pants and he slapped my bare ass. My phone was now ringing, and he had two missed calls. We quickly dressed, but made no efforts to conceal what had just happened as we walked out of the supply closet and went back to the room backstage where the band was getting ready to go on stage.

We caught a few knowing looks, and Sergio added a whistle. I felt my cheeks heat, but carried on to grab a bottle of water.

By the time the guys finished performing, we'd packed up and returned to the house. I was getting drowsy. I took a shower and packed the few items that weren't in my bag so that I could head to the airport for my early flight back home.

After making it through security and to our gate, I was damn near asleep on my feet. "I'm fucking beat," I mumbled to Silas as if he hadn't noticed me nod off a few times. He directed me to a chair and I practically fell in.

"Yeah. You've been awake for days. You're gonna sleep for a long time."

I leaned my head on his shoulder and he put his arm around me. "Can't. I have...something to do when we get back."

"We'll see about that."

I fell asleep on his shoulder waiting for our turn to board. I was barely conscious when we landed in New York. Although the deal was that Silas would just walk away when we got off the plane, that wasn't really possible. He had a difficult time waking me up and basically had to drag me up the jetway. Some helpful person at the airline brought a wheelchair and Silas pushed me to the exit where Mason waited in an Uber to drive us to meet our plane.

I vaguely registered Mason coming over and introducing himself to Silas. "Mason. You must be Silas. Thanks for getting her this far." I was vaguely aware of Mason pulling me into his arms from the wheelchair and helping me into the car.

They exchanged a few more words I didn't quite catch, then Mason and I left.

That was Monday morning.

Nine

I woke up Wednesday morning in Mason's bed without a clue how I got there or what day it was. His alarm was going off. I started hitting his side of the bed to make him make it stop, but I was alone. I grabbed the phone and turned it off, realizing the shower was running in the bathroom. That's when I noticed the day.

"Oh shit. I fucked up." Did I sleep through Monday *and* Tuesday? Worse, did I go through Monday and/or Tuesday and completely forget everything about it and land in bed with Mason? I heard the shower turn off, and I reached for my phone. It was dead, but I stared at it as though the act of holding it and giving it a dirty look would magically charge the battery and also provide me with the answers I sought.

"Ah, Sleeping Beauty rises." Mason emerged from the bathroom clad only in a towel around his waist. "I figured it would be better if you couldn't see the carnage as soon as you woke up." He pointed to the dead cell phone in my hand.

"Carnage? What the fuck happened?"

"From what I understand, it involved some stimulants and days of no sleep, but your friends aren't exactly being forthcoming with the details. I just showed up to collect you as required." There was a hint of bitterness in his voice.

"Let's not pretend the roles have never been reversed here, Mace. I've picked your sorry ass up far more than you have mine." I was in no mood to have this conversation.

"This is true. But I never had to be carried off a plane in public."

"Wait. Did I?" I asked, horrified.

"What do you remember?"

"Sex in the supply closet; things got fuzzy after that. "Packing for my flight?"

"Well, after Silas had to drag you off the plane, you were basically sound asleep. Rather than fight with you to keep you awake, he met me with you in a wheelchair. There are pictures online of me taking you out of said wheelchair and helping you into the car."

That was worse than I expected. Pictures of me being pushed through an airport? Mason watched me process the information. "What does dad know?" We'd circle back to the Silas thing.

"The world believes you came home with a terrible case of the flu; this includes the governor." He started pulling pants on and looking for his belt.

"You met Silas?" That must have been awkward for Silas.

"Get up and get in the shower. I can only cover for you so long without them sending a doctor over. Yes. Silas dragged you off the flight from California."

I peeled myself out of bed and grabbed some clothes from Mason's closet.

"I'm going to grab coffee and breakfast. Be ready when I get back; we have to head into the office this morning for a campaign meeting."

There was no chance that was happening unless he planned on grabbing those things outside of the city because my hair was just a giant knot and that was going to take time and conditioner. I plugged in my phone and hopped in the shower. By the time

I emerged, I could see there were many notifications that I absolutely knew I didn't want to deal with. I needed my hands to work through my hair with a brush so I dialed Mish and put it on speaker. "Duchess! You're alive!" She shouted into the phone.

"Barely. I literally just rolled out of bed ten minutes ago. Give me the highlights of whatever your billion messages say."

"Most of them were just checking to see if you were alive. Mason responded a few times on your behalf to confirm you were still breathing, but also still passed out. And then there were some about your sexy pictures in the tabloids speculating all kinds of crazy shit. Have you seen those?"

"Literally just rolled out of bed, Mish," I repeated. "Though Mace mentioned being taken from the plane in a wheelchair and claiming I had the flu."

"Right. So there were the pictures. The world was pretty excited to see the princess of Boston looking less than regal, let me tell you." Mish prattled on while I processed the situation. My father was going to have my head. Perhaps I shouldn't bother with the hair? Nope, all the more reason to reappear looking perfect. If duchesses can pose with perfect hair and make-up immediately after giving birth, I could do the same after a few days of stimulants. "...and I don't know what happened with Silas, but Connor says he's in a raging mood."

"Silas was mad at Connor for giving me the pills to begin with. It was a little too paternalistic, if you ask me. I'm a grown-up, I can handle myself."

"Says the woman who had to be escorted home, but I get both sides. Can we just talk about how you're fucking that handsome specimen? SiLen is the talk of the group chat." I could imagine her waggling her eyebrows on the other end of the call.

I was about to ask why I am not on this group chat, but was interrupted. "No. We cannot," Mason said from behind me. I was just finishing up brushing out my hair and he handed me a coffee and held a cup of oatmeal. "Eat this." He shoveled a spoonful into my mouth as I started pulling out makeup and hairpins.

Mish said a quick, "gotta go, bye," knowing there would be no more substantial details with Mason there.

"So bossy this morning, Mason."

"Well, now you know how it feels to be on the other end of this." Honestly, having someone else be the responsible one was kind of nice, even if he was pushy. I gathered hair to put it into a bun as drying it was out of the question at this point. He spooned more oatmeal into my mouth.

I managed to get make-up on and look presentable in ten minutes. Mason dropped some heels at my feet and put his suit jacket on, ushering us toward the door. "Let's go, Sleeping Beauty."

As predicted, my father was *pissed* even though he completely bought the bullshit line that I had gotten sick in Puerto Rico. Apparently, having your picture taken while being so sick you had to be escorted off a plane in a wheelchair is not an excuse to have your hair in a messy bun. *It was a lie, but still. What the fuck?*

Noted. I tapped out a message to my younger sister, Catherine.

> **Me:** *Burn the House Down*, AJR
> **Catherine:** *Ha! I saw you in all your "sick" glory. That song is perfect. Burn, Ellie Goulding.*
> **Me:** Also on point. Should I be concerned that both songs are about something burning?

"Eleanor, can you please pay attention? What the hell is so important you can't focus right now? We have a disaster on our hands here and you're socializing!" My dad roared from behind his seat at the head of the table in the conference room of Mason's election headquarters.

Uninvited

"This is hardly a disaster, dad. People saw me ill; I didn't have some kind of public breakdown. Even politicians' wives get sick while traveling." I resisted the urge to roll my eyes. I already said more than I normally would.

Mason's campaign manager, a man in his mid-fifties named Cliff, cleared his throat to remind us of his presence. Mason was mere months away from a seat in the U.S. Senate. He was polling well, would have the requisite wife before election day, and all things looked like I was about to spend more of my days in D.C. Certainly my "illness" wouldn't completely derail this campaign. He was a fucking Davis in Massachusetts, for crying out loud. They were basically political royalty. Hell, people *expected* lady drama with his family.

I was antsy. I had slept off the last 48 hours and had a ton of texts, emails, and voice messages that I needed to deal with. Interestingly, the ones from Silas ended Monday morning. Unsurprisingly, many of them had been from Michelle, and then Catherine, who heard about my weekend from Michelle. Since I had proven my living status to both of them, I deleted any of the messages that came from those two.

"Cliff, where are we with announcing the wedding date?" My father continued to growl. I snapped my attention back to the room.

"I thought we'd agreed that we were announcing just before to limit the security issues." I tried not to whine or yell, but the topic of my wedding was triggering me.

"I think given this last weekend, we need to change that. Cliff will need the names of the people in the wedding party."

"No," I stated simply. All three of them stared at me like I said something horrifying. "I do *not* want a media circus. I agreed to move up the wedding to make Mason a married man for election day, but I don't want to have visible secret service and media scrutiny. Family and *close* friends only. Mason and I agreed that Robert and Catherine would be our *tiny* wedding party and that's it.

Those are my terms."

My father looked over at Mason to see who he'd side with. Mason shifted uncomfortably in his chair. "I think it's best if we keep the wedding as quiet as possible until it's over. My father's security agrees. And we don't want it to look like a campaign stunt instead of an actual marriage."

My father turned to Cliff. "He has a point, sir," Cliff said, looking up from his phone.

"Fine," my father grumbled. "But pick someone other than Catherine. We don't need to slice open old wounds."

"Dad!" I raised my voice, outraged. "She. Is. My. Sister."

"She's a liability."

"She is your *daughter*," I bit back. I was never this openly aggressive with him, but I was sick of the games.

"And I love her, but she's an unwed mother, Eleanor. She's bad for your image."

I sat in stunned silence. This one-sided feud between my father and my sister had gone on longer than I had ever imagined it would. "You *love* her? Dad. You haven't spoken to her in four years!"

"It hasn't been that long; don't be dramatic. You are acting like Catherine. Immature and selfish."

"Dad. Wyatt is three and a half. It's been four years. She changed her name and basically lives in obscurity in the middle of Nowhere, Massachusetts, to 'protect your image'." I put air quotes around the last part. "Your grandson is *three and a half years old* and you have *never* seen him to protect yourself. You are the selfish one here. I'm done moving my life around to pretend my only sister ceases to exist." I picked up my notebook off the desk in front of me and stood to leave. Mason stood up beside me and placed a hand on the small of my back to remind me to act like a damn lady.

I took a cleansing breath and walked out of the conference room with Mason hot on my heels. As usual, we walked in silence back to his office before he commented, "That did not go well." I gave him the side-eye and dropped myself dramatically onto the chair in the room's corner. His assistant followed in with a cup of tea for me and a coffee for Mason, already knowing that we'd need a few minutes to gather ourselves after a heated meeting with The Governor. She closed the door behind herself on the way out.

I hugged the tea in my hands and willed my blood pressure to return to normal. "You're a Davis. There must be things more scandalous than Catherine on your side of the family."

He laughed into his hands. "Fuck, yes. Some may be true and some are absolute horseshit. Somehow, they have tasked us with selling a more pure generation of Davises free of faults and scandal. As if there is any family on the planet without faults." He took a sip of the coffee. "You know, no pressure or anything. My dad? He thought he could start the next great Davis legacy."

"Right."

"So, listen, this isn't the time or place, but we need to talk about last weekend. Dinner at my place? I'll pick something up."

"It's Wednesday, I have Wyatt for Cee. I'll be out at her place."

"Right. Well, I will co-babysit and we can talk after he goes to bed?" he offered.

"Sure. If it's that urgent to lecture me about being irresponsible, you can join Wyatt and me for dinner."

"Elle," he sighed, "that's not my intention. We need to get our stories straight because, unfortunately, we weren't as under the radar as we would've liked. I don't blame you at all for letting loose for a weekend away from this shitstorm. And we have to go over some wedding stuff."

"Wedding stuff? I thought we delegated most of that out?"

"We need to talk about what happens between us when we get married. It seems there are some terms to commit to that I didn't think would be a problem."

We really needed to have that talk, but I suddenly felt nauseous.

"Right. So, see you this evening at Cee's house. Just don't let any media know you were there because apparently, it's 'bad for your image'. Wouldn't want to lose the election because you visited your fiancée at her sister's residence."

Catherine shared a house with her boyfriend Elijah and her son Wyatt. Wyatt isn't Eli's son; I did not know who Wyatt's father was. Eli and Cee had been best friends since high school, but only recently became a couple. I didn't pretend to understand their dynamic, and I didn't throw shade because I am betrothed and that's far more drama than dating your best friend after years of swearing it "wasn't like that."

As promised, Mason picked up Thai food for dinner, which was even more appreciated since Wyatt was hell on wheels and making dinner while watching him was an Olympic sport I had little to no actual training in. Wyatt sat at the table trying to negotiate rice with his fork because he was, and I quote, "not a baby" and absolutely did not need help or a spoon. He was really adamant that the rice would succumb to his will on the fork, but there was more rice on the floor than had made it to his mouth. At least he managed the chicken.

"So, let's talk about the logistics for the next few months. Obviously, on the home front we continue as we have been, but do you have any, uh, plans with others between now and then that we need to work in there?" Mason asked.

I put my chopsticks down. "Are you asking me if I plan on hooking up with someone between now and the wedding?"

Mason looked at Wyatt. "Should you be saying that in front of him?"

"Mason, he's three. He does not know what that even means. Not even remotely."

"Then yes, I'm asking about your sexual plans."

"What's sect yull?" Wyatt asked. Mason glared at me with an *'I told you so'* look.

"Sectional is a kind of couch," I responded, redirecting Wyatt to his rice. "I think I have a few quick trips between now and then to work for Connor."

"What do you mean, 'work for Connor'? Connor who? I thought his name was Silas?"

"Connor is Mish's boyfriend. The singer?"

"Ah, yes. Him. You work for Connor?" I could almost see him trying to put the pieces together in his head.

"I figured you knew, honestly. You seem to come by details of my life without me being the one to tell you all the time," I sassed. He just returned a glare, expecting an actual answer. "Just some promotional stuff. It's basically the same as politics, but a different audience. Actually, it's terrifyingly *just* like politics."

"And Silas is?"

"The band's manager."

"The one you're hooking up with."

"Yes, also the same guy."

"So, who... got you the medicine?" Mason chose his words carefully as he watched Wyatt get more food onto the floor than into his mouth.

"That was Connor. Silas wasn't drugging me to," I glanced at Wyatt, "to hook up, if that's what you are worried about."

"Good to know."

"Auntie Elle, who dunked you?" Wyatt asked, now dunking his chicken in my water.

"Auntie Mish did, can you believe that? Right in the pool!" I exclaimed. Seeing that Wyatt had finished with dinner, I started wiping him down so he could go play with his cars until it was time to get ready for bed.

I swept up the rice from the floor while Mason tucked the dishes into the dishwasher. "You know that you'll have to quit when we get married, right? It would be impossible to hide that if I win the election."

"You will win, and I will hand over the job to someone else soon. I just need to convince her to do it." Cee didn't know it yet, but this was definitely her new job. "But while we're discussing our extra-marital life...." I didn't know how to ask if this was a monogamous marriage or if we'd be like most marriages in politics and there would be standard affairs with other people.

"Listen, I know this happened faster than we intended. Settling down will be an adjustment."

This wasn't the answer I wanted from him. I wanted to know what the parameters would be. I wanted to know if he'd be sneaking off with other women for the duration of our marriage — however long that ended up being. We'd been discussing getting married our whole lives, but it wasn't until recently that I realized once that happened, maybe it was temporary. A few years? Forever? I had no idea what the plan was.

"Mason, are we getting divorced?"

"We aren't married."

"No, I mean… Is this a real 'to death do us part' thing, or some kind of holdover until, I don't know, until some other thing?"

"I have never contemplated we wouldn't be old and ugly together. It's just the plan, isn't it?"

I didn't know. Clearly, he didn't either.

I moved into the other room and spent the next forty-five minutes getting Wyatt ready for bed. Mason was surprisingly good at helping Wyatt cover the bathroom floor with water during bath time, but Wyatt was *thrilled* to have someone who was such fun to play with. *Is this my future? Do I want this? Mason and I putting our kids to bed together?* We had always planned on kids, it was part of the expectations, but I had never really thought about what that meant.

I helped Wyatt into his pajamas and with brushing his teeth, and Mason took the honor of reading him a story. Once tucked in, Wyatt just came bouncing back out every three minutes for another hour. Mason and I took turns getting him back into bed until he finally crashed around nine.

I couldn't fathom the idea of potentially having children with Mason. I needed answers to questions I had never thought to ask. "I just need to know what the expectations are here," I asked.

"I'd like to get through the first year without scandal. Whatever that takes, that's what I expect. You'll be off on my father's campaign after that."

"So, then you start fucking around?"

"If that's what you want. Maybe by then we'll have become a real couple or something. Who knows?"

I didn't know what to say to that. He wasn't giving me any clear indication if that was what he wanted. A real relationship. Mason and I had dated in high school, but that ended ten years ago and we've never felt the need to pick it back up. I wasn't jealous of the women he fucked on the side and, until recently, he'd never acknowledged that I did so as well. We've operated as friends in the background despite the show we put on for the public.

We both sat on the couch discussing mundane work-related things for the next few hours until Cee came home from work. My father's paranoia about Cee's ability to ruin images must have rubbed off on Mason as he never really stayed in the same place she was. Even when there wouldn't be a chance of people seeing. We met Cee in the kitchen as Mason grabbed his keys from the counter, ready to head out. "Hey, Catherine, nice to see you."

"Oh, ah, hey. It's been a while. I didn't know you'd be here," she replied without making eye contact.

"I'm headed out. Elle, I'll see you at home," he said to me and then kissed my cheek. Cee gave me a sideways glance, wondering what the display of affection was all about, and Mason all but ran out of the house.

"What the fuck was that?" She asked as soon as the door closed.

"Mason being Mason."

"I meant the kiss, Elle. Were you not screwing some dude

named Silas all weekend? Are you fucking Mason now, too? How am I the wild one?"

"Exhibit A would be the child sleeping in the other room. Exhibit B is that I'm not sleeping with Mason. Everything there is quite platonic. Just like a married couple."

"Yeah. I don't understand you two."

She asked questions about Silas, and I used the opportunity to lay the groundwork for convincing her to take over for me with the band. The Handheld Ninjas were blowing up much faster than expected and needed more help than I had time to provide.

"So, I just arrange things from here?" She asked, intrigued. The server life wasn't one she wanted to live forever.

"Mostly, yes. They just need someone to keep up with their real lives when they are on tour. Tell them where they are, where they need to be. Connor is the only one who requires assisting when they aren't touring. There may be some short trips here and there, but we'll figure those out as we go."

"And do I get to bang the hot manager?" She waggled her eyebrows at me teasingly.

"I think Elijah would be a bit upset. Also, it won't be Silas for much longer; he's just filling in, so if he was your incentive, you may want to reconsider."

Ten

Things escalated on the home front the next day when someone (obviously my father) let it slip at an event that Mason and I were getting married in the fall. Imagine our surprise while at a formal dinner honoring the retiring senator the focus suddenly became us. We were just sitting at our table chatting with some colleagues and noticed a shift. My father laughed jovially across the room and everyone looked over at us.

Mason excused us from our table to work the room. As any doting fiancé would, he took my hand in his to escort me toward a state representative, Camila Rodrigues, and her husband Joe. "Mason and Eleanor, how lovely to see you," Camila greeted Mason with a handshake and me with a hug.

"Hi, Camila, it's so nice to see you," I responded. I really liked Camila; she was one of the more *real* politicians in this room.

"I hear you two are making it official soon."

Thanks, Dad. "Yes, this fall," I responded with what I hoped was the appropriate amount of excitement.

"Finally got her to nail down the day," Mason added jovially, pulling me closer to him and kissing my forehead.

"Well, it hasn't been easy, what with coordinating with Secret

Service so that Mason's father can attend, but I'm still trying to get us married before the election so I don't have to spend my honeymoon in D.C." We all laughed the way you are supposed to when making light conversation. A forced "hahaha" followed by an obligatory smile with too much teeth. *This is such bullshit.*

Repeat this encounter at least fifty times over the next two hours.

I had been attending these events and playing this role for years. It was always a carefully orchestrated dance, but I had never been so internally annoyed at the whole charade as I was as we ensured that we spoke with just about everyone in the room. I felt the mask of Eleanor weighing heavy in my brain.

I spent my whole life carefully following The Plan. We intimately tied my career to Mason's from what seemed like birth. I worked my ass off to earn my doctorate in political science, and to make the connections required for a successful career in politics.

And we were so close to hitting our stride. But it felt like it was crushing my soul tonight. The meaningless chatter, the fake smiles, and the posturing was making me feel trapped.

The news of our wedding became the topic of discussion as we made our rounds and resulted in quite a few pictures of us gracing the news for the next few days. While I was happy to have the wheelchair picture fall down the list of recent photos, the announcement didn't thrill me.

Two days later, I got the first text from Silas that wasn't about work.

>   **Silas:** *Can we talk?*
>   **Me:** Yeah, I can call you in a couple of hours?

I was sitting at home working on band stuff, but really needed to get it done before I lost my momentum. Just seeing a text from him had me distracted enough. My mind flashed to us on the floor of the recording studio and I needed to fan my face to read his response.

> **Silas:** *I was thinking more like now. You alone?*
> **Me:** Yeah, I'm at home by myself. I'm just working on something.

There was a knock at the door. I looked at the camera app on my phone and saw Silas standing at my doorstep. I was equally excited and suspicious. I slipped into my 'Eleanor' mask and I got up from my desk to let him in. "What are you doing here?" It came out more aggressive than I intended.

"When you said your father wanted to be *like* a Kennedy, or a Davis, what did that mean?" He said as soon as I shut the door behind him. I didn't have a response. I was positive he must have finally Googled me and seen pictures of Mason and me together. "Because from what it looks like, *you are literally marrying a fucking Davis,* Len. Like the fucking Vice President's son, *that* Davis."

I didn't like how my worlds, and identities, were colliding. "Indeed, I am. Can I get you something to drink?"

"What the actual fuck? I assumed you were exaggerating a bit!" He was angry, but not yelling. I kind of wanted him to yell. And maybe have his way with me. *What the hell is wrong with me? Get your head out of the gutter, Eleanor. This guy isn't here to fuck you.*

"I'm sorry, did you come all the way here, from *California*, to give me shit about this? Because I was very clear that I had a very different life. A life that included a fiancé. And after our last conversation, I wasn't exactly hiding a political background. I didn't say it word for word, but I hardly lied and you didn't ask."

"I don't know that 'clear' is how I'd describe it since you left out every detail and I literally had to fuck you before you'd even give me your real first name. You left out some pretty big pieces. Like you are *Doctor* Eleanor *Roberts*, not Fuller, and that you are literally engaged to *the* Mason Davis."

"Does any of that information really change anything, Silas? My PhD in political science is hardly worth mentioning when it isn't at all relevant to touring with a band. And does it really matter that my father is so weird that he intends to marry off his eldest child to a wealthy politician for political favor? Because it's not something I wanted to talk about, Silas. This is my world, and I wanted to escape it for a bit. In this world, they cultivate female children to be the perfect wives for high-profile men. I wanted to have a somewhat normal, low-key escape from my soul-crushing reality. I intended nothing else."

"Soul-crushing?" he asked incredulously. Honestly, the phrase surprised me when I said it, but was that how I felt? He pulled up a picture from the dinner where my father announced our wedding plans on his phone. "Fooled me. Because you look every part the doting wife-to-be who loves her future husband right here."

He wasn't wrong. The photo showed Mason in his tux and me in an emerald green evening gown. Mason had me tucked closely into his side and it appeared he was kissing the top of my head, but I knew for a fact that wasn't the case. The photo was taken at the moment he was covertly assuring me we'd get out of there as soon as possible. Though, there had been a kiss or two to the temple that evening, so I suppose the exact moment of the picture was subjective.

I looked at the photo, trying to see it from his point of view. Our practiced smiles and masks of happiness glimmering. "We put on a good show. We've been doing it our whole lives. This is who I am, Silas. This is why I didn't give details. Because the public evidence paints a very clear picture of the lives we've worked very hard to convince people we have. I don't know what else to tell you."

I turned and walked toward my kitchen. I needed tea. Well, I needed something with alcohol, but I still had a long day ahead of me and the tea was my version of meditation. I needed to calm down. I did not expect to see Silas standing in my house, or for him to be so obviously angry. He followed behind silently and watched as I quietly put water on for tea. "I'm having tea. Would you like some tea, Silas?" I said, forcing myself to even out my voice.

"No, I don't want tea, Len." He stared at me as if I was an alien. "You are like a fucking Stepford wife. Jesus." He ran a hand through his hair. I desperately wanted to kiss him. I wanted his hands all over me. *Super inappropriate right now.* I just stared at his handsome face and, for the first time I could remember, I wished I had a normal life. I had long since been made aware (mostly from Mish) that the expected trajectory of my life wasn't what most women my age had in mind, but it wasn't until this moment that it felt like I was losing anything. He took a deep breath and more calmly said, "So when you were talking about Uncle Teddy, did you mean, like Ted Kennedy?"

"When did I do that?" I asked, confused.

"When we were on the plane. You were mumbling something about not being what Uncle Teddy had in mind when he said you'd do great things."

"Then yes, the same guy. I'm sure you can find photos of Mason and me together at his funeral. The Davis, Roberts, and Kennedy families are all good friends. There are photos of Mason and me together all over the internet. I'm the daughter of the governor and he's a damn Davis who is currently running for United States Senate. People have been taking our pictures since we were born, Silas." I dipped my tea bag into the mug of hot water.

"Oh, I've seen," he practically seethed. "There are entire corners of the internet dedicated to the love story of Mason Edward Davis and Eleanor Myra Roberts. Pictures of you both

being baptized on the same day. First birthday. Graduations, prom. Oh look, at his boot camp graduation you're kissing. And my personal favorite, your engagement photos; from Valentine's Day when he proposed," Silas made a gagging motion, "and then the official announcement just before our flight to Florida. I've gotta say, it doesn't look fake to me, Len."

"Then I've done my job, haven't I? It's just that, a job. People call me Eleanor or Elle. Len doesn't exist in this world. This is me, Silas. I have my hair and makeup done and I'm dressed for work even though I haven't left the house today." I gestured wildly at my outfit in front of him. "Ironically, that is in case someone shows up unexpectedly and, would you look at that, I have an unexpected and uninvited visitor. In my reality, I can't let anyone catch me looking anything less than perfect." I took a deep breath and tried to resume a calm demeanor. "I know you said you don't want to share, but I warned you that having me all to yourself wasn't a possibility."

He just stood there and stared as if he was trying to find Len under the Eleanor character in front of him. *Is Eleanor just a character, or is Len?* To be honest, it was working. The longer he stared, the less I wanted to play the part of Eleanor and the more I wanted to strip our clothes off and fuck him right in my dining room.

"I know I should walk away immediately." He stepped right up close to me. "But I really just want to mess up that perfect hair and makeup." He let his fingers play with the hair on my shoulder. "What if I strip off those clothes right here? Would you be too much of a lady to let me fuck you on that table?" His voice was low, his eyes staring deep into mine.

Well, we were definitely on the same page there. I squeezed my legs together tighter. "We're alone here, Silas. We can do whatever the fuck we want to do. I'm not ready to stop whatever this is, but that's up to you at this point." I rested my hand on his chest, no longer capable of keeping it to myself. "I can't give you anything other than casual. I need you to tell me you understand."

He kissed the top of my head. "Why do you smell so fucking good?"

I resisted the urge to melt into him.

"Silas, tell me you understand that this won't ever be more. I can't offer anything but a casual fuck."

He cupped my face in his hands, his thumbs gently brushing against my cheeks. "Why can't I stop touching you?"

I moaned softly at the contact, but tried to focus. "You don't get to be angry when I live my life exactly the way I told you I would."

He leaned down to brush a kiss to my mouth. "Why do I lose all self-control around you?" he asked against my lips, continuing to ignore everything I'm saying to him. Anger, frustration, and confusion drove his mouth as he held my head in his hands and kissed me deeper. I slid my hands under his shirt and started inching it toward his head while he moved his hands back to tangle his fingers through my hair. He removed them for a second to pull his shirt off, then mine, before returning his lips and hands to their previous vocation. I let out another involuntary moan. Never in my life had I been this incapable of keeping my damn clothes on or my hands to myself.

I closed my eyes and felt his mouth travel down my jaw, stopping in the crook of my neck — a spot that always caused me to tingle all over. I moved my hands to unbutton his jeans, and he looked down to unbutton my pants. He grabbed my left hand and put his fingers around my engagement ring. "This has to come off too, Eleanor." I nodded, and he slipped it off and put it down on the table behind me. The moment we were both finally naked, he lifted me onto the table.

"Oh, you were serious about the table thing, huh?" I asked, surprised.

"Quite." His hand made its way up my inner thigh and my whole body shivered. I took his hard cock in my hand and he moaned. "Jesus. What am I gonna do with you?"

I smiled wickedly, no longer worried about the complications of this arrangement. "You're gonna fuck me on this table."

"Am I now? Is that what you want?" He traced a finger lightly over my folds. "Tell me that's what you want." The request was far more loaded than sex on the table and I didn't have it in me to care at that point. My heart was racing, and my body consumed with desire.

"Silas, I'm begging you to hurry up and fuck me on this table." He slipped two fingers inside me, causing a hitch in my breath. He used his other hand to lower my back onto the table and then ran it down my chest, stopping to circle each nipple with his thumb.

The way he looked at me with such desire lit me up inside, made me feel sexy in a way I'd never experienced. He kissed the top of my knee and then lifted my leg over his shoulder, his body between my legs. He removed his fingers and teased his cock around my entrance. "I swear to all the gods if you don't use that cock of yours to fuck me stupid in the next second, I will never forgive you." He grinned, satisfied that he was in control of the situation, and then pushed inside me hard. "Yes. Fuck, yes."

"This, Duchess, is not what I came here for, but holy shit, is it exactly what I needed." He pushed in and out slowly, using a hand to run his fingers up and down the leg resting on his chest slowly before nipping my calf. I caught my breath and laid back to enjoy the feeling of him inside me, our eyes meeting. "There's that fucking irresistible temptress I can't get enough of."

"It would be a hell of a lot of fun for you to try." With every move he made, I was losing all control. I wanted to fuck this guy forever, and that was a problem. I needed to remember this was a short-term thing, but in that moment, all I wanted to do was get lost in the feeling of him inside me.

Growing impatient, I wrapped my other leg around his back and pulled him in closer with it, prompting him to fuck me harder. He pulled the leg I had around him up onto his chest, making another string of expletives and some incoherent words pour out of both of us.

He slowed and rubbed his thumb in circles over my clit. "You want to come, Gorgeous?"

"Yes," I begged. I felt my orgasm start in my toes and take hold of my whole body. "Damn Silas," I panted as pleasure came over me in almost violent waves. As I lingered in the afterglow, he picked up his pace, chasing his own. He came with a groan a few seconds later, my name on his lips. *Why is it so much hotter when he calls me Lenny?*

I slid my legs off of his chest, one on each side of his body so I could sit up. He pulled my ass to the edge of the table and kissed me like it was his only job. That's when I heard it: a cough from the other room.

"The fuck?" I whispered. I hopped off the table, which was not where it was a short time ago, and peeked around the corner into the other room. "Mason, what the fuck?!" I screamed when I saw him sitting on the couch.

I saw Silas quickly pull his pants back on out of the corner of my eye as Mason explained, "I, yeah. I'll give you a minute to, uh, put something on." I turned and Silas was standing behind me, holding my clothes.

I yanked on my pants. "Mason, why are you here?" I asked, still only half-dressed. Silas was just looking from Mason to me and back like he couldn't believe what was happening.

"Why is *he* here?" Mason pointed his chin toward Silas. This caused Silas to step in front of me while I finished putting my clothes on. "She's my fiancée, man. I've seen her naked."

I saw Silas ball his hand into a fist and I moved between the two men. "There's no need to be an ass, Mason."

"How am I the one being an ass? I just came home to this guy fucking my wife on the damn table."

"He lives here?!" Silas piped in, grabbing my hand.

"No. He doesn't. Nor am I his wife." I shot a death glare at

Mason. Both men stared each other down with clenched jaws.

"*Yet.*" Mason qualified. "You can't be here, Silas. This house is off-limits."

I didn't want to agree with him because I knew it was going to piss Silas off. I turned to face him, anyway. He slid his hands around my waist. "I'm sorry, but he's right. I can't risk having someone see you here this close to the election and wedding." I could see anger fill his eyes. "You've got to go. I'll call you later."

"Yeah, sure," he agreed. Without taking his eyes off Mason, he leaned in to place an angry, panty-melting kiss on my lips. When he lifted his head back up, he said to Mason, "You may see her naked, but I'm the one making her come so hard she didn't even notice you walked in, asshole." With that, he took my hand and gently kissed the inside of my wrist.

I could tell he was livid at the idea that Mason was winning this war, but not about to let Mason see he was at all deterred. I walked him to the door and as he walked outside, he turned and said, "This conversation isn't over, but I have to head out tonight." I just nodded.

As I was shutting the door, Mason came up behind me, so I spun to face him. "Allow me to ask again, Mason. What. The. Fuck."

"How was I supposed to know you moved on from sex in a bed, Elle? If I'd known screwing on the table was your thing, we would've done it years ago, but as your boy toy pointed out, we don't fuck on the table."

"No. No, we do not. But if I walked in on you fucking someone, I would have *left the fucking house*! Why the hell did you stay in the next room? What is wrong with you? How long were you there?"

"Right around the time you told him to fuck you on the table. Which we totally have to burn now, by the way." He looked at the table with disgust.

"It's not your table. This is not your house." I was so angry with him I was vibrating. "We have had an understanding since I went to college that we don't acknowledge each other's sex lives and we certainly don't hang out in the next room while the other is having sex with someone else."

"And that understanding was also that we don't bring this shit home, Elle."

I took a deep breath because I had to acknowledge that he was right on that point. I would've flipped out if he had brought someone to his house. "I apologize for that. He just showed up. I don't even know how he knows where I live. It pissed him off because he found out who we both are. It wasn't really supposed to play out that way."

"Can we trust he isn't going screaming to a tabloid?"

"Oh, for fuck's sake, Mason, he won't tell anyone about our fucked-up situation. I wouldn't have let him get this…" I searched for the correct word, "*close* if I thought that was the case."

"Did you not tell him he was a casual fling?"

"Of course I did. He ignored that part, I guess. He knew I was engaged and until the day he met you in the airport, he did not know to whom I was engaged. I was just another normal woman that no one knew."

"He doesn't see this as casual, Elle," he pointed out, softer. "I know we've kind of left the topic of extra-marital relationships open for future discussion, but by relationship, I was thinking more like *actual* casual. That guy wants way more than that."

I didn't respond. He was right, and it was a problem. It was also a problem that seeing him walk out the door a few minutes before caused my stomach to flip. I didn't do love, but clearly, Silas was more than a casual fling and that was not allowed.

Silas: *She's So Mean.*
Me: Matchbox Twenty.
Silas: *I should've known you'd get that one in seconds.*

Me: Believe it or not, you are not the first person to quote "She's So Mean" to me via text. But I know, and I'm sorry. I tried to tell you that my life is complicated.

Me: I'm also sorry that Mason is a psycho.

Silas: He's just protecting what is his.

Me: Again, I'm not property. But we've intimately tied together our reputations and my actions can have very real implications for his life and career.

Silas: Just how intimate? He sees you naked? I thought this was a very platonic thing.

Me: He platonically sees me naked. We dated for real years ago. Every once in a while, we get shitfaced at some kind of event and end up having very... unexceptional sex. But it's been at least a year since the last time that happened.

Silas: Right. Got it. So what's in it for him?

Me: Marriage?

Silas: Yeah. Why does a guy agree to get married to someone who isn't his choice? I can only assume that there isn't some million-dollar dowry involved.

Me: No dowry, no. It's not quite that Victorian.

Silas: He's in love with you then.

Me: I told you, Silas, it's not like that. It's just how people do things in my social circles.

Silas: No, Len. It's the only reason he'd go along with this.

Me: Does it matter?

Silas: Do you love him?

Me: I told you I don't know how to do that. It's all bullshit. If it helps, there's no lust there at all. He's been in my life since he was born. Yes, we have had sex. We tried dating years ago, and it didn't work out. It didn't really change the expected outcome.

Me: Our arrangement is for career purposes. That's it.

Silas: *Spell it out for me, because I don't see how that works.*

Me: He's young. In order to appeal to voters, he needs to give the air of stability. Being married gives him a leg up on that. Being married to a woman who knows how to behave in his social circles is crucial. For me, these connections mean amazing opportunities in my field. I worked on the last Presidential campaign and they have asked me to do so again next election cycle. The reality is, even though we'll be married, Mason and I will rarely be in the same city at the same time for the next thirty years. It's convenient. That's all. But it's also the reason I'll never be able to give you more.

Silas: *Sorry. Flight is taking off. Gotta turn off the cell service. I'll call tomorrow.*

Two days later:

Me: "Be Careful What You Ask For" – Everclear.

Eleven

Silas didn't call after his flight. Nor did he text or respond to emails. He ghosted me, which was an impressive move since we worked for the same band. I resigned this to be the end of whatever it was we had been doing, which was for the best, really. It was not fair to drag him into the madness that was my life.

Mason and I didn't speak for a week after the incident with the table. Eventually he had to speak to me because we not only worked together, we were supposed to be getting married in three and a half months. The show must go on, after all. That said, we did not speak of the incident again and we were only putting on that show when we had to.

> ***Mish:*** *So I know you said things got weird with Silas when Mason decided to lay his claim to you, but I'm surprised you aren't here.*
> **Me:** Why would I be there? Is "there" CA?
> ***Mish:*** *Yes. Because his fucking brother died, and I thought that would kind of transcend any awkwardness.*

I clicked Mish's name to call her, but she didn't pick up. She responded via text.

> ***Mish:*** *We are literally at the funeral.*
> **Me:** Whose brother died? Silas's?
> ***Mish:*** *Yes. How did you not know this?*
> **Me:** How would I know it? Last I talked to Silas, he was on a plane.
> ***Mish:*** *That must have been when he was bringing Kyle back from rehab in MA to a halfway house nearer to his family. Clearly things didn't go well because he OD'd a couple of days ago.*

Holy shit.

> **Me:** I'll be there as soon as I can.

I called Megan and asked her to arrange for me to be on the first chartered flight humanly possible to Los Angeles. She didn't ask questions, both because she didn't want the burden and because she was a damn professional, but did note that I had some things that I absolutely had to attend that Friday and Saturday. It was Tuesday, which gave me a small amount of wiggle room. I asked her to get me a return flight for Thursday night and text me all the details.

While I gathered some clothes and necessities, I worked through the information in my head. I vaguely remembered Kyle from the times I saw him with the other band. I had forgotten that he was Silas's brother, but that wasn't shocking because while Silas was constantly grilling me for details about my life, I really knew little about his. It was a defense mechanism. I didn't want to get close to anyone, especially not the incredibly attractive guy I was supposed to work with but couldn't keep my hands off.

I made the connection that the first time I saw him on the

flight to Florida he said he had been here for "business". I now wondered if that business was Kyle. I took Silas's explanation that Kyle needed a vacation at face value but there were signs I'd missed along the way. Mish, who was close with Kyle, hadn't mentioned him in months. Silas's mood changed after speaking with Kyle, always privately.

Mason and I knew more than a handful of people we grew up with who had been trapped by addiction. Cee's boyfriend, Eli, was one of the ones who recovered and was living sober, but so many people never found their way out of that hole. My heart broke for Silas. Losing friends to this disease was hard, but it must be downright horrible to lose a sibling.

I arrived in Los Angeles that evening and took an Uber to the hotel where Connor and Mish were staying. Mish told me to just come straight there, since she wasn't sure what was happening with Silas and his family. I tried texting him twice with just quick messages. The last one was just, "I'll be there soon. I'm so sorry."

Unsurprisingly, he did not respond to any of them. I didn't even know if he had his phone on him, but we had said nothing to each other since the night he fucked me on my dining room table. I wasn't expecting a response, but the lack thereof was making me nervous. Mish had confirmed Kyle's death devastated him and noted that he had iced out everyone, not just me, but I was still on the fence whether my presence would help or hurt. The only reason any of them knew Kyle died is because Silas's older sister had texted Connor and let him know. Silas never said a word to anyone about it.

In my haste to make it to Los Angeles, I had traveled in full "Eleanor" gear: black dress pants and a red silk blouse with a black blazer adorned with gold buttons. I wore my typical neutral makeup and perfectly blown out hair. While I have accustomed

Mish to my everyday look, I noticed Matteo and Tom taking in this very different version of the person they thought they knew when I entered the hotel suite. Of course, they wore clothes much different from their usual tour attire, as they had attended the funeral earlier that day, but that was more expected than my business attire.

"Where is he now?" I asked anyone who would tell me.

"Home, I guess," replied Connor. I could see that he hadn't slept well in at least a few days, and that he was recently crying. Everyone in the room looked the same. Mish looked downright horrible and I felt like a bad friend leaving her to go see Silas when I knew how close she and Kyle were, but it just felt like he needed me more.

"Someone give me their keys and an address," I demanded, holding my hand out for a set of keys.

"Are you sure that's a good idea?" Mish asked quietly.

"Nope, not at all. Keys, please."

She pulled the keys to her rental car out of her purse and tossed them to me and told Connor to text me the address.

I gave a quick hug to everyone there and drove to Silas' apartment.

My whole body was shaking with nerves and probably a sign of dehydration mixed with hunger, but I had this deeply rooted need to make sure he was okay.

There was no way he was okay.

I arrived at his address and parked the car. Taking a deep breath, I walked up to the door and rang the bell. A woman about five or six years older than me answered the door. She had clearly been crying for quite a while.

"Um, hi. Is Silas here?" I asked awkwardly from the front step.

"You must be Eleanor. I recognize you from your photos." She attempted a welcoming smile. "I've heard a lot about you. I'm Silas' sister, Gia. Come on in." She waved me in the door.

"I'm so sorry for your loss, Gia," I said as I stepped into the entryway.

"Thank you. Don't take this the wrong way but, the way he was speaking of you made me think you wouldn't be here. But he's been fairly drunk for two days now, so he's at a point where making sense isn't really in the cards."

"Well, I just found out about Kyle this morning and he isn't the one who told me, so I'm not shocked you weren't expecting me. Where is he?"

She led me to the living room where Silas was sitting on the couch in most of a suit. The jacket was slung over the back of the couch and his tie undone. He sat with his elbows on his knees and a glass of something in one hand. He didn't look up when we walked in.

"Silas," Gia tried to get his attention, "there is someone here to see you."

"I've seen all the people today, Gia. I just want to wallow alone," he slurred back, still not looking up. Gia gave me a look that said, *see what I mean?*

"Silas." I said quietly. He still kept his gaze on the floor.

"Gia, is it Eleanor or Len?" he asked. Gia looked at me, confused.

I walked over and kneeled in front of him. "Whoever you need me to be today, I'll be." I took the glass from his hand and placed it on the table beside the couch. "You should've called, Silas. I would've been here."

"This? This is too scandalous for Eleanor and too real for Len. And I didn't have the energy to deal with either." It was a punch to the gut. I hated that he felt like that, but understood why. It's how I wanted him to see me. How I *needed* him to see me.

"I'm sorry. C'mon. Let's get you out of this suit."

He looked up at me. "You look like Eleanor, but she would

never try to get me naked."

"You should know by now that Eleanor is like that Usher song, both a lady in public, but also down to get naked."

He cracked a smile. "*Yeah*," he both agreed and guessed the name of the song. I stood and pulled him up to meet me there. He was a bit wobbly, but on his feet. "Are you real?"

"I really don't know the answer to that, Silas." The whole situation felt surreal. All I knew was I needed to be there. "Which way to your room?" Gia pointed in the correct direction and I led him to the bedroom. Once there, I sat him down on the bed and removed his shoes and socks, setting them beside the bed. I slipped the tie off his shoulders and placed it on the bed beside him. "Are you hungry?" I asked him as I unbuttoned his shirt.

"No. You are beautiful." He pushed some of my hair behind my ear. The feeling of his fingers against my skin calmed me. I undid his belt and unbuttoned his pants, pulling the shirt out of them and off his shoulders. I thanked him and told him to lie back so I could pull the pants off. I took his clothes and set them on top of his dresser across the room.

"Come on, up onto the pillows and under the blankets. You need to rest." I held up the corner of the blankets for him to crawl in.

"I'm not tired," he protested. I disagreed with that and once again asked him to get into bed properly. "Only if you are, too," he mumbled.

"I will in a minute. I'm going to get you some water and Tylenol for the raging hangover you're going to have tomorrow." I draped the blankets on top of him and kissed his head. Seeing him so upset was breaking me in a way I didn't know was even possible. He had dark circles under his eyes from what I could only assume were days of no sleep mixed with all the emotions of losing his brother. I went out to the kitchen where Gia was putting some dishes in the dishwasher. I opened the fridge and grabbed two bottles of water, then reached into my purse for a bottle of

Tylenol. I noticed Gia had tears streaming down her face, so I went over and put my hand on her shoulder. "You should lie down, Gia. I'll get this in the morning." She wiped under one of her eyes and nodded.

"Thank you so much. I've been trying to get him to do that for hours." Thinking about it made her sob, so I pulled her into a hug, this woman I had just met, and let her cry on my shoulder for a few minutes. At some point, she noticed my blouse. "Oh, my gosh. I'm so sorry. I totally just ruined this."

"Gia, it's fine. Go lay down. Get some rest." She nodded again and retreated into what I assumed was a second bedroom. I returned to Silas, expecting him to be asleep, but he was lying exactly as I left him on his back, staring at the ceiling. "Here, drink this." I handed him the water. "These are Tylenol. You should take them."

He took them from my hand and sat up to swallow them with some water. "Please don't leave." I had no intention of leaving the apartment, but I had planned on sleeping on the couch.

"I'll be right in the living room."

"Len. Please." He sounded defeated and exhausted. "I'm so tired. Can you just come lay with me so I can sleep? I've wanted to just lay with you for so long, but there's never really been an opportunity."

I didn't have the resolve to say no, so I crawled into the bed, fully clothed, and laid next to him. "Come here," I said, pulling his head onto my chest.

He did as I asked and I pulled the blankets up around us and ran my hands through his hair.

"A week ago he was fine, Len. Better than I've seen him in so long. The whole flight home, he wanted details about you because he thought you were so hot. And now he's just...gone."

I could feel tears falling from his eyes to my shirt. There weren't any words that would make it better, so I just let him say whatever he needed to say and was silent when he didn't know what to say.

"I told him you were already marrying that douchebag politician. He told me I should fight for you anyway. He talked about hanging out with you this summer with the guys. We were going to go to Europe in the fall. Why the fuck did he do it? He knew. He knew it would kill him and he did it anyway. It was too little too late and I feel like it's all my fault. I've seen this coming for years. I should've been more insistent. How could he fucking do this?"

It was all things I'd heard before, so many times from the people left behind. Family and friends of addicts who tried desperately to save their loved ones but in the end weren't able to keep them alive. Silas was speaking of the overdose in a way that seemed to imply Kyle had done this on purpose, but was that true? "Shh. Go to sleep now." I kissed the top of his head, tears threatening the backs of my eyes. "We can talk tomorrow." Within a few minutes, he fell asleep, and I fished my cell phone from my pocket to text Mish and let her know I would call in the morning. There were texts from Mason, but I didn't bother to open them. Whatever he wanted wasn't really important.

The next morning, I awoke before Silas. I slid out of bed and made my way to the kitchen where Gia was sitting at the table with coffee. "Morning," I said.

Gia went to stand. "Can I get you some coffee?" She asked. I motioned for her to sit.

"Just point me to the mugs and I'll get it."

She pointed to a cabinet in the corner and I made myself a cup of coffee and sat with her at the table. I was still in my clothes from the day before, and I never had the chance to wash my face before we went to bed. I cringed at the thought of how I must look and then realized that Gia likely didn't give a fuck at all. Her brother had just died.

"So, I have to head back down to San Diego today. My husband needs to go back to work and my kids aren't quite ready to return to school. Will you be here? I don't want to leave him alone."

"I have to leave tomorrow, but I agree. He shouldn't be alone."

"He can come stay with us then."

Silas came wandering out of his room. "Gia, who are you talking to? I had the weirdest dream." He stopped when he saw me at the table. "Len? I totally thought that was a dream."

"Hey, Silas. Gia and I were just talking about what your plans are for the next few days."

"Uh, I don't have any. Why?"

"Maybe you should come home with me," I said, surprising all three of us.

"I am uninvited to your house. Permanently."

"Well, technically yes, so I have a backup plan. You can stay in exile with my sister Catherine." Cee didn't know this yet, but she wouldn't say no when I told her the situation. Gia glanced between us with a confused expression.

"There's an island of misfit toys where you send those who don't fit the narrative?" He snorted. That hit me harder than I would have liked, but I appreciated I had him back to being mad at me instead of devastated about Kyle. At least for a few minutes.

"The island is relatively uninhabited. There is one house with 3 occupants. Two males, one female. Full disclosure: one of those males is a preschooler who *thinks* he's grown."

Gia chuckled. "I have one of those, too, but the female version."

"Well, to be honest, he may be the most mature person in that house," I mused. "Certainly more so than his mother, anyway. Regardless, you can stay there out of Mason's sight."

"No, thanks. I'll stay here."

"Then you can come home with me," Gia stated, using a tone that made it clear these were his two choices.

"You know I am an adult, right, Gia? I don't need my big sister babysitting."

"Awesome. Then you'll go with Len. Let me know when you've

made it there safely." She put her coffee cup in the sink and left the room.

Without waiting for him to agree, I started planning for him to fly back east with me. Since we would get back late Thursday night, I threw caution to the wind and planned to have him stay at my place that night. With that in mind, I had to let Mason know what was happening and why.

Mason was reasonably understanding, especially considering I had up and left without giving him more than one word text responses for the last twenty-four hours. I arranged for Cee to pick Silas up at my place Friday afternoon, so if someone saw him, it was with her and not me. Generally, Cee didn't go to my place, but it had been a long time since she was really in the public eye and she was good at going undetected.

Silas continued to put up an argument for about an hour. He resigned himself to needing to get away when he saw something that triggered a memory of Kyle and punched a hole in the living room wall.

Connor and Mish popped by in Matteo's car to drop off my bag and take possession of the rental car. Silas didn't talk, and they didn't force any engagement. They left fairly quickly, followed by Gia.

Hours went by and Silas just sat on the couch, holding his injured hand. I gave him space and tried to get some things done on my laptop. I ordered takeout for dinner, and he ate it in silence. For some reason, the silence wasn't uncomfortable. He needed to work through things in his head without my interference, but I needed to know that he wasn't punching more holes into the walls.

After dinner, I suggested he take a shower, and he wandered off to do so. After about twenty minutes of hearing no water, I went to check on him. He was sitting on the side of the bed, holding a towel in his hand. "I punched a wall."

"Again?" I asked.

"I hit the same spot and it's bleeding again."

I hadn't realized it was bleeding earlier. I stooped down and held out my hand for his so I could look at his injury. Sure enough, he had cut open the side of his hand and a bruise was already forming across his knuckles. "Come on. We've got to clean this up, so it doesn't get infected." I led him into the bathroom and put his hand under the running water in the sink. I soaped it up and made sure it was clean before drying it gently with a paper towel. "You should put ice on this. Did you still want to take a shower?"

"Only if you're coming with me."

It wasn't what I expected him to say at all, but all things considered, I also needed a shower, so I agreed. I didn't have it in me to argue with him about it. What I didn't expect was that somewhere after getting in, he grabbed some soap in his hands and lathered them up. Instead of using it on himself, he ran his hands down my arms, back up and over my shoulder, then down my back.

The hot water sluiced down both of our bodies as he continued rubbing the soap all over me. Despite being insanely turned on, I tried to remain neutral. I grabbed the soap and started washing his body, noting the hard-on he had, but trying to focus on getting clean instead of getting dirty. It was at this point Silas slipped his uninjured hand between my legs and gently brushed his fingers along my center. He used his other hand to bring my face to his for a kiss.

"Mmm, Silas," I whispered, trying to gain control.

"I need this. I need you. I need to have control over something right now, and that's going to be making you come." He inserted two fingers and slid them in and out gently. I moaned and reached for his dick, stroking it to match the pace he was using. And then he banged his injured hand into the wall and winced.

"Let's move this to somewhere safer before you break that hand," I suggested. I turned the water off and had planned to dry off, but Silas pulled me right back to his room before I could even grab the towel. He laid in the bed and pulled me in with

him, getting the whole thing soaked, but I wouldn't notice or care about that for a while.

His uninjured hand went back to exploring my body while he kissed me urgently. I tried to reach out and touch him, and he took my hands over my head with his injured hand. "Don't struggle, Len. You'll injure my hand," he said with a mischievous smile. His free hand went back between my legs and he rubbed my clit with his thumb while sinking two fingers inside me. My hips rose off the bed and he smiled at the reaction. The tension of the last day eased, replaced with desire. He continued his ministrations until I came on his hand.

Before I had even caught my breath, he moved down the bed and positioned his face between my legs, licking me. My only thoughts were of the amazing feeling of his tongue moving in a slow, torturous way around my pussy. My hands curled into the sheets and I tingled from head to toe. "Please don't stop, Silas. I need you to make me come." He slipped two fingers inside me and gave my clit a teasing lick before sucking on it until I came a second time, writhing with the pleasure. As I caught my breath, his fingers danced between my legs. "Silas I can't. It's too much." I panted.

"I can't help it. You are so fucking sexy when you come. I just want to watch you do it all damn day."

"As excellent as that sounds, that's only going to lead to a UTI, so how about you let me return this favor?" I pulled him back up to the pillows. I kissed down his chest while stroking his length until my mouth could join my hands. His hands tangled in my hair and I nearly came unglued. I took him into my mouth as far as I could. His breath hitched, and I heard him say "holy shit" under his breath. Satisfied that this was going well, I began moving him in and out of my mouth, licking and sucking. His hands in my hair gently guided my head up and down his length. "I'm close. You have to stop," he said, tugging at my hair. I had completely planned on continuing until he finished, but he had other plans.

He sat up to pull my face back to his. "Control, Len. I need the control."

I nodded, understanding. He reached next to him and grabbed a condom from the nightstand, rolling it on. He pulled me under him and slammed hard inside. I gasped in pleasure at the sudden intrusion and he moaned. I wrapped my legs around his back, my fingers scraping down from his shoulder to his ass as he continued to fuck me hard. My orgasm built and I could feel myself clenching around his cock. "So fucking good," he groaned just before we both came.

As he was discarding the condom, I started thinking about the day in my kitchen. I was almost positive we hadn't used one, and I didn't notice until now. And the day in the storage closet we didn't either. I was on the pill and relatively certain pregnancy wouldn't be a concern, but never in a million years would I have ever considered sex without a condom, and I was pretty sure that ship had sailed with Silas.

He came back with water for both of us and a bag of chips. "I have a long-standing rule about eating in bed, but I am breaking that rule because I need you to rally for round two. I have you to myself all night and I don't plan on sleeping." He handed me the water, and I noticed his hand bleeding again.

"We really should wrap and ice that. You're making a fucking mess."

"We can wrap it, but the ice will impede my plans."

"Your plans can wait for twenty minutes."

He sighed and went back to the kitchen for some ice. He sat up on the bed next to me, holding it in his hand. "So, after our last chat, I definitely didn't see a time in which I'd have you in my apartment, much less my bed."

"Hell, a bed in general," I joked. "I'm sorry, Silas. I didn't even think before getting on the plane. Mish told me what happened and I just — got on the next flight. I only barely stopped at their hotel."

"If I didn't know better, I'd think you cared, Len."

I sighed. "Of course I care, Silas. But I feel like that only makes this more...."

"Fucked up? Because you're choosing him over me?"

I felt like he just stabbed me in the chest. "I don't get a choice."

He huffed. "Ignoring the fact you have a choice is making a choice. There's no gun to your head. You can just say no. But you won't because you are choosing him over me."

We sat in silence. After a few minutes, his hand reached for mine and he intertwined our fingers. "I'm sorry. It's been a tough week. I never would have asked you to come, but I'm glad you did. Come on, let me cuddle with you." He pulled us down under the covers and assumed the position of "big" spoon.

I hated how relaxed this made me feel. I've never been someone who cuddles. I don't like the invasion of space unless it's for sex, but here I was, wishing we never had to leave this bed. I reveled in the feeling of his warm chest against my back.

I woke up the next morning exactly where I fell asleep. I tried to slip out from under Silas' arm without waking him, but he hugged me tighter.

"Don't get up," he whispered in my ear. He moved his hand to my breast and started kneading it. His lips connected with the side of my neck, just below my ear, and a very contented sigh escaped my lips. I felt his hard cock rubbing against my ass.

"Fuck me, Silas," I whispered.

He wasted no time flipping me onto my stomach and pulling my ass back into his front. "I love it when you beg me, Duchess." He reached his hand in front to rub my clit a few times and then slipped his fingers in.

I squirmed back to rub my ass along his length. "Please. I need you inside me." He removed his fingers and replaced them with his cock, sliding in painfully slow. I groaned and pushed my ass back into him further to take him as deep as possible.

"Fuck," he rasped. I felt him move away and heard him open the drawer of the nightstand for a condom. He tore open the packet, rolled it on and slid back into me. "You are seriously killing me," he moaned as I pushed back again, rolling my hips. He grabbed my breast again and gave my nipple a pinch between his fingers. I gasped, goosebumps running down my body, and he started slamming into me harder. He would pepper kisses on my back and then fuck me hard again. The rhythm pushed me to the edge quickly. I reached down to circle my clit, and he grabbed me by my hips. "Come, Duchess," he commanded as he pulled my ass back onto him, hard.

I saw stars.

Waves of pleasure rocked through my body. He pumped into me, joined me, finding his own release.

We collapsed onto the bed, breathless.

"Good morning to you, too," I said with a satisfied smile.

"Can't say I've ever enjoyed waking up more." He sat up to get out of bed. "I don't know how you do it, but I lose every ounce of control when I'm with you." He went into the bathroom to deal with the condom, wash up, and brush his teeth. Coming back in, he brought me a towel, placed it on my stomach, and kissed my forehead. I felt like I was melting. "So much so, I nearly fucked up. I apologize for that."

"About that," I said. "Pretty sure we've forgotten a condom before."

"I don't think so." He looked up to the ceiling in thought.

"So the closet?"

"Definitely had a condom, and not surprised you don't remember. You were awake for *days*."

"Okay, cool. But um, my table?"

Shock hit his face as he realized I was right. "Oh fuck. Holy shit. You're right. That has never happened before.

I always remember."

"I mean, I'm clean. And on the pill, so we should be good on that end."

"Me too. Clean, not on the pill. Though if they worked that way, I would be. Christ, I'm rambling. I'm really so sorry." He ran his uninjured hand through his hair.

"Silas, it's fine. We're good."

"Why do I lose all ability to think around you, Duchess?" He ran his fingers down my bare shoulder.

"The feeling is mutual." And it terrified me. I've always been in control. The second this man was around, he was all I could think about.

Twelve

We grabbed something to eat and showered, which led to some really amazing shower sex, followed by more sex on his couch after lunch.

It was a fantastic day.

Sadly, the bubble popped when we had to put clothes on and head to the airport. I packed with Eleanor in mind, not knowing how close I would cut my return, so I donned a very modest, long-sleeved brown dress with white dots. It hit about the knee and flowed at the bottom. Since my hair was not tamed well enough to be worn down, I put it up in a twist with the very few bobby pins I found lingering around the bottom of my purse. We would arrive in Boston at about ten at night, so I wasn't terribly concerned about it, as there would be very few people around. I just couldn't handle a second airport scandal.

Silas eyed my outfit with a bit of noticeable disdain, but said nothing, knowing that I literally threw clothes in my bag and got to the airport with little thought. The flight home was quiet, and we arrived at my house shortly after eleven. Without even turning on the lights, we dropped our stuff at the door and went into the bedroom, as if the eight hours with clothes on were setting our bodies on fire.

We hopped into the shower together to get the air travel off of our skin, both of us soaping up each other thoroughly before I dropped to my knees under the water and took him into my mouth, licking and sucking until he came. There was a sense of... rightness. *There's a word for this. Not quite fate, but contentment mixed with the realization that this felt* right. He pulled me to my feet, taking me out of my contemplation. Stepping out of the shower, he wrapped me in a towel and then toweled himself off before doing the same for me.

We were tired from days of emotional overload, sex, and travel. I was overwhelmed with the need to comfort him. *This is new.* I had to head into the office the next morning, so we crawled under the sheets of my bed. I laid in the crook of his arm with my head on his chest while he played with my hair. To my surprise, he just unloaded. Quietly, he told me about his father dying about six or seven years ago. "Kyle always flirted with the line of recreational drug use and addiction, but once Dad died, he was high in some manner every time I saw him. Adderall to stay awake, opiates to fall asleep, repeat. Hanging out on the road managing Connor's band, with all the drugs and alcohol, wasn't helpful."

Silas' rage at Connor for supplying drugs to me suddenly made so much more sense. "So when they had that handful of Northeast shows, I came to stay at his house and talk to him about how concerned we were. It took a few months of being back and forth between here and California before he agreed to rehab. I offered to take his place with the band temporarily, though I really didn't think he would be returning; the environment was not what he needed. I was willing to say anything to get him help.

"I dropped him off two days before we flew to Florida together. That's why I was in town. Kyle had been living here since Connor started dating Mish. They shared a place in Hopkinton. Though, between touring and appearances, Connor was rarely there.

Uninvited

"Anyway, he came out of rehab clean and we agreed he'd go to a kind of halfway house between my house and my mom's so we could support him. The first week went really well, but then I noticed subtle signs of something brewing a couple of days before he died. I guess he scored some cheap heroin, and that was that. They found him in his room, already gone."

"I'm so sorry, Silas. I've lost friends to addiction. I can't imagine losing Cee."

"I haven't been taking it well."

"I think you're doing fine, all things considered."

I could hear a smile in his voice when he held up his injured hand and said, "I literally punched a hole in the wall. Pretty sure that's a sign of not handling it well."

I looked up to kiss him. "Sleep, Silas. You don't have to process it all at once. But thank you for telling me."

I left Silas sleeping in my bed around eight the next morning. It was a late start for me, but luckily Megan worked it out so that as long as I showed my face before ten, no one would care. I got ready, wearing my usual attire: a knee-length dress. It was off-white with a paisley-type print in bright blue with elbow-length sleeves. I added a complimentary bracelet and a strand of pearls. I was pulling on my nude heels when Silas wandered over.

"This," he said, pointing to my outfit, "does not fit with my version of you." I stood and gave him a quick kiss on the lips.

"Well, she's who I am most of the time. Behold, Eleanor in all her glory." I spun slowly for effect. "I'm headed to the office. Cee will come get you around noon. I have an event tonight which I'll try to leave as early as possible and then I'll head over, but it is a campaign thing and it will probably be late. I'm sorry I have to leave."

"It's fine," he said, though it didn't look like it was. "Am I going to run into Mason?"

"No. He's likely been at the office for quite a while at this point. He knows you are in town and has promised not to start any shit." "Promised" was probably too strong of a word here, but I was confident he was going to stay on his own side of the state.

I left and headed into Boston. Every time I made this commute, I remembered why I was moving out of my house once Mason and I married. Mason would be splitting time between D.C. and Boston and I really hated sitting in traffic. It was such a waste of time.

It was just before ten when I walked into the building, heading first to Mason's office. I dropped a coffee off on Megan's desk as a small thank you for helping me out (espresso was her love language) and was on my way to my office down the hall when I encountered Mason.

"We have the governor in five," he said as he walked by me without a glance.

The day was brutal. I bounced from one meeting to another regarding Mason's campaign and then had to get ready at his place for the fundraising dinner. I was tired. I was worried about Silas. I resented the need to wear a gown to this event when I wanted to wear leggings and a tee shirt. Keeping up the act was really draining me. I couldn't remember it being this *hard* to just move through my everyday tasks. I may be in a fake relationship but my job was always something I thought I genuinely enjoyed. Today it felt like an extension of my farce with Mason instead of my own identity.

I'm just overtired. It's been a crazy few days.

But I put on the gown. I did my hair. I did my makeup. I arrived at the venue on Mason's arm and smiled like everything was amazing. We played the part of a young couple in love and on our way to doing big things. I could tell it was bothering Mason as well. I knew he hated I was spending so much time with Silas, but I didn't actually care.

As I predicted, it was a late night. I didn't leave Boston until almost midnight, not arriving at Catherine's until after one. I let myself into the house and quietly went to the spare room Silas would be in. He was sitting on the bed, going through emails.

"Well, that's not what you left the house in," he said, looking at the gown.

"This here is peak Eleanor. True duchess regalia. I am, after all, the princess of Massachusetts," I joked as I kicked off my heels and sat on the edge of the bed.

"I hate it, take it off." A mischievous grin took over his face.

"Let's not wake my sister."

"Man, she is a trip."

"Isn't she, though?" I laughed. I could only imagine how his day went with her. She's a bit of a loose cannon and I know she would've been deep into making Silas forget why he was here. "Girl has no filter and gives zero fucks. She takes no shit and has no shame. I love her, but it's weird that we came from the same gene pool." I started pulling pins out of my updo.

"That's a solid nurture versus nature issue right there. And I have to say, Len exhibits those same characteristics. It's Eleanor who is straight laced."

I don't know when Silas referred to my double life as two different people as I do, but there was something about it I found comforting. Like he understood I had a "real" life and a "just for fun" life that was not at all the same.

"Maybe. But Cee will break your legs if you fuck with her and I'm relatively non-violent."

"She has that energy. Good to know she'd follow through. I will stay on her good side." He set his laptop on the nightstand. "Are you wearing that dress to bed or what?"

I was dead tired. I motioned for help with the zipper on the back of the gown and stood to let it pool at my feet. Any other day I would've put it back on a hanger destined for a dry cleaner, but today I stepped out of it and crawled between the sheets, leaving it in a heap on the floor.

Silas turned off the lamp beside the bed and pulled me close to him. I relaxed into his embrace and fell asleep.

If things weren't awkward enough making Silas stay with my sister, I had to have my wedding gown fitted Saturday morning, and then a variety of wedding-related things on the agenda. Meanwhile, Silas hung out with my nephew and my sister's best friend.

When I returned to Cee's house in the afternoon, Wyatt was literally running circles around Silas, babbling on about his latest obsession: trains. Eli watched from a distance, certainly counting down the minutes before my mother came to get Wyatt so he could go to work. Since my mother and I were coming from the same place, I knew it would only be a few minutes before she arrived.

"Wyatt. Hey, buddy!" I tried to divert the boisterous child's attention. When he didn't stop running, I positioned myself close enough to pick him up as he passed me. "Hey, Energizer Bunny, it's almost time for Nana to get here and you need to make sure you have your stuff together."

Of course, either Eli or Cee had packed the essentials for Wyatt, but he was currently going through a phase in which he also had to pack a bag to take for his sleepover with Nana. This bag contained mostly toys and sometimes a random item of clothing. I watched as Wyatt sped off to his room to stuff a bunch of trains into the bag, along with a lone shoe, his favorite stuffed lion, and what appeared to be two blocks. Three was clearly a magical age.

My mom arrived as Wyatt came out of his room, proudly wearing the backpack. "Great job, Wyatt!" I praised.

Mom opened the door and Wyatt shot off in her direction,

screaming, "Nana! Guess what?! My new fwend Siwis likes twains too!" My mother looked over at Eli and me for help.

"Mom, meet Wyatt's new friend Silas. He's visiting from out of town." Silas shook my mother's hand.

"Nice to meet you, Silas. It's good to know you like trains. It's basically a requirement around here," my mother laughed while Wyatt continued to bounce around between us. There was a minute or two of small talk before my mother and Wyatt left, with Eli following suit almost immediately after.

"Whoa, that kid has energy," Silas commented once everyone left.

"He does. He exhausts me." I started picking up random toys left around. "I don't think I have the stamina to live with a toddler. They completely lack an 'off' button."

"Hey, you be nice talking about my new 'fwend', Auntie Elle." We both fell onto the couch with exhaustion. "So Eli is not his dad?"

"No. Though he loves Wyatt like a son, and clearly my sister has him wrapped around her finger. Alas, the identity of Wyatt's father remains a secret."

"Does Mason have a brother?"

"Weird question, but yes. His name is Rob."

"I only mention it because Wyatt looks so much like Mason. Maybe it's Rob?"

I thought about this for a few minutes. I'd never made the connection, but Wyatt *did* look just like Mason. "Maybe? Rob is gay, but he only came out about two years ago. Maybe he experimented with Cee? I don't know. But now that you mention it, he looks like a Davis. But damn, that family is large, so I suppose there are a lot of options there." We were quiet a few minutes before I ran my hand up his thigh. Decent house guests would have at least moved to the bedroom, but we weren't feeling decent.

Late that night, Cee and Eli came home from work and we hung out with them for a bit before going to bed.

"So," Eli asked, "how did you meet?"

"You've heard I have an alter ego who is currently working with Mish's boyfriend's band?" I asked. He nodded. "Silas is their manager. We were on the same flight to Florida a few months ago. So about two hours after we met and maybe fifty words spoken to each other, this guy kisses me on an airplane."

Silas gave me a confused look. "Well, that happened, but it isn't when we first met. I was feeling bold, but not *that* bold."

"Meeting over email doesn't count," I laughed.

"No, really. We met in January. You made out with my brother."

Cee and Eli were now the ones laughing.

"Silas, I've never made out with your brother, and I definitely did not know who you were when I got on that plane."

"The night the band played in Boston? I was staying with Kyle. I *literally* brought you drinks half the night."

"That was you? I don't remember. Those drinks seemed to just magically appear."

"No, I brought them. And after the show, in all your drunken glory, you made out with Kyle."

"I definitely did no such thing."

"Oh, but you did, because I had to fork over twenty dollars to Sergio when it happened."

I had no recollection of these alleged events. "And then you decided to kiss me when you saw me because?"

"I'm crazy sometimes. And I was pretty sure you had been flirting with me via email, text, and phone calls for weeks. I was slightly concerned you thought I was him, but quickly dismissed that."

"Isn't there some kind of 'bros before hoes' protocol you are breaking here?"

Silas laughed. "You literally don't remember kissing him at all."

"You didn't know that until just now!" I practically yelled.

"Well, I probably overstated the situation. It was a very short, very chaste kiss. And to be fair, you were like the third person he kissed that night. After a few days of Adderall he'd get very affectionate. We literally had him in time out half the night. So while he remembered you being there, I'm not sure he remembered the details of kissing you."

"So I'm fairly forgettable then?" I teased, remembering just how much I couldn't remember from my own experience with stimulants. It was a blur. Makes sense Kyle may not have remembered the kiss that I, myself, didn't remember.

"No way. One reason he was considering *not* going to rehab was because you'd be on the next trip and you were, and I quote, 'fucking hot'." He smiled at the memory. "As his brother, it was my duty to inform him I had been laying the groundwork already to make my move. He called me an asshole, but made me promise to tell him the details."

"And did you?"

Silas feigned shock. "Kiss and tell? Why I would never!"

"So that's a yes."

"Absolutely it is." He kissed my cheek. "Rubbing it in his face was my brotherly duty," he said proudly.

Thirteen

After a few days of crashing at my sister's place, Silas decided he needed to go back to Kyle's condo. "He made me promise to keep this place for him and not let Connor break the lease while he was in rehab. For some reason he preferred it here to his house in L.A.. I want to clear out Kyle's stuff so Connor doesn't have to worry about it," Silas explained as we walked into the house.

"Silas, you don't have to do this right away. Give yourself some time to heal."

"I need to do this to move on, Lenny." He kissed the top of my head and put his bag down in the living room, looking around.

I could tell it was a former bachelor pad that was sometimes inhabited by a female. I noticed several pairs of Mish's shoes by the door and there were lavender scented candles on various flat surfaces. Lavender was her favorite scent. "Well then, I guess I'll assist."

Armed with iced coffee and a Bluetooth speaker, we went into Kyle's bedroom. It was relatively neat. The bed was made up with a navy comforter and a couple of pillows. He had a desk in the room with a notebook sitting on top and a bookcase filled with books. On top of the bookcase were several framed photos. I picked up one that had Silas, Gia, and Kyle on it. Silas was in a cap and gown and all three smiled triumphantly.

"What did you major in?" I asked Silas, holding up the picture.

"Business. Accounting. I'm a nerd."

"Lucky for you, I find nerds irresistible." I slapped his ass to keep the mood light. "So, I assume we're donating things like clothes?"

Silas nodded. "There's a hoodie in here somewhere that I'm supposed to get for Gia. But we can donate the rest of it."

"Go grab some bags and we will start there." Silas left the room briefly to retrieve some garbage bags from the kitchen. I started emptying the dresser and Silas took the closet. Starting at the bottom, I encountered a drawer filled with several pairs of jeans. I pulled them all out and placed them in the bag. The next drawer up held sweatpants and gym shorts, and they followed suit.

Before I could move to the next one, I heard Silas angrily mutter, "That fucking idiot."

I got up to see what was going on. "What's wrong?"

He held up a baggie.

"Is that…?" I didn't want to say it out loud.

"Fucking meth. Why, yes, it is. I don't even know what to do with this."

"Maybe Connor knows someone who wants it?" I shrugged my shoulders.

"I'm not contributing to the addiction of another person. But I know you aren't supposed to flush it because it gets into the water. If we toss it in the trash, we will probably get arrested. Leaving it here seems careless." He was getting agitated.

"Maybe we should take a walk," I suggested, trying to redirect the situation.

"Let's just finish with the clothes. We can drop them off and check it off the list."

I took the baggie and put it on the desk so Silas could finish what he was doing. "Go back and check the pockets just in case. I found that in a shoe, but who knows what else is hiding in this place." I pulled the clothes I had put into the bag back out to check the pockets. As much as I hoped we wouldn't encounter any more drugs, we found a few loose Adderall in the pockets of other clothes. We piled them on the desk next to each other and just kept moving until all the clothes, minus the hoodie for Gia, were in bags for donation.

We loaded the bags into my car to drive them to the local shelter donation bin. When we pulled back into the driveway, he quietly said, "We came back here before heading to California. I should've torn through his room while he was in rehab. He must have grabbed the heroin when he was here."

"How would he have gotten that past TSA? It's not likely. He probably got it in California. Either way, this is not your fault. If he wanted it, no matter where he was, he would've found a way."

"Fucking bastard. I'm so fucking mad at him." He slammed his hand on the dash.

"He was sick, Silas. I'm so sorry he's gone, but you did everything you could." I hopped out of the car and met him on the passenger side, kneeling to look him in the eye. "It really sucks. And I don't know how to help you, and I know there's nothing I can say to make it go away." A tear fell from one of his eyes. It gutted me to see him this way. "Do you want to go in or leave? We can stay somewhere else. Just tell me what you want."

"Just stay with me," he said, staring at the roof of the car. "I just need a minute." He looked at me crouched beside the car. "Come here." He pulled me into the car and across his lap. I curled into his chest, legs dangling out of the car in the breeze while he held me close. "This is the only thing that makes it a little better. I know that's not what is supposed to happen with us, but I just need you to be with me right now. Just for a little while."

I knew him needing me this way was dangerously close to being too close, but I was worried about him being alone here.

Alone in general. I didn't think he was suicidal, but he definitely wouldn't be acting like a rational human for a while. No one in these circumstances would. The real problem was, I couldn't tear myself away if I had to at this point. "Yeah. I'm here." I kissed his cheek and got lost in his gaze.

This was such a bad idea.

After a few more minutes of sitting in the car, we moved back into the house. I made him sit on the couch while I got us both some water. "There are a few things in there I need to find. Some things my mom wanted, a few I swore I'd destroy in the event this ever happened," he said.

"Do you want me to find them? Just tell me what I'm looking for and I can do it."

He shook his head. "We can look together. Let's just hope we don't find any more surprises. I have to warn you though, the evidence I'm here to destroy is sex-related."

"Isn't it always? Did you erase evidence from his phone?"

"Deleted the browser histories from his laptop and all the inappropriate things off his phone. Motherfucker had a lot of different tits in his photo app. Luckily, I got to it before my mother. Or my sister. There are some things sisters and mothers shouldn't have to see, you know?"

"Agreed."

"We should eat dinner before going back in there," I added. We ordered food from an Italian place a couple blocks away. While we waited for it to be delivered, Silas insisted on looking for the evidence needing destruction. There was a stash under the bed (how predictable) which I was not allowed to see. He placed it directly into a garbage bag. He then went back into the closet where he found a bag with something else unknown inside; that also went right into the bag.

He sat down at the desk next. Without opening the notebook, he picked it up and asked me to put it in his bag. "I'm going to need some boxes, I guess. There's some stuff here I should probably look through before getting rid of it, but I'd rather do it at home."

"We can put it in a stack in the corner and grab boxes tomorrow when we know what we need."

He handed me a few more notebooks, and I put them in a pile. I wasn't sure what made these different from the one he put in his bag, but I also wasn't inclined to ask.

He picked up the framed photos and put them in the pile and then went to the bookcase in search of some very specific titles. The doorbell rang with our food and we went out to eat it on the couch. I turned on *New Girl*, my go-to show for shitty days, and we ate in comfortable silence..

We continued watching long after we'd finished eating. He pulled my head onto his lap so I could lay down and ran his fingers through my hair. There was nothing I loved more than the feeling of Silas's hands in my hair. It was sometimes relaxing and sometimes a total turn-on, but always, always gave me goosebumps in the very best way.

We fell asleep on the couch, with Silas sitting up but slightly bent at a weird angle. I hated to wake him, but if I didn't get him to move, he would be very sore the next day. "Hey, Si." I reached up and brushed his cheek. "You need to lie down before you break your neck."

He tried moving his head side to side, making pained faces that made it clear he was already stiff from sleeping with his head dangling. "Yeah. Bed." We moved to Kyle's bed, which I didn't think he registered in his exhaustion. At that moment it was just a place to lay down. He was asleep almost immediately. Emotional overload will do that to a person.

I woke up with Silas's arm over me and our legs tangled together. I never did things that resembled cuddling and the fact that I seemed to do this with Silas was something I was acutely aware of. I needed my personal space to sleep, and yet, more often than not, if I was sleeping with Silas, there was no distance between us. He was just…comfortable.

I tried to disentangle myself without waking him so I could use the bathroom, but he tightened his hold. Looking at his face, I could see a smirk. "Listen, buddy, keep squeezing my middle and I will pee all over this bed." He let go of my waist and grabbed my hand to kiss it before releasing me completely.

While in the bathroom, I brushed my teeth and hair before returning to bed. "Do not leave this bed while I'm in the bathroom," Silas commanded as he got up. I covered my head with a pillow in response.

He crawled back into bed and tangled himself back up with me. "If I had my way, I'd always wake up to a gorgeous woman in my bed."

"I think you could pull that off. You are a very attractive man. Of course, today you're not even in your bed."

"That is true. While I've slept in this bed before, it's always been alone. But I'm damn glad I made the bed last time I was here."

"That was you? I just thought Kyle was neat."

"Oh, fuck no. I wouldn't get into his bed without washing sheets. Ever. While *I* haven't been in this bed with a woman, I do not want to know how many times he was. It's not something I want to think about."

"So, are we getting out of bed now?"

"Oh, hell no. But I am getting both of us out of these clothes." He pulled his shirt over his head and shimmied out of his shorts and boxers. I stared at his naked body. Until recently, circumstances did not afford us the time to appreciate the details of each other's naked form. He was an average build, with bigger arms than you'd expect from an accounting major, and was hotter than hell. I traced the compass tattoo on his chest. I never had the inclination to lick someone's entire body before seeing this man naked, but for some reason, I just did. He was already hard, and I was looking forward to this kind of morning greeting.

"See something you like, Duchess?"

"Eh, maybe." I tried my hand at nonchalance. He laughed and sat me up to remove my tank top, kissing a trail across my collarbone. I tingled all over.

I made a move to rid myself of my shorts, and he grabbed my hands. "Allow me," he said, moving off the bed for leverage. He tugged them down my legs in one pull. "Damn, seeing you naked never gets old. It should be a crime for you to wear clothes." His hands ran up and down my legs as his eyes ran up and down my body. He pulled my legs so that my ass was on the edge of the bed and I wrapped them around his back, desperate to feel his erection against my clit. We both hissed at the contact. "Not so fast, gorgeous."

I groaned with frustration as he pulled my left leg up to his chest and ran his fingers down the inside of my leg, stopping just before reaching where I needed to be touched and moving back toward my ankle. He did the same with my right leg and I squirmed to make contact between his length and my center. He wrapped both legs back around him and leaned over me to go in for a deep kiss, palming my breast as our tongues slipped around in each other's mouths.

I ran my hands down his chest, reaching for his waist, lower to stroke his cock, and he groaned into my mouth. I rubbed the crown over my wet slit.

"If you keep doing that, this is going to be over before it begins," he said against my mouth before moving his down to suck my nipple. In doing so, he moved back out of my reach.

"But I need to feel you," I pouted.

He lightly bit my nipple. "You can't feel that?" he teased.

"Yes, I can, which is why I need to feel you inside me."

In response, he slipped a single finger inside me, causing me to moan deeply. "Better?" he asked as he worked it in and out.

"Yes, but I want more, Silas."

He kissed me and pushed in a second finger, creating more

pressure. "How about now?" he teased, keeping a steady pace with his fingers.

"Silas!" I groaned.

He licked and sucked down the side of my neck, removing his fingers, and then moved to kneel in front of me. He pulled my legs around his face, but didn't make a move. "You're killing me here." Silas groaned.

He slid his fingers back in slowly and as my hips lifted as a result, he took my clit into his mouth and sucked hard.

"Fuck Silas, yes!" I screamed, an orgasm building quickly. His tongue licked me relentlessly until my whole body tensed, toes curling, fists pulling at the sheets. "*Fuckfuckfuck*!" I panted as he used his fingers and tongue to coax my release until it waned.

"Better?" he smirked up at me.

"Yes, but I still need you inside me."

He moved back up and lined his cock up to my entrance. He paused, looking for his bag. "I'm good without it if you are," I said, knowing he was looking for a condom. He slid into me slowly, and we both moaned.

"Fucking amazing," he breathed once he was all the way in. I wrapped my legs around him tighter and rolled my hips, making him groan some more. He met the rhythm for a few seconds before taking over, fucking me hard, his fingers digging into my ass for leverage.

It didn't take me long to feel my orgasm build again. Nonsense spilled from my lips between pants as my nails scraped down his back.

"Shit," he breathed as he felt me come undone beneath him. "So fucking amazing," he murmured before surrendering to his own orgasm. After a minute of catching our breath, he pulled us back into the bed properly, holding me close and peppering kisses on the top of my head. I relaxed into his arms and fell back to sleep.

When I woke up, he was packing the stack of items he was

bringing back home into some duffel bags he must have found somewhere around the house. When he noticed me watching him, he just started talking. "So, I'm going home tonight. Well, to my mother's with this stuff. But I need to know when I see you again."

"I don't really know. Cee is taking over for me with the band. The campaign is gearing up and I'll need to be around here most of the time." I tried to review my summer schedule in my head. "I need to see our calendars to figure out where we will be when and find time to sneak away."

"I will be anywhere you will meet me as often as you can," he said, walking back over to the bed and sitting on the edge.

"You must have to work, Silas. Shows with the band?"

"I'm a financial analyst. I work wherever my laptop is. And fuck Connor and his schedule. If you are free, that's where I want to be."

His insistence set off alarm bells deep in my head. The part of my brain that knew the more time we spent together, the harder it was going to be to cut off contact when I got married. There was a completely different part of my brain, the part that was thinking with my libido instead of logic, that noted this meant I had few opportunities left to spend fucking Silas.

I really, really enjoyed fucking Silas.

"Mason and I have a week off in July that we usually take separately. Definitely that week; you name the place. We have a second week off in early August, but we will be in Hyannis, staying on the family property. I may be able to find a reason to leave early or arrive late, but that would have to be local because we're talking a day or two."

"That's a start. Send me the dates. We will drive up to Maine the week you have off."

"A start? We're talking 24 hours or fewer the rest of the summer."

"I'll take it."

I gave him a quizzical look.

"I'll live here for the summer. Connor will be in and out, but that's not an issue. I'll be within driving distance. I have one summer with you and I plan to spend every minute I can fucking you senseless."

The alarms screamed louder in my head. This was such a horrible idea. "When will you be back?" I asked, ignoring my logical self. But my stomach fluttered with excitement.

A smile spread across his lips, knowing he was getting his wish. "A few weeks." He leaned down and kissed me.

Fourteen

Silas made a temporary move to Connor's apartment over the week of the Fourth of July; however, he and Connor switched bedrooms for Silas's sanity. The plan was that he would stay there through the summer so we could be within driving distance for the rare unscheduled chunks of time I had. He lived there a full week before I could meet up with him.

The first night I saw him, I had been at an event until about midnight before getting home. I texted him to ask how moving was going and he responded with a phone call. "I haven't gotten a non-text message in two years," I answered, quoting a line from *New Girl*.

"He most certainly did. He got calls from Cece and Elizabeth in the second episode of season three."

"You've made it to season four!"

"It's a long flight to Los Angeles. And then back. I've watched a lot of *New Girl* recently. The only reason I've watched it, though, is because you and your sister are constantly making references I know I'm not getting."

"Do you feel left out?" I laughed.

"Maybe just a little. How was your day?"

"Long. I'm breaking in a new pair of nude heels and my feet are killing me." I looked down at my blistered feet with a frown. "Which also means my hips and back hurt from trying to discreetly shift my weight off my feet. It's a whole thing."

"How many pairs of basically invisible heels does a woman need?"

"At least two broken in. Same with black. Other colors or styles I just have one. It's like coat dresses; I have them in all kinds of colors and patterns, but I have two black."

"What is a coat dress, exactly?"

I sent him a picture. "It's a coat that looks like a dress. Just look at the picture. For reasons I'll never understand, men can wear the same damn dress coat every day, every winter, but I can't wear the same one twice in a row, or even in the same week, really. So *my* coats look like A-lined dresses that button down the front."

"That's the stupidest thing I've heard so far."

"Fucking patriarchy. Men can have one fucking suit and wear it every day and no one bats an eyelash, but I need multiple outfits per day that have to be worn far enough apart that people won't talk shit. Being a woman is exhausting, Silas." I sighed.

"And apparently painful. If only I were there to help alleviate that."

"That sounds magical."

"You would have to take off your top and bra for this to be done properly. You're there alone, right?"

"Yes."

"Say yes and I'll be there in twenty minutes, massage oil in hand."

I briefly considered countering and saying I'd go to him, but I really had no desire to put shoes on. "Take Mish's car and promise you will leave before morning when someone might see you."

"Done. I'll be there in twenty."

"Silas, you live at least half an hour away."

"I've been in the car since I called. I've been so close, but so far for way too long." I could hear the smirk in his voice.

"What if I said no?"

"I would've turned around and we would get creative."

Nineteen minutes later, I greeted Silas in the doorway, completely naked. "This right here? This is worth all of it–moving for the summer, driving half an hour in the middle of the night, and the sneaking out in a few hours. Absolutely perfect. You are absolutely perfect. Now get that beautiful ass somewhere horizontal so I can begin the rubdown. I can't wait to get my hands all over you."

He kicked the door closed behind him and followed me to the bedroom. My body buzzed with anticipation. "I wasn't sure if you were serious about the oil, but I was serious about the massage and I have some there by the bed. You're gonna want to strip down to keep from ruining your clothes."

Before I finished the sentence, he was pulling clothes and shoes off frantically. "On the bed, face down," he ordered, and I happily complied. He straddled my body, but stayed on his knees. Starting at my shoulders, he started kneading the tension away with strong hands. I moaned in appreciation, melting into the bed. His fingers moved down my spine kneading the tired muscles and then spent some time working the knots from my lower back, every so often brushing a hand lightly over my ass. "Seriously, your ass. How the hell do you have such a great ass?"

"It's the heels and barre. And if you keep massaging my cheeks like that, I'm going to die of sexual frustration."

"We have *hours*, Len, and I plan to spend all of them ensuring I take care of every part of your body."

I moaned in frustration. "Patience is not a virtue of mine, Silas. Not when it comes to sex." My clit thrummed with need and my nipples pebbled, wanting attention. His hands moved down one leg, rubbing the arch of my foot deeply. I had no idea a foot rub could make me so needy, but it felt absolutely amazing. He moved to the other foot, and then up my leg, millimeters from where I needed him, but continued back up over my ass and onto my back.

He pressed his body flush to mine, and I could feel his erection in the crack of my ass. He kissed the back of my neck, and I pushed my hips back to have more contact with his cock.

"So impatient. I haven't even done the front yet."

We were at least twenty minutes into this massage, and I was desperate for it to change course. He made me turn over, and he started the torturous, sensual process all over. When he again came to my legs, I whimpered when he barely touched my center. "Silas, please."

He gave me a sexy-as-fuck, teasing grin. "Please what, Len?"

"I need you inside me. I can't wait anymore."

He trailed one finger down my slit. "Here?" He slid one finger in and held it there, unmoving. "Is that what you need?"

I rocked my hips into his hand. "More Silas, I need more."

He added a finger and pushed them in and out slowly, using his thumb to rub my clit.

"Yes, there." My hips continued to rock in rhythm with his fingers. My whole body was on fire from being touched for so long without the release I needed. I could feel it getting closer with every stroke. Silas took his cock in his hand and began fisting it as he watched me climbing toward the peak. The visual had me worked up. I was jealous of his hand.

"I'm here now, Len. Let go." He added pressure to the thumb on my clit and my whole body shook with release. He continued rubbing until it was over. "Yes, just like that," he rasped, slipping his fingers out of me and positioning us so that he had access to my pussy with his tongue. I had barely recovered from the orgasm and I was still so sensitive that just the tip of his tongue touching me had me clawing at the sheets, unable to control the needy sounds that were coming from my mouth as he dipped his tongue inside me. "Fucking hell you taste good, Duchess." His lust-filled voice was doing me in. His teeth nipped my clit and in less than a minute I was coming again, this time thinking I may actually crush his skull with my thighs.

"Oh god," I cried. "Shit, that's so good." He continued to lick up and down slowly as I came down. "Come here," I said when I caught my breath. Silas moved up to the top of the bed to lie next to me. I reached down to palm his cock, and he let out a hiss. I moved down the bed and took it in my mouth.

He groaned as I licked him up and down before taking as much of his cock as I could into the back of my throat. His hands twisted in my hair as I alternated between sucking and licking. "Len, I need to fuck you."

I kept at it another minute, taking him to the edge before moving up. I straddled over him and slid down onto his cock slowly. We both moaned. I stilled, needing to focus on the feeling of him filling me. Thinking about this feeling had consumed me for the weeks since I had seen him last. He grabbed my hips, pulling me down while pushing his hips up, burying himself all the way. I rocked my hips, and he moved one hand to my ass cheek and the other palmed a breast. His touch and the rhythm of his cock in and out of me caused me to tremble with building need. We rocked into each other frantically until we both hit the peak.

I laid down beside him, and he kissed my forehead. "Damn, I have missed that," he said, pulling me into him. Hell if I didn't feel exactly the same. But even more, I missed the feeling of him holding me tightly to his body, his breath moving over the top of my head. The way his thumbs rubbed back and forth along my lower back. The sound of his heartbeat returning to normal.

There were two weeks before our trip to Maine. I had put Mason on notice of my plans and we coordinated a way to make it look like we'd be leaving and returning together from a lover's retreat. Those two weeks required turning my life into something that resembled calendar acrobatics. Most nights, after work, I went to Silas for a good fuck and then made the drive home in the wee hours of the morning.

I was getting very little sleep, but I had no plans to change this pattern. He came with me on Wednesdays to babysit Wyatt. It overjoyed the kid to have his friend "Siwas" there to tear shit up with him. One night, after Wyatt went to bed, Silas and I were post-fuck on the couch when he asked, "what's the deal with your sister?"

"How do you mean?"

"She's not in an arranged marriage."

"No. She and I weren't really raised on the same level. By the time Cee came around my mom had decided that she wouldn't allow my father to run her life the way he did mine. He blames my mother for the way he treats Cee. Says mom is the reason Cee turned out how she is."

"What's wrong with Cee?" his face scrunched up with confusion.

"She is a secret unwed mom, Silas. When she refused to give up Wyatt after being sequestered far away for pregnancy, my father basically banished her to not ruin the family reputation."

"Are you serious?"

"Quite. Governor Roberts cannot have unruly children. He wrote her off like the youngest kid on Family Matters. There one season and never spoken of again."

"That's fucking weird, Len. You get that, right?"

"It's fucked up. I don't agree with any of it. It doesn't seem to bother Cee, though. She's always been a wild child who openly expressed her free will whenever possible. I think she is happy to be out of the whole circus."

"Speaking of leaving the circus, we get to leave your circus Friday for an entire week. Alone." He waggled his eyebrows suggestively.

"You aren't enjoying my circus?" I asked coyly.

"I enjoy the few hours here and there I get with you, but it will thrill me to see the whole duchess persona take a back seat for a week." He gave my work attire a side eye. "I enjoy the dresses for obvious reasons, but wouldn't mind if they showed a little knee," he winked.

"Scandalous. I'm perfectly happy to wear nothing but a bathing suit for the whole week. Secluded in Maine sounds magical."

"Are you even allowed to wear a bathing suit? Doesn't seem very regal."

"In the water only. Otherwise, I typically wear some kind of linen cover up."

"Rules for Maine include no cover-ups and absolutely no bathing suit in the water." I laughed. "Oh, I'm quite serious," he added.

"Have you seen my very pale, freckled complexion? I will turn to burned toast immediately and you won't be able to come within feet of me for the rest of the week."

"I will liberally apply high spectrum sunscreen many times a day," he said with a wink. The sound of that made my pulse quicken, recalling the night he gave me a massage.

"That's an offer I can't refuse. Friday can't come soon enough."

"How long is this drive again?" he asked, looking me up and down from the driver's seat. I had tossed the modest blouse I was wearing into the backseat in favor of the tank top underneath.

"Five hours?"

"How is that remotely possible?"

"We're basically going to Canada. It's all in the name of bikinis and solitude."

Silas groaned. "I will not make it all the way there before getting you out of those clothes, Duchess."

"Better get moving then," I said, putting a hand on his thigh, causing him to tighten his grip on the steering wheel.

We made it about three hours north before needing to stop to use a bathroom. On the way back to the car, Silas was ever-so-slightly behind me, apparently checking out my ass in the linen pants I was wearing. It was dark, so I wasn't really sure how much he could actually see, but I knew it was what he was attempting to do. "Of all days to wear pants, Duchess."

I turned back. "Huh?"

"If you were wearing one of those godforsaken dresses, it would be very easy to take care of this need I have to fuck you without having to wait another *two hours* to get to our destination."

I looked around the rest stop. There were picnic tables off to the side, barely visible in the dark. "Come on." I grabbed his hand and pulled him toward them. I led him to the back side of the table, facing the woods instead of the parking lot. "Take out your cock and sit, Silas." He gave me a quick questioning look before deciding he didn't care about the public nudity. I sank down to my knees in front of him. "Do not make a sound, Silas." I said and then wrapped my mouth around his hardening cock.

His hand went to the back of my head and tangled into my hair. I moaned softly, causing him to hiss. I licked around the crown and then took him back into my mouth and sucked, using a hand to cup his balls. His grip tightened in my hair, slightly pulling. Desire pooled between my legs, and I doubled down on his cock. He rocked his hips deeper into my throat and began fucking my mouth. I could feel him getting close and trying to pull back. "Len, I'm gonna come," he said in a quiet voice.

I gave another quiet moan and slid his cock to the back of my throat. He took that as his cue to come. A few more seconds and he stiffened and came into my mouth with a jerk. I swallowed as much as possible, trying to minimize any mess since we were basically in public. When he was done, I sat up, wiped my mouth and said, "That should help get you to our destination."

We both stood. "You are un-fucking-predictable sometimes." He kissed me in appreciation and we walked back to the bathroom so we could clean up a bit and get back on the road.

We got to our rental around midnight. No sooner had I dropped my bag on the counter than Silas pulled me toward the bedroom. I laughed as he pushed me gently to the bed. "Blow job not enough?" I asked seductively.

"Oh, that was fucking incredible. Most unladylike of you." He pulled my pants and underwear off, tossing them behind him. "But if I don't get a taste of you soon, I'll lose my damn mind." His tongue made a firm pass up my slit.

"Yes. More of this," I pleaded, my hand holding his head to my center this time. He licked and sucked like I was the very best kind of ice cream cone and melting fast. He dipped a finger into my wet pussy and pulled it out, trailing it down to my ass, rubbing circles around the tight ring. "Fuck, that feels good," I moaned, rocking against his tongue. His finger pressed into my ass slowly, and I stopped breathing.

"Breathe, Duchess," Silas reminded me. His tongue moved over my clit as his finger pumped in my ass. Everything around me felt like it was shaking as I came hard against his tongue, inhaling large gulps of air and moaning loudly as I did. "That's my girl," he kissed my inner thigh.

He got up, cleaned himself up and brought back a damp towel to clean me up as well. It was just as well because my legs were still shaking and it would be awhile before I could do it myself. "You see those bedposts, Duchess?" he rasped.

"Yes," I replied, still out of breath.

"At some point this week, I want to tie you to them and fuck you senseless. What do you think about that?"

"I think as long as you are giving me orgasms like that last one, I won't give a shit how we get there."

"Good to know," he chuckled.

Fifteen

We woke up very late on Saturday since we didn't actually get to sleep until earlier in the morning. We made a run to the nearby market to get some essentials for the week. After returning, we made quick work of making eggs and toast for breakfast, even though it was noon. We cleaned up and got ourselves settled into the adorable rental cabin.

I needed time to decompress, so we took some iced coffee to the back and settled on a blanket in the sand in front of the porch. I pulled up the reading app on my phone and did some much needed mindless reading. "Are you *working* right now?" Silas asked about twenty minutes later.

"Nope. Reading a book."

"Remember when people used actual, physical books for that?" he teased.

"It was terrible. Everyone knew what you were reading."

"What are you reading that is so secret?"

"It really never mattered. If I was in public, you know, at the beach or on a train, anywhere, my choice of reading material was scrutinized and talked about as if it was actual news. The *only* books I've read in physical book form since I was about twelve are textbooks. I don't need people that deep into my personal space."

"Makes sense," he conceded, "but what are you reading? I need to know what someone such as yourself reads for fun."

I could feel my cheeks heat. "It's fiction. I like to get away in my head when I can."

"What's it called?" he prodded, sensing I really didn't want to tell him.

"I don't know," I lied.

He laughed and reached over to grab my phone from my hands. "Well, it's got to be right here," he tapped the screen a few times. "Hard Contact?" he looked up at me. "Why Eleanor Roberts, are you reading smut?" he smiled like he won a prize.

"It's romance." I tried to deflect a bit, my cheeks heating.

"Why on earth does someone who doesn't believe in love or romance read a romance novel?" he mused. He read a few pages, clearly getting to a spicy part as his eyes went wide. "Len, this is straight up porn."

I feigned shock. "No way. Can't be. Porn is visual. That's just words."

"Nope. This is porn. Word porn. You naughty Duchess."

"Whatever, give it back," I held out my hand.

"Oh no, I need to study this. Maybe I can learn a thing or two about what gets you all hot and bothered."

"Pretty sure you do that just fine without the tips from my book. Download your own reading material. That one is mine."

"I'm going to do that. I need to know what the proper young ladies are reading while they are having very clinical missionary sex for the purpose of procreation."

"Ugh, you're awful. Totally killing my lady boner."

He threw his head back with laughter. "Your what? Did you just say 'lady boner'?" I just stared, waiting to get my reading material back. "I feel like I just unlocked a whole new door to your personality. Here I thought you were more... reserved."

"Really? What about our exploits has screamed reserved?" I

raised an eyebrow.

"Absolutely nothing," he smoldered, clearly recalling something specific. "For some reason I just never pictured you as the type to read 'romance'," he used air quotes.

I laughed. "To be fair, I have very little time for this type of reading. Typically, it's boring work shit, but when I get a chance, yes, I read the 'word porn'." I used air quotes right back at him.

"Well, it's giving me a guy boner."

"Silas, that's just a boner," I rolled my eyes.

"I don't care what you call it, I just know *I'm* all hot and bothered reading and talking about your book, so we're going to need to take care of our boners together." He put the phone in my lap, stroking his hand up between my legs and pressing. "Yup, wet. We need to take care of that," he said seductively before pulling me to my feet and bringing me inside to strip me down and fuck me.

So far, this was hands down my favorite vacation ever. The next time I picked up that book, we were sitting on the beach. I caught him watching me, and when I got to a particularly provocative part, I squirmed a little, knowing he knew what I was doing. I kept reading for a minute, shifting because the scene had me quickly riled up. Silas noticed my discomfort and said, "read it to me."

"Wh-what?" I asked, not sure I could even do such a thing.

"Whatever you are reading right this second, start reading it out loud so I can hear it."

"You want me to read you the smut?"

"I absolutely do. No need for context, just start reading, Len" he leaned in close. "No one but me can hear you."

This was very far from my comfort zone, but I went ahead.

He slid his hands into my shorts, feeling how damp I was. "Mmm," he said appreciatively, dipping a finger into my pussy slowly.

Silas did as the character in the book did, and I had an even harder time reading aloud. "Keep going. I need to know how to proceed." His blue eyes twinkled with a mixture of lust and mischief. I groaned, trying to focus on just reading and not on what I was reading or what he was doing *while* I was reading.

His other hand trailed up my back under my shirt and unclasped my bra. His hand came to the front and pinched a nipple. My hands ran down his back and the finger in my pussy sped up a bit. He ground his erection into the side of my thigh and I reached to unbutton his shorts. His mouth came down on mine as my hand made contact with his hard length, moaning.

Silas stopped me. "I can't do both parts, Len. You have to participate."

"I'm holding the phone. I can't unbutton your shorts with one hand. You'll have to improvise."

"Tell you what, I assume all the clothes are coming off, so let's just take care of that now," he started unbuttoning my shorts.

"Um, sir, we are on a beach in public."

He contemplated that a minute. "Yes, a little bold for mid-afternoon to be fully nude on the beach. Get in the house." He pulled me up from the blanket, abandoning it there, and smacked my ass. "Now."

We were barely in the back sliding door before he started reaching to pull off my shirt and his own. He took off his shorts and when I didn't take mine off he did it for me. "Now, where were we? Ah yes, your hand is supposed to be on my cock. Keep reading."

"Is that really necessary? I think we know how this goes." I used my free hand to stroke him up and down, and he slid a finger back in me as we stood in the middle of the kitchen. He kissed my neck– little nips here and there that were making me crazy with need.

"Maybe you know, but I've never read this kind of book before and I need to know what happens next. Read." His voice was low and rough in my ear.

"Spoiler alert," I whispered, bringing my mouth to his ear. "They are going to fuck, just like we are." My plan was twofold: stop reading this book out loud and get fucked. The latter was inevitable, as we were already naked and touching. The first depended on how serious he was about following through on this whole game.

"Might become my favorite kind of book. Read it, Len," he added a second finger and moved them in and out.

I moaned. I read further as the man in the story, Jake, undressed the main character, Alison, and himself. Silas continued to fuck me with his fingers, while licking and biting my neck, which was a departure from the story. I became more breathless and speaking became difficult as the book went into detail about Jake getting Alison off with nothing but his fingers while she jerked him off. "Silas," I moaned, "I can't read and let you do that. You have to choose one."

He smiled, clearly pleased with himself and the direction this was taking. "Gotcha. Let me just read ahead so I know what comes next," he took the phone from my hand.

"Me, Silas. I come next." He smiled diabolically and scrolled through a few pages while still fingering me. I stood there, enjoying the feeling, but also slightly concerned my whole body was about to fall to the ground if I came.

"I think I got this from here," he said, as if he needed an instruction manual. He picked me up and carried me to the bed. "Hand and knees, ass toward me," he instructed.

No sooner had I gotten in the required position than he brought my center to his face, licking me front to back. I shuddered with pleasure. "Yessss!" I hissed. He continued fucking me with his fingers and tongue until I came almost violently. He flipped me over before I could even recover, trailing open-mouthed kisses up my stomach to my neck, biting lightly when he got there.

"Don't move," he commanded. He went to his bag and retrieved

a tie. "Last minute thought," he explained as he tied my hands over my head to the bedposts, as previously promised.

"I don't think this is part of the story, Silas," I mused.

"Better than that. Fucking hell you are going to be the death of me," he slammed into me to the hilt. He groaned, and I cried out. I wrapped my legs around his back, the only thing I could do to pull him closer with my hands bound. "You like my cock deep inside you, Duchess?"

"Yes," I uttered, desperate for him to move. He kissed me deeply, his hands tangling in my hair. He used one hand to pull the hair at the nape of my neck, licking and sucking as I tried to pull him deeper.

"Yes, what, Len?" he teased.

"Yes, I love your cock inside me Silas. *Please.* I need you to fuck me now."

"That's good because being inside your pussy is my favorite place to be." He pounded into me relentlessly until he came, causing me to come again right behind him.

We both cleaned up in the bathroom and he pulled me into the bed with him. "I approve of the books," he said, "not that I'm suggesting you need my approval, of course, more like I'm actively encouraging it."

"Yeah, I don't know that I'll be able to read a spicy book again without thinking about this day."

"It's like that Taylor Swift song, but instead of seeing me in a nice dress, you'll remember me reading your lady porn in your wildest dreams."

Somehow, I had forgotten that Silas was temporary. This was all going to end and I would indeed only have dreams and memories. My eyes stung slightly at the thought. It was more than mind-blowing sex (though this was not to be removed from the equation) I really just enjoyed being with him. Shit, we were cuddled up in a bed together, naked, and I was *really* comfortable. I would never have considered there would be someone in my life that I *wanted* to be this physically close to *all the damn time.* I refocused. "Well, I'm glad you recognize the value of my reading material."

Though we had only been up a few hours, I drifted off into a post-coital nap in Silas's arms and I swore as I was falling asleep I heard him whisper, "I love you, Lenny." When I thought back on it as I woke from my nap I wondered which was worse, dreaming he said it, or him actually saying it. Dreaming it meant I wanted it, and him saying it meant it was real and both were out of the question.

I slipped out of his arms, leaving him asleep in the bed, and grabbed my phone.

> **Me:** I think he told me he loves me. WTF!
> **Mish:** *You think?*
> **Me:** It was real, or it was a dream. I can't tell. I was falling asleep.
> **Mish:** *So you weren't drunk or having sex?*
> **Me:** Sex adjacent? It was like a few minutes after.
> **Mish:** *Gray area. It doesn't count if you're drunk or having sex, but it could be leftover sex hormones.*
> **Me:** What if it happens again outside of those parameters, Mish? I can't let him think he loves me.
> **Mish:** *Calm down. If he said it when he thought you were asleep, if he even really did, he won't be saying it while you're awake. He knows you'd run like, well, like he told you he loved you.*

I sighed.

> **Me:** Let's just hope it doesn't happen.
> **Mish:** *What if it did someday, though? Would that really be so awful? Because that guy looks at you like*

you are a goddess to be worshiped. The thought made my hands shake.

Me: I don't believe in it as an entire concept. I'd feel awful that I can't even pretend to reciprocate such a thing.

Mish: *You are impossible. Love exists. I am proof.*

Me: You are proof you believe in love. And while I agree Connor would move the earth for you, I don't know how to reconcile that with my worldview. But thanks for talking me through this crisis.

Sixteen

When Silas woke up, I didn't mention what I may have heard. It still shook me. I had been clear, hadn't I? It was a month until I married Mason and here I was hoping like hell I imagined Silas saying he loved me. This was supposed to be a casual fling. Sure, his mere presence made me feel things I never thought I would, but that was lust, right? It was all sex and hormones. If given the opportunity, I would've chased them longer, until it all wore off, but that wasn't reality.

We spent the next few days having sex, hanging out at the beach, and just being in close proximity. Neither of us had any commitments and reality seemed to be a far off land. It was blissful.

Until it was nearing time to leave. The last day we were there, Mason started texting with real-life issues that needed resolutions. I noticed every time my phone vibrated to signal a new text, Silas got increasingly more irritable. "I'm sorry. It's just we have this event and I still haven't worked out all the details with Mason and Megan."

"There's always an event, Len. Can't Megan handle it? She's his assistant, not you."

"She's his assistant, not *mine*. And faking a relationship with someone takes a certain amount of coordination."

"Right." He walked outside, letting the screen door slam in his wake.

Knowing he needed time to cool off, I started packing up some things. We were leaving first thing in the morning, and I really had a tight schedule once we were back home. As is my nature, I had already put this trip, and Silas, into a box categorized as 'the past' and left my emotions along with it. I didn't have the time or the luxury to wallow in self-pity for all the amazing sex I was about to miss.

Or just missing Silas, generally. That line of thought I had to shut out completely. I was wondering if I should create a bit more distance once we got back. If he thought he loved Len, I needed to shut that down.

I watched him sit on the edge of the water, looking over the sea. The waves would sometimes creep up and get him wet, but he didn't seem to notice. I wanted to go out there and hug him, but in the interest of not making things more confusing, I just sat and watched. There was an ache in my chest, knowing that I was hurting him. Both of us weren't ready to let Len go, but the time was flying by and she'd disappear into the ether soon.

It sucked.

We spent the most of that day in silence, near each other at times, but only stealing glances. There was a palpable heaviness in the air. It wasn't until dinnertime that Silas spoke again, to ask me what I wanted to eat. There weren't many options left since we were leaving soon. While he made burgers, I prepped the salad using the variety of leftover ingredients we had.

Instead of sitting across from me, he sat down right next to me at the table, his leg brushing mine. "I had a great week with you, Len."

There were so many things I wanted to say. That I did too, and I wish it didn't have to end. I wished we had more time to spend together. That I was sorry it had to end, and that things

Uninvited

got too involved. Instead, I just replied, "It was one of my favorite vacations ever." It was the truth. I'd realized in the last week I had felt a freedom that was only present with Silas. I couldn't decide if that was because I leaned into my "Len" persona, or if Silas just made me feel that way, but it was another thing I was going to miss. The freedom to just *be*.

He put a hand on my thigh, and we continued eating in silence.

After dinner, we cleaned up and finished packing for our morning departure. We took a final stroll down the beach before heading to bed. The ocean breeze in my hair, Silas holding my hand, and only the sound of the waves brought a peace I didn't feel often. I tried to absorb as much of it as I could, knowing my life was about to take a sharp turn back to reality.

We returned to the rental and got ready for bed. As I was pulling my sundress over my head, Silas came over and quietly assisted. Then he ran his hands down the sides of my mostly naked torso. He leaned in and placed a soft kiss on my lips before reaching behind to unsnap my strapless bra and let it fall to our feet. He pulled my naked chest close to his and went in for a deeper kiss.

It was a slow kiss. Usually, we were frantic and impatient. This was different. Much like I was savoring our walk, this was a kiss to savor. I wanted to live in this moment and commit it to memory for when memories of my time with Silas were all I had. I wrapped my arms around his waist tighter. He moved a hand to my cheek and brushed his thumb back and forth, pulling back slightly and just staring into my eyes intensely before bringing his mouth back to mine.

There were tears behind my eyes that I wasn't expecting at all. To ensure he didn't notice, I trailed my lips down his jaw and across his shoulder, hugging him close. His hands tangled into my hair, eliciting a soft moan from my lips before he tugged on the hair to bring my face back to his. "Don't look away, Lenny," he said in a soft husky voice.

His hands resumed their path up and down my back and sides as he just stared at me, as if he could use his stare to see into my thoughts, and maybe even change my mind.

He moved us over to the bed, where he laid me back and removed my panties, removing his boxers after. He trailed kisses up my leg, my stomach, over each breast and back to my mouth. He laid his body half over mine and half on the bed while he continued to kiss me slowly and let his hand roam up and down my body. The feather-light touch of his fingers released oxytocin in large amounts.

I let my hand roam his chest, down his side and over his ass. His mouth went back to exploring the rest of my body as I lay there, taking it all in. It was slow, and we took turns just kissing each other all over for so long I couldn't take it anymore. "Silas, please," I whispered into his ear as he kissed my shoulder.

"Anything. I'd do anything you ask, Len." He looked up at me as he dragged his fingers slowly down my body before inserting two inside just as slowly. He pulled them out and spread my wetness around, causing me to arch back with need.

Silas grabbed my leg and hitched it up over his hip and lined his cock up with my entrance. Slowly, he pressed in while staring into my eyes. His pupils dilated with desire and my whole body flushed with heat. I whispered his name against his lips.

"Fuck, Len. Why does this feel so good?" he groaned as he slowly rocked in and out of me. A hand massaged my breast and his mouth went back to mine, this time with a ferocity. My fingers were digging into his ass cheeks as I wondered the same damn thing.

Despite the slow pace, I felt an orgasm building quickly. I tried to meet his stare, but it was so hard to do when it felt so good. "Let go, Len. Come."

My eyes fluttered into the back of my head and I let the feeling build higher and higher. "That's it, beautiful." Silas urged. The stars started appearing behind my eyes as I let out a moan. Silas leaned down and kissed the spot on my neck that always sent pulses straight to my clit and I came undone. Wave after wave of pleasure poured over me as he slowly pushed in and out, a moan escaping his lips as I shattered under him.

He kissed me deeply and then rolled onto his back, pulling me on top of him. I took my time kissing along his collarbone and up the side of his neck before sinking down onto him once again. His hands went to my ass cheeks. My head fell back as I slowly rode him. One of his hands moved to my breast, and he pinched my nipple, causing me to gasp.

My speed picked up in response and Silas muttered a quiet, "shit," moving a hand between us to rub his thumb in circles over my clit. Another orgasm was building and Silas was bucking up against me, his also close. I whispered, "Silas, yes," and his movements stiffened as he came below me, sending me over the edge right after him.

With him still inside me, I laid on him while we caught our breath. His arms went around my back, pulling me to him tightly. He kissed my temple and sighed. I lifted my head to place a kiss on his mouth. "This week was amazing, Silas. And I wish it wasn't already over," I said softly.

He stared up into my eyes. "But it is, isn't it?"

"The week is over, but we don't have to be yet. I still have a few weeks." He didn't respond. I rolled to the side, one leg slung over his, and he tucked me under his arm. He continued to hold me close, his nose in my hair. "I understand if you need to walk away."

He tensed. "And I don't understand why you need to walk away."

"I know," I admitted, "and I'm sorry. I didn't expect this, Silas."

"Whatever," he mumbled, pulling away.

"Don't do this. You're mad, so say it."

He rubbed a hand over his face and sighed deeply. "I'm not mad, Len. Frustrated, yes. But if I'm mad, it's at myself. I knew this had an end that doesn't include a happily ever after for me.

But like a fucking idiot, I let myself forget about that."

I laid there silently for a few minutes before letting my hand search for his. "I need you to be the one to decide here, Silas. We can walk away tomorrow if that's what you want."

"That's the problem. I don't want to walk away, but I need to." I tried to pull my hand back, tears pricking at the back of my eyes, but he held tightly to my hand. "Tomorrow, Len. Tonight I can't lay beside you and not hold you." He pulled me back close to his side. I closed my eyes and tried to memorize how it felt to be in his arms.

We said nothing the next morning as we headed home. When we got to the parking lot, he got my bag out of the trunk and put it into mine. Mason was waiting to leave, looking annoyed. We were taking his car into the office and grabbing mine later. I didn't know what to say to Silas. Not just because Mason was staring daggers at him, but because he made it clear this is where we ended. Silas placed a very chaste kiss upon my cheek and said, "Have a good day, Elle," before returning to his car and speeding off before I even got into Mason's car. His calling me "Elle" felt like a punch to my gut.

"What did you do, Eleanor?" Mason chastised as I buckled into the passenger seat.

I wasn't sure what he meant by that; he knew damn well that I'd been with Silas all week. "Same as you, I assume. Fucked."

"Sure. But that's not what I'm talking about. That dude is pissed."

"Yeah, well, he knew the score." I tried to play it tough, but Mason had known me far too long for that act.

"As did you, and look at how fucked up you are right now. Is this going to change our plans? I need to know before you leave me at the altar."

"No change in our plans. Just fucking drive and shut up."

"I'm dead ass right, now, Ellie," he said, pulling my chin toward him. "I need to know you will not bail on this."

"You know I wouldn't do that to you. Please just drive, Mason," I whispered.

He did.

Later that night, I got a text from Silas.

> **Silas:** *I need to see you.*
> **Me:** Are you sure?
> **Silas:** *I'm literally parked down the street.*
> **Me:** Come in the back door.

A few minutes passed, and I heard the back door open and close softly. "In here," I called out from the couch in the dark living room.

He switched on a lamp as he entered the room. "Lay it on me. Show me when I get to have you and when you absolutely walk away." He was holding a printout of the month of August, which he set on the coffee table in front of me with a pen.

"Silas. I think this is a bad idea."

"I'm a fucking masochist then. Because I want every minute."

I shifted forward and took the pen marking an X just after August was over. Two days before my wedding. "This is the day we leave for the wedding. But it's a busy month with the campaign and final wedding plans. We have a standing date night on Tuesdays. The days are basically booked solid." I circled a long weekend we had committed to spending at the Davis residence for our annual trip. "I'll be on the Cape with Mason and our families this weekend. We share a room like a couple. People take pictures of us." I needed him to understand exactly what was happening.

"Awesome," he said sarcastically. "Other than your trips away and *date night*, you're mine at night."

I was reluctant to agree. It was a bad idea with all the makings of a horrible ending, but if I could have a few more stolen hours with Silas, I was taking them.

So I spent the next few weeks playing Eleanor during the day, and on Tuesday nights, and allowing myself the luxury of being Len every other night with Silas. Having him there felt far too comfortable for something that was only temporary.

The days were getting harder. I couldn't focus on my "real" life. I needed to be focused on this campaign and things that normally came naturally to me were difficult. I found myself thinking about Silas instead of working toward a goal that was years in the making.

The goal was simple: get Mason into office and launch my career as a political strategist. I never wanted the spotlight as the politician. I craved the satisfaction of plotting the moves that made for victory. I was good at it. Working on the Presidential campaign as senior staff was going to be a game-changer for me. I was so close to getting across that goal line.

I had made promises to Mason and our fathers. I got opportunities to work on the Presidential and gubernatorial campaigns with the understanding I would make the perfect trophy wife for Mason. It was win-win (-win, if including our fathers). Power couple goals. I never thought twice about wanting this.

Until now.

Before Silas, I never thought I was giving anything up. Suddenly the reality that I had committed myself to my career so fully was feeling like the wrong move.

The weekend Mason and I spent down the Cape, I tried to remain "present" with the Davis clan, hanging out with them and my father. (They did not invite Catherine to such family gatherings.) It was a difficult task. Silas and I spent most of the time texting, sending song lyrics back and forth, and I explained it all away as wedding or campaign business. If any family understood the demands of political life, it was this one, so no one blinked when I would excuse myself from time to time for a private conversation.

Mason did notice, however, and knew exactly what I was up to. He never said a word to me about it, though. He played the part of doting fiancé the whole weekend effortlessly. Years of practice were coming to a head and anytime someone questioned my preoccupation, Mason would tell them that our wedding was fast approaching and I was being a "typical" bride.

Just two long-time lovers looking to tie the knot before Election Day.

On our last night there, I was moving things around our room while Mason took a shower and his phone flashed with an incoming message. I caught the name of the person texting out of the corner of my eye:

Silas Browning

What the actual fuck? Why did Mason have Silas in his contacts, and why were they texting? A sick feeling rumbled through my stomach. I wished I had the passcode to his phone, but we weren't that kind of couple. I'd never give him mine, either.

Instead, when Mason came back into the bedroom, dressed only with a towel around his waist, I asked, "Why do you have Silas's number?"

A guilty look flashed across Mason's face, but he recovered quickly. "You remember when I had to basically carry you through a couple of airports? We needed to coordinate. I guess I just never deleted it."

"Why is he texting you now, Mason?" I remembered him and Silas texting during the weekend in question, but this didn't explain why they were communicating now. That was months ago.

"You can look if you want, Elle. I'm not trying to hide anything from you." He held the cell phone out for me to take. I didn't accept it.

"Just tell me this isn't some kind of power play or attempt to get him to back off. I promised you it would be over before the wedding, and it will be." I threw myself onto the bed and under the blankets.

"It's not like that. But do you really think this guy will just disappear in a couple of weeks?" He pulled on shorts and slid into bed next to me.

"I have it under control, Mason." I turned off the light next to the bed, leaving us in the dark.

"We do not need some kind of scandal weeks before the wedding. I just need to know what he's thinking."

"You need to trust that I have this under control. Going behind my back and contacting him is an insult."

"Maybe so, but I need you to focus, Elle. This guy is getting under your skin and I need to protect what's mine."

"I'm not property, Mason," I scowled.

"No. But you gave an outsider the power to derail *my* life, and I'm ensuring that doesn't happen."

I secured one full day for Silas and me to have to ourselves before my "big day." Against my better judgment, we spent the day at a lighthouse in Jamestown, Rhode Island, just sitting on the rocks, swimming, and chatting. There were only a few people really wandering around, and I felt relatively incognito in my big sun hat and oversized sunglasses. It was supposed to just be one last good day before going our separate ways. For the most part, it was exactly that.

The problem came at the end of the day.

We had finished packing up, and we were walking along

the side of the roadway with the ocean beside us but down a steep cliff. Without preamble, Silas put down the cooler he was carrying and tugged my hand to hold me back.

"What's up? Did we forget something?" I asked, turning to face him. As I caught his eye, I realized shit was about to get real in a way I wouldn't like. I knew *something* was going to happen, I just didn't know what.

He took the bag from my arms and put it on the ground beside the cooler. I removed the hat before the wind took from my head and he pulled me against his chest. "I love you, Len."

I pushed away before he even had all the words out, my whole body suddenly shaking uncontrollably. "Take that back. You don't mean it," I demanded.

He looked at me like I lost my mind. "What the fuck do you mean, I don't *mean* it? Of course, I mean it." He tried to reach for my hands, but I backed even further away.

"No. You don't. You need to go. Just. You need to go."

"We came here together. I'm not leaving you a hundred miles from home. That's insane."

"You have to go." Tears pricked my eyes and adrenaline surged through my body. Though I was terrified of heights, I considered jumping off the cliff into the ocean and rocks below to avoid this conversation. "I'll have someone come get me. Please, just go." I pulled out my phone to text my sister to come to my rescue.

"Who are you texting? Just get in the fucking car and let's go."

"Cee will come to get me. I can't do this anymore, Silas. You have to go."

"Well, then I'm staying until she gets here."

"Can you just wait in the car or something? Look, she is sending Elijah. He'll be here in an hour. It's fine. I'm fine. This just has to be over." I started walking away from him, toward the lighthouse, to wait for my ride. After mumbling something, he picked up the cooler and stomped off to the car. Just as he said, he did not drive away.

It was over an hour before Elijah pulled up to my rescue. Over an hour in which I could see Silas sitting in the car. Sometimes he appeared to be yelling, sometimes his head was just resting on the steering wheel and I couldn't figure out what he was doing or saying to himself. He did not get back out. As soon as Elijah's car passed by, Silas sped out of the parking lot like he was late for something important.

I hopped into Elijah's car, and he just stared at me.

"Thank you for rescuing me, but can we please not talk about it?"

"You don't owe me an explanation. But your sister is definitely going to want to know what's up."

I didn't doubt she'd ask me about it repeatedly, but I held no interest in recapping what just happened. Elijah turned up the volume on the stereo and we just drove without speaking for about half an hour.

"Silas told me he loves me."

"I take it you didn't say it back?"

I laughed nervously. "Actually, I immediately demanded he take it back. Needless to say, things did not end well."

He let out a low whistle. "And I thought your sister was the prickly one."

"She has abandonment issues. I got the attachment issues." I fiddled with the handle of the bag in my lap.

"I get that. She's afraid of everyone bailing on her, and you let no one get close enough to care if they do. But you should probably make some exceptions to your rules. If the guy says he loves you, he does. At least, I'm pretty sure I know Silas well enough at this point to say with certainty he isn't lying."

"I don't doubt that he thinks he loves me. I just think he's confusing lust with something that doesn't exist. It doesn't really matter, anyway. I'm literally getting married next week to someone else. It's over for Silas and me." With this thought in mind, I called Mason.

"Can this wait?" he answered.

"Sorry. No. Are you busy?"

"Depends. What's up?"

"I need your help. I'm on my way back from Rhode Island. I need you to pop over to my place and make sure Silas and his stuff are gone."

"On it." He mumbled something to someone.

"Are you sure? It sounds like you're in the middle of something." I figured it would piss him off that I interrupted him and that Silas had himself and/or stuff at my place.

"She can wait. This can't." He hung up.

"Need me to take the really long way?" Eli asked.

"You're one of the good ones, Elijah."

Seventeen

I had just a few days to wallow privately before my wedding weekend.

Mason and I arrived in Hyannis Port on Saturday morning with a very large entourage of people. It was quite clear some kind of gathering involving the Davis family was occurring because they were basically everywhere. Our "small" wedding was really anything but that, just because of the sheer number of family members in attendance. We had delayed telling anyone other than our very immediate family and close staff members who were assisting with the planning until two weeks before, hoping that it would reduce the number of guests and the likelihood that press would show up.

I think we miscalculated.

Saturday evening was the rehearsal dinner. We went through the motions of the wedding, noting cues and what should happen, and I felt ill throughout the whole exercise. Reality was staring me in the face: tomorrow I was getting married to Mason.

Following the rehearsal came the dinner portion of the evening. We kept this fairly intimate: his parents, my parents, our siblings, and what I can only describe as members of the Davis family who had contributed generously to Mason's campaign. There were fewer than twenty people, which made acting like I felt fine much more difficult.

Of course, I was the bride, so naturally there was a minimum amount of attention to our guests that was obligatory, but once dinner was over I was hoping for a quick escape. It took considerably longer than I had expected, but seeing me in distress, Mason told everyone that we wanted to grab some time alone together before the "big day", which seemed to be acceptable to the group.

Walking down to the beach, we set a blanket in the sand. We laid next to one another, looking up at the stars just as we used to when we were kids and we'd come here. I felt uncomfortable and uncertain about our future. I needed to know what he was thinking. "Mace. Are we doing the right thing?"

He looked over at me, confused. "Ignoring our guests?"

"No. Getting married. My father is crazy. I mean, I guess yours is, too, but I just need to know what you are thinking here."

He grabbed my hand and interlocked our fingers. "Elle, I've loved you for as long as I can remember. No one is forcing me to do this. I want to."

Tears fell down my cheeks. I wasn't prepared for that.

"But we can't back out now. There's the election and a fuck-ton of people here for a wedding. I just need you to fake it until you make it at this point. I know you don't love me. It's a transaction." He squeezed my hand. I was silent for a long time. Mason had never said he loved me, something that typically precedes one's engagement, never mind the day before the wedding.

"I care about you, but I don't love you. I won't ever love anyone. I don't know how." I wanted to vomit. Telling him I didn't love him was almost as hard as hearing he loved me.

"I saw how he raised you, Ellie. I get why you are so closed off. And who knows, maybe once the pressure of having your dad dictate your life is over, you'll let go a little."

"I don't want you to hold out hope for that."

Uninvited

"I want to marry you. I've *always* wanted it. Knowing I was marrying you made getting to this point so much easier for me." He paused. "I know that's not how it has been for you."

"Okay." I knew he was trying to make this easier for me, but the pressure was just doubled. Maybe if he was an asshole, I could just call it off without a doubt that I was doing the right thing. And hey, there was always divorce, I guess. All the things I had been telling everyone else about this relationship, and telling myself, were all true. He was a nice guy, with a good job, who was good to me. I trusted him implicitly, which was something I didn't really do with ease. Apparently, he loved me, though I doubted he truly did. I was pretty sure he just talked himself into it over the years. Maybe I should have done the same? Would starting now help?

I took a deep breath and blinked away the tears. He leaned up on his elbow to look down at me. "Ellie, I need you to promise you're going to be there tomorrow."

"It'll be fine. I'm just stressed out. I'll go make some tea and calm down."

"Tea will not fix what's wrong here. You are crying. I haven't seen you shed a tear since the day that dog bit you when you were five."

"That's because my father read me the riot act for crying in public, despite my need for a dozen stitches. I learned to shove that shit down."

"Exactly my point. Stress doesn't cause *you* to cry. A year ago, this wouldn't have caused you to be so stressed. You *wanted* this."

"What are you talking about, Mason? A year ago, we weren't about to be married and in the middle of you being elected to the fucking Senate. We weren't even engaged." I was choosing to ignore his acknowledgement of the tears streaming down my face. I wasn't supposed to cry. Ever. That's not what the wives of politicians did. As long as I ignored it, it wasn't happening.

"And a year ago, you weren't in love with someone else, Elle.

This isn't about you and me and the crazy life we planned. This is about the one you're giving up."

More tears fell down my cheeks because, while I wasn't certain he was right about me being in love with Silas, I definitely missed him already. I also just plain resented the life of "Elle" and wanted the life of "Len." I hated that in one breath Mason was acknowledging what I was giving up for him, but in the next, he was asking me to do it, anyway.

"I'm sorry you're stuck with me," he said more quietly.

"I'm not in love with anyone. I just thought I had more time to just be me. We figured it would be another term before this seat came up. This is making us real adults and I'm mourning the loss of my carefree youth. We're...old."

Mason laughed. "You shut your mouth. We are still young. I refuse to even entertain the idea of adulthood until after we turn forty."

"You probably shouldn't let the voters hear this."

"Right. The voters. Shit, we are old." We sat with this knowledge in silence for a few minutes. "I think we both knew that our marriage wouldn't be the forever kind. It's the business transaction kind. So, with that in mind, I say we set the terms of this deal, *including* a termination date."

"Mason, you literally just told me you wanted to marry me."

"But I'm being realistic. I love you; you are literally my best friend. I can't think of anyone else I'd rather be married to, arranged or not. You are a consummate professional, but it was never going to work long term. At some point, one of us will crack under the pressure and explode. But if we have an end date in mind, as well as expectations along the way, I think this is doable. I just need you to do this with me for now."

"Mason Davis, you are quite the romantic. What are you thinking?"

"One year. No external relationships for the first year and then all bets are off. The relationship can remain a marriage on paper only or split up when it becomes glaringly obvious to the outside world that we aren't really together."

"Is a year long enough?"

"We can extend if necessary, but I think so. In a year you'll be off on the campaign trail, I'll likely be in D.C. It'll be normal for us never to be together. We can discreetly do as we please at that point until it becomes an issue." Mason kissed the back of my hand and gave it a squeeze. "Agree to my terms, Ellie. Please."

I stared up into the sky. He was a good friend. I didn't disbelieve him when he said he loved me, but I also knew he believed in happily ever after and he deserved a shot at it with someone who also believed in those things. "Okay. One year. We will assess the situation after that and see where things are. But literally, we tell no one. Plenty of people know this is an arranged marriage, but they don't need to know *this*."

"I agree to those terms."

I could see my skirt being blown about by the wind even though I was staring upwards. "I should probably go in before I end up with a head full of sand the night before the most important day in my hair's life."

"I didn't realize your hair was this serious about getting married."

"These pictures will follow us forever, Mason. It must be perfect. It all must be perfect. If it's itchy with sand, you'll be able to tell in all the pictures."

"How on earth would that be possible?"

"I mean, I'll know. I'll see them and think *'ugh, so much sand'*."

He laughed, and we both stood up. He picked up the blanket, careful to lift it so the sand blew away from us, and we walked back to the house. Upon getting to the door he said, "So, I guess I'll see you tomorrow." His voice shook a little like he was feeling the imminent pressure of getting married.

"I'll be the one in the white dress," I said. He kissed my cheek, and we walked inside and to our separate bedrooms.

Silas: *Can you meet me somewhere?*
Me: I'm on the Cape. I'm getting married this weekend.
Silas: *I know. I'm in Hyannis.*

My chest tightened. We hadn't spoken since the afternoon I had Mason evict him from my home.

Me: Silas.
Silas: *5 minutes, Eleanor.*

I cringed at his use of my full name. I knew better than to do this. This was an exercise in self-torture, but I knew I was doing it. I needed just one more minute with him.

It wouldn't be enough.

There was no way I could escape the compound unnoticed alone the night before my wedding. I tiptoed down the hall to the room Cee was staying in and knocked lightly. She opened the door and let me in. "I need a favor."

"Why Eleanor, are you about to do something controversial the day before your wedding? If so, I'm ready. Are we running away? Getting rip-roaring drunk? Do I need our passports?" She said excitedly while pulling on shoes.

"I just need you to go for a ride with me, no questions asked."

"Bride card activated."

I texted an address to Silas and told him to meet me in twenty minutes. Cee drove us to the dark beach. "Tell me you're running away," she pleaded with me.

"Don't be ridiculous, Catherine. Silas wanted to talk."

"The night before your wedding? Girl, he wants you to run away with him. Do it."

I rolled my eyes at her. "You and I both know it's not that

simple. Running away with Silas means burning every damn bridge I've built for my career." We hopped into her car and drove to the beach where I was meeting him.

"Would it set you back a bit if you leave Mason at the altar? Yes. Absolutely. His father is the damn Vice President. So I guess if your career is more important to you than Silas, it makes perfect sense."

I didn't actually know that her last statement held any truth. My career was important to me, and I was damn good at it. I already sacrificed so much for it that another year didn't feel like too much more to ensure job security. If it weren't for Silas, I wouldn't even be bothered by the situation, as much as that shocked everyone who knew. But I couldn't throw away the future I'd been building for a relationship that may not last another month. It always ends. Hell, even my arranged marriage wasn't forever. I didn't want to break Silas's heart, but I needed to protect myself more.

Selfish bitch.

I saw Silas pull up beside us. "Wait here," I instructed Cee and got out of the car.

Silas got out of the car and followed me down to the shore. I took my sandals off and wiggled my toes in the cool sand.

"You shouldn't be here, Silas." I didn't look at him as he stood at my side, but watched the waves coming ashore in the dark.

"Neither should you." I kicked at the sand as he continued. "Please don't do this."

"Silas." I dared to look at him. His eyes instantly connected with mine and it felt like he was trying to stare a place into my life.

"No, let me talk. I love you, Len—"

"Silas, it's just lust, there's no such thing as—" Tears spilled down my cheeks.

"Don't tell me how I feel!" He ran his hands through his hair in exasperation, cutting me off.

"Look, Silas, I've been very clear that we can't happen. I'm getting married. To someone else. Tomorrow. I don't doubt that you love Len, but she isn't real, Silas. Eleanor is just another politician with a ridiculous set of expectations. She's boring. Always polished. Always says the expected thing. Eleanor doesn't run away. I'm not the person you think I am. I'm her. I'm Eleanor and I have obligations. I can't just drop them because you think you love someone who doesn't even exist."

"Eleanor is the fake one. Who I see is who you really are. Not the robot you pretend to be."

We weren't going to agree on this. It was time to take a different approach. "Maybe so, but she's who I have to be."

"You're being ridiculous."

"No, Silas, you are. I told you this had an expiration. I knew we took this too far. *Sonofabitch*. I don't expect you to understand, I just need you to accept it."

"Never."

I let out a sob. I never cried; emotions like that are forbidden and here I was crying for the second time in as many hours. Silas stepped in front of me and wiped the tears with his thumb. I felt weak. I held his hand to my face as another tear fell. I had gone and dug myself in too deep.

"Just run away with me," he pleaded softly.

"I wish that was possible. I promised I would do this before I met you. I didn't know…" I sobbed so hard that it was becoming difficult to talk. "I'm so sorry. I never meant to get this attached."

He pulled me into his chest, wrapping his arms around me. I inhaled his comforting scent deeply, trying to memorize the way it felt to be in his arms. We stood there a few minutes, trying to stop time. Breaking his heart was killing me. *Maybe even breaking my own heart in the process.* He held me tight, and I cried into his shirt while he ran his hands through my hair.

The wind blew through my hair and he lifted my chin for a kiss. "I love you," he reiterated before kissing me with unspoken desperation. The kiss went from frantic to slow as we stole as many precious moments as we could. He pulled back slightly, but I wasn't ready and I crashed my lips back to his. It wasn't fair to either of us but I knew the second he pulled away it was all over and I wasn't ready to let him go. His hand tangled in my hair as he gave in to the kiss for another minute. "I have to go," he whispered against my lips, tears in his eyes. I nodded and watched him walk back to his car.

I fell to my knees in the sand and continued to sob uncontrollably. It felt like I was losing everything. My chest ached and my head felt unnaturally heavy. Everything just felt so wrong. Something inside me was broken and it had less to do with getting married to Mason than it did watching Silas walk away. For the first time in my life my head and my heart were at war. I didn't notice Cee walk up to me and sit down. She said nothing but rubbed my back until I was all cried out. "Can you ask Mish to find him and make sure he doesn't do anything stupid?" I sniffled.

"Already done," she said. I stood, brushing the sand from my legs and arms. We quietly went back to the car and drove back to the house in silence. I walked back in wearing her oversized sunglasses, went directly to my room and laid across my bed.

Cee shut the door behind me and sat on the floor. "So, are you ready to call this madness off? Because it doesn't look like Mason is the one you want to marry."

"I don't *want* to marry anyone, and you know that." I threw a pillow at her head. "He told me he loves me."

"What?! Wait. Mason or Silas?"

"Both of them, just a couple of hours apart."

"And these were words previously unsaid?"

"Mason, yes. Silas, a few days ago and again down at the beach."

"Were either of them drunk?"

"No."

"Were you having sex?"

"First, I haven't had sex with Mason in at least two years. Silas and I were in public. I bolted when he said it."

"Listen, I hear stories. I assumed you were banging."

"Fucking Sergio." The thought of him running his mouth to my sister made me smile. "If our upbringing has taught me anything, it's that Silas has a lust issue, and Mason has a guilt issue. Though Mason said he loved me more like a friend, I think."

Cee scoffed. "Right. That guy loves you, Elle. So much that he would lie to you because he knows you can't handle that level of emotional commitment."

"Not helping, Cee."

"And Silas, well, I'd say the lust goes both ways there."

"I definitely have a hard time keeping my clothes on around him." I blew my nose. "Like, they fucking fall off all on their own the second he enters the same space as me."

"So, for tomorrow, we institute a safe word. You say the word, and I get us the fuck out of there."

"I'm not running away, Cee."

"Just say 'apricots' if we need to go."

"That's your second *New Girl* reference of the night."

"I just can't stop watching it on repeat. It's like hanging out with old friends. Fun fact: I was fucking a dude who looks a lot like Nick Miller," she mused.

The next morning, the morning of my wedding, I awoke to my mother bursting into my room with a cup of tea and a banana. "Eat this," she instructed. I sat up in the bed and watched my mother flit around, rearranging random things.

"Mom. Stop. You aren't even the one getting married," I pleaded, taking a cautious sip of my tea.

"Right," she said. "So, the car will be here in half an hour to take us for hair and makeup."

My stomach turned. Despite there being plenty of space here

on the compound, I was getting ready at a hotel near the church. St. Francis Xavier Catholic church. Because I was marrying a Davis in Hyannis and *obviously* I'd be getting married in the "family" church. My father would not have it any other way. How he managed this on such short notice I'll never know, but alas, my church wedding day was here.

Cee bound into the room, coffee in one hand, some kind of pastry in the other. "So, who is ready to get this shit over with?" she asked. My mother shot her a very stern look. "What?" Cee said with a mouthful. "We've been preparing for this day for as long as I can remember. And personally, I'm slightly terrified to step foot in a church after all this time and all of my misdeeds."

"Misdeeds that most of these people know nothing about because your father is a complete asshole, and you went along with it," our mother spat in disgust. Our parents officially called it quits after Cee got pregnant and he insisted she go into hiding. If he had it his way, she would've put Wyatt up for adoption and carried on without a backward glance. But my sister wasn't having that. So they agreed she could do whatever she wanted as long as it was as quiet as possible. She adopted my mother's maiden name (as did my mother) and they moved into the western part of the state after she gave birth in Maine.

There was no love lost from those two for my father.

"Eleanor, this is what you want, right?" Mom started speaking rapidly. "I guess I just assumed, since you and Mason have always been so close, that this silly arrangement wasn't the reason for the wedding." A look of sheer terror blanketed her face as if she realized that this was as bad as what happened with Cee if it wasn't what I wanted.

"Of course, mother," I answered, "Mason is my best friend." From behind her, Cee put a finger into her mouth to imitate gagging. Our mother seemed to bounce back from her brief guilt.

The entire morning passed by in a blur. I had a mimosa in my hands at every opportunity, with Cee making sure I balanced it

with water. If I didn't pee on myself at the altar, it would be a miracle. We moved on to the hotel room, where we met up with one of the photographers who took pictures while we continued to get ready.

"If you glare at it any harder, it may burst into flames," Cee warned. My gaze had been on the white satin gown being steamed across the room. The bodice had beadwork that must have caused the poor seamstress many sleepless nights to complete on such short notice, but it was gorgeous. I just resented actually having to wear it.

My mom, my sister, and Megan got me into the dress. I flat-out refused a veil, and there was a big debate about a tiara. In the end, I wore an intricately beaded headband. Once I was put together, they brought me before a full-sized mirror.

I really wanted to vomit. I think Cee could tell because without asking or even looking at her; she held out a mimosa, and I swallowed it all in one gulp. She followed suit. It was the upscale version of shots.

And then it was time. The wedding coordinator handed me a bouquet and positioned me at the back of the church, ready to walk down the aisle. Just before being shooed down the aisle by the wedding coordinator, Cee turned to me and asked, "Do you want an apricot?" I shook my head, and she proceeded down the aisle.

It was a long aisle, and the church really was pretty, with its columns leading to the altar. I could see Mason standing up at the altar with the priest and his brother Rob acting as Best Man. I took a couple of deep breaths to calm myself and at the last moment, my father joined me to give me away.

You know, like the property that I swore I wasn't.

When we got to the altar, my father kissed my cheek and shook Mason's hand before taking a seat in the front pew. As it was a Catholic mass and wedding, it was far longer than I would've liked given the fact I really had to pee; I was also pretty tipsy, and somewhat convinced I'd fall over in front of everyone.

None of those things happened. We repeated the obligatory vows and afterwards, the priest declared us married. There was a kiss to seal the deal, and I leaned heavily on Mason's arm as we went back down the aisle. To onlookers, it probably looked like a cute display of affection, but in reality, I was holding on for dear life. "You look absolutely stunning," he said softly as we made our way back down the aisle.

As we came to the back of the church, I saw *him* sitting with Connor and Mish as we passed. I made brief eye contact with Silas as we exited the church. My heart slammed in my chest. *He looked like hell.* I stumbled a bit, but recovered without anyone noticing, thanks to Mason's tight grip on my arm.

Once alone in the car, Mason and I finally took a deep breath. "Well, that's over," Mason sighed with relief. "I hated being stared at like that for an hour."

"You. Are. Going. To. Be. A. Senator," I reminded him with a giggle.

"And you are drunk. Did you eat today?"

"A banana. My mother made me do it."

"I'm going to go ahead and call all the alcohol on a mostly empty stomach the reason I thought for sure you were going to puke when the priest told us to kiss, and *not* that you find such a thing that disgusting." He chuckled as he handed me a bottle of water. "Drink this."

I drained half the bottle, wishing it was alcohol after seeing Silas in the church. "Just a few more hours and we can retreat to joint solitude under the guise of consummating a marriage."

As was customary, we needed to stop for a million photos before heading to the reception. While the men of the family had their photos taken, I pulled Cee aside. "He was fucking there, Catherine!" I tried to keep my voice low, but I was having a bit of an internal meltdown that was making staying composed very difficult. The alcohol wasn't helping.

Jillian MacGregor

"I know," she responded. "We tried to talk him out of it. He said he needed to see it for himself for closure. I'm so sorry."

"It's fine," I lied. It was anything but fine. "If that's what he needed, then I hope he got it." More lies. Catherine gave me a knowing Look as the photographer called us over to be in the shots.

I forced myself through the motions of the reception. Despite a steady flow of champagne my head was pounding from a sleepless night of crying, dehydration, and fake smiling. I was tired both physically and emotionally. Mason and I made our rounds during dinner so I was also working on an empty stomach, but I had no interest in food. The closest thing I had was the tiny piece of cake that Mason neatly fed to me.

After a few hours of acting like a blushing bride, we said our farewells and made our way to the hotel. "Three hundred and sixty-four more days," he said just before we crashed for the night.

There was no consummation of the marriage.

Governor Roberts Announces the Marriage of his Daughter Eleanor to Mason Davis.

The pair were wed in Hyannis at Saint Francis Xavier Church, with a reception held at the Davis Estate. The couple had only their families and a handful of friends in attendance. Please join us in congratulating the happy couple.

-New York Times

Eighteen

Because of the campaign, there wasn't a honeymoon, not that I cared one way or the other. We went back to work Tuesday morning like nothing significant had occurred over the weekend.

Megan texted me to let me know that Mason and I were supposed to meet with my father. I dropped my purse in my office and joined Mason to walk across the street to see him. Right away, I could see it was not our usual kind of meeting. First, it was just the three of us, which always meant we were going to talk about things that were more confidential than usual. We almost always had a staff member there. Every interaction ended up needing someone in on the conversation to execute the details on our behalf.

Usually, a meeting of this type meant one of us had displeased my father, which, quite frankly, was very easy to do. I assumed this had something to do with the wedding, but I couldn't figure out what we could have possibly done wrong.

Mason and I walked into the office and closed the door. My father motioned for us to sit in the chairs across from him at his desk. He barely looked up from the material he was reading.

"I'm leaving office," he said, as if he was talking about what he had for breakfast.

Mason and I exchanged a look of confusion. "Leaving the office…like, resigning? Or just not running next term?" Mason attempted to clarify.

"Resigning. I've let Alex know already. We've been working on a transition plan for a while now." Alex was the Lieutenant Governor.

"Dad, what are you talking about? Why are you resigning?" I asked, concerned.

"Oh, right, buried the lead there, didn't I? I'm dying, Eleanor. I have stage four pancreatic cancer." He said it without looking up from the damn paper he was reading, as if he didn't just drop information that felt more like he slammed a brick into my face.

"*What*?!" Mason and I exclaimed at the same time.

"Keep your voices down, damn it. No one will know for a week still, but unfortunately, I can't quite wait until after the election. I have things I want to do before I die."

We sat in stunned silence for a few minutes before Mason spoke up. "Have you gotten a second opinion? Can't you do chemo or something?"

"I've seen the top doctors in the state. They say the same thing, it's too far gone and already spread to other areas. I have about six months at this point." Again, he said this factually, as if we were overreacting to this news.

Mason went into full politician mode while I remained dumbfounded. "We will work on the statement and timelines with Alex's office." He stood to leave, gently grabbing my hand to indicate I needed to join him. In my shocked state I just followed behind without question. As was customary after a meeting with my father, we retreated to Mason's office and shut the door.

"I'm so sorry, Ellie. You okay?" he asked, pulling me into a hug.

I was still stunned into silence. My father and I spent a significant amount of time together, especially since I started working with him after graduating, and I couldn't fathom him not being there watching my every move. It was frustrating and annoying, and I felt some guilt that there was this tiny part of me that felt relief knowing I wouldn't have to live my life to his standards anymore. My father was ridiculous, but I loved him anyway. "Can you imagine life without my father staring over our shoulder?"

"No. Not at all. Any chance he refuses to die because he'd have to give up controlling everything?" He was trying to lighten the mood a bit. I appreciated the attempt.

"Or just haunt us from the grave?" I mused, though I was mildly concerned that was a possibility. "I wonder how long he's been hiding this?"

"Probably a long time. At least since he told us to get married this summer. He knew then, he had to. I bet it caused the sudden urgency."

I stepped away from his embrace and took a deep breath. "Well, on with our day then, eh?" I didn't want to continue this discussion. I had things I needed to do, and they didn't include obsessing about whether my hasty wedding had something to do with my father being terminally ill and the fact he hid it from us to ensure we followed through with it to further his own agenda.

Governor Roberts Announces he has Terminal Cancer.

> *Just a week after his daughter's wedding, Governor Roberts has announced he will resign from office before the end of his term due to a diagnosis of stage four pancreatic cancer. The Governor and his family ask for privacy at this time.*
>
> *-Boston Globe*

Jillian MacGregor

An hour later:

Silas: *You knew. You knew he was dying and you married Mason, anyway. What the actual fuck?*
Me: I just found out, I swear. But it changes nothing. What's already done is done.
Silas: *Matchbox Twenty, Disease.*

October

> **Silas:** *Lying is the most fun a girl can have without taking her clothes off. Panic! At the Disco.*
> **Me:** I never lied to you, Silas. And for the record, you are absolutely the better fuck.

I shouldn't have included the last part, but the gut reaction was to fight somehow.

> **Silas:** *And yet that's not enough, is it? It's not me you lie to. It's yourself and everyone else.*

This guy knew how to punch me in the gut. Missing Silas the way I did was both unexpected and painful. He wasn't wrong. I lied to myself repeatedly.

Uninvited

November

Mason Davis Wins Senate Seat!

Davis is the son of Vice President James Davis, and grandson of former longtime U.S. Senator Ted Davis. Senator-elect Davis recently wed Eleanor (Roberts) Davis, daughter of former Massachusetts Governor Roberts.

-Boston Globe

Silas: *[link to Boston Globe article] Congratulations, Post Malone.*
Me: Thank you. I hope you are well. I truly do.

December

Silas: *Normal Like You, Everclear.*

I didn't know how to respond. The song was about a woman walking around like everything was normal when it just wasn't. It was pretty spot on. The fact he still sent random texts caused me to spiral into confusion and miss him more.

I never missed someone like this. Ever. I went away to college for years without a single minute of homesickness. But every day without Silas was slowly killing me. I wanted to go home, but "home" was no longer a place, it was a person. I didn't know what to do with this, but as long as I was married to someone else, I needed to leave Silas alone. It wasn't fair to him for me to keep engaging with him. I'd made a choice, and it was much harder to come back from that now.

Me: There's nothing normal about me.

I'm a bitch. Why can't I just leave this guy alone?

January

Silas: *Soundgarden - Slaves & Bulldozers.*

Nineteen

Former Massachusetts Governor Roberts Dies

Just five months after announcing he had stage four pancreatic cancer, former Massachusetts Governor Roberts passed away in his home. His daughters, Eleanor and Catherine, along with Eleanor's husband Mason Davis, were with him in his final days. Funeral arrangements are being prepared.

-Boston Globe.

My father's last few days were hard on all of us. The day the hospital released him into hospice care, the press swarmed like vultures. Mason returned from Washington D.C. early, just prior to this, and the press knew this was *the end*.

Like the robot Silas had once accused me of being, I didn't shed a tear. Catherine, on the other hand, was a blubbering mess. The day before we released the statement about my father's

condition to the press back in September, I called her to let her know first, at my father's request. He wanted to "make amends" before he died, and this was an item on that list. (I did not, however, tell her she was an item on his to-do list.)

My father met Wyatt briefly on Thanksgiving and Christmas, though we just told Wyatt this was a friend, not wanting to get into the details of what a grandfather was and why he just appeared after almost four years. There's only so much a small child can understand.

My father was in and out of the hospital in January until finally relenting to hospice care. He spent eight days at his home before dying in his sleep. I felt both sad and relieved. His last few months had been torture on him, and therefore incredibly hard to witness as well.

I sat in his home office, finalizing all the arrangements with the various parties. People were coming and going, leaving food, flowers, and condolences. Mason did the majority of the greetings while I hid away, making phone calls. There were just so many people in the house taking care of various things. I needed peace and quiet.

There was a knock on the office door, and it opened slowly. "Come in," I replied. Silas stood in the doorway. My breath caught in my throat. "Um, what are you doing here?" My heart pounded in my chest. Emotions flooded my senses and I was having trouble forming words. There were so many. *This is a horrible idea. I need you. Please don't leave.* I couldn't say any of them but they echoed in my mind.

"When a friend loses a family member, you visit the friend and see if you can assist in any way. In your married life, they still permit you to have friends, right?" He flashed a cheeky grin. *This man. Damn, I've missed him.*

"Shut the door, Silas."

He complied.

"Yes. Many friends have been through the house in the last few days, but this is a little... awkward." I tried to appear neutral but everything in me wanted to run to him and feel his arms around me. *Oh you want more than his arms around you.*

"Why?" He asked earnestly.

"Because all I want to do right this minute is fuck you on my father's desk and there's no way on earth I can go through with that because I'm fucking married to someone else." *Probably not the right thing to say, Eleanor.*

He smiled wickedly. "So, if I give you a hug, would that help or hurt this situation?"

"I don't know how to answer that because I'm not sure which sides 'help' and 'hurt' fall."

"Well then, I'm going to hug you, and I will not let you in my pants because you're married. But I really am sorry for your loss, even though he was the reason you're married. Because losing people sucks. I'm not here to upset you. I just want to offer to help, however that is, and let you know that I'm here if you need me."

Stop being so fucking nice to me. A tear escaped my eye. The first since the last time I saw him, despite the fact my father just died. The second he walked in the door my suppressed emotions were hitting like bombs. "Thank you. I appreciate all of that. I will accept the hug. This sucks even though he was such a huge pain in my ass."

Silas closed the distance between us and took me in his arms. I inhaled his scent deeply, letting it comfort me. For the first time in months, I felt like I could breathe and I just wanted him to hold me forever. Before the embrace could be anything other than a friendly hug, he kissed the top of my head and backed away. Immediately, I felt cold and alone. "I am going to head out. But I mean it: Please let me know if there's anything I can do."

And then he left. He was there less than five minutes, and it

had me riding a rollercoaster of emotions. I was happy I saw him; even happier to have been able to hug him; and fucking devastated that he had to walk away. *It's only seven more months. If you are still this miserable then, you can get out of it.*

My father laid in State while the citizens of the Commonwealth and various dignitaries paid respects. Mason and I stood stoically, accepting condolences for an entire day. There was a funeral, a long funeral in a Catholic church filled with so many people I didn't even know.

Then came the private burial with just family. Of course, that was still many people, more so since the wedding, but at least I could identify them all. In the car on the way to the cemetery, Cee burst into tears. She mumbled to Eli that she hated being upset about this because "that asshole" had never even seen her house and only met her kid twice. Eli hugged her tightly and whispered things I couldn't hear. Mason squeezed my hand, knowing I was just as pissed about the same thing.

We held a graveside service. Once it was over, everyone dispersed except Mason and I. We stood in front of the casket with Cee and Eli. It was absolutely freezing and while I wore my thickest pair of wool tights with a heavy wool coat dress, scarf, and gloves, I was going numb every time the wind blew. I had to take off a glove, my fingers stinging with the sudden exposure, to pick up a fistful of frosty dirt and sprinkle it on the casket. Mason followed suit, and we walked back to the car, leaving Cee and Eli alone. They were there a few more minutes before Eli all but carried her away.

I was so glad she had him. In some odd way, it made me miss Silas, even though Mason was one of my best friends and had known my father as well as I did. He was being so supportive, and I felt guilty that I really just wanted Silas to wrap his arms around me again.

I slid my phone from my pocket when the car pulled away from the cemetery.

> **Me:** Thanks so much for coming to see me, Silas. I miss you so much.
> **Silas:** *I'd do anything for you, Len. Even open a bank account.*
> **Me:** A *New Girl* reference!

I smiled for the first time in days.

> **Silas:** *I've been studying. I need to keep up with Cee. And it makes me think of you. I know you literally just buried your father, but I'm hoping I can see you somewhere soon while being totally respectful of the whole married thing. I just need to see you.*

I felt a stab in my gut. I should not have told him I missed him, even though I truly did. Not even because I hadn't been laid since August. I just really missed being around him. I felt alone and adrift without him for the last five months. Our occasional texts were both a lifeline and a curse. It was totally selfish, but I just wanted to make sure he was still there when this stupid sham of a marriage was over. I decided that the year was all I could handle. I couldn't even ask Silas to wait because I wasn't about to reveal my divorce plans until I knew it was a given. I couldn't do that to him if, for some odd reason, Mason and I ended up extending the marriage.

A few hours after we got home, I was still thinking about Silas asking to see me.

> **Me:** Meet me at my father's house.
> **Silas:** *Really?*

Me: Yeah. Give me about an hour. Text me when you get there and I'll let you in.

This was one of my more outlandish ideas, but it seemed like safe enough ground. People have been coming and going from my father's house for days, including me. "Hey, Mace," I called out as I grabbed my nude dress boots.

"What's up?"

"I'm going to head over to my dad's for a few hours. I just need to go through some stuff without all the distractions and people coming and going."

He eyed me suspiciously. "You okay?"

"I guess? Kind of grief numb." I reached into the closet to grab a winter coat.

"Is Silas going to be there?" I gave him a look. *How did he know that?* "I saw him earlier. I'm the one who showed him to the office. I don't care. Do what you need to do. Death sucks and if he makes you feel better, go for it."

I didn't know what that meant. Was he just talking about seeing Silas, or was he telling me to do more than just see him? "Mason, he's a friend. I just need someone who isn't so close to this."

Mason sighed. "No, he isn't. And I don't expect you to act like friends right now. If you need to fuck him to get through this mess, I say go for it."

A look of shock took over my face. "Are you saying you're off to fuck someone to relieve the tension?"

"It's not a quid pro quo kind of thing, but it has crossed my mind."

"If you're asking permission, you don't need to. Normal married people would probably fuck each other, huh?"

"Let's not complicate this. Especially right now."

I nodded, giving him a kiss on the cheek, and walked out the door.

My father's house was lit up like the damned sun with all of his outdoor lighting. I let myself in the front door and set my clutch and keys on the table, hanging my coat in the closet. I left my boots in the closet and walked around the house in my tights. It was the closest they'd ever been to walking barefoot on these floors that I could remember.

I went into the kitchen and put the kettle on for some tea. I looked around the room with a critical eye, wondering how much of this my mother chose, and what was chosen by some assistant or hired interior designer. My mother hated this house. She called it a museum and, to be fair, she wasn't far off. Everything was for show, and virtually nothing, including the floors, were meant to be touched.

The kettle whistled, and I poured the water into a mug and dropped a bag of some herbal tea that smelled like cinnamon into the hot water. This tea definitely didn't belong to my father. He didn't drink tea. As I walked toward his office, I wondered who brought it into the house. Maybe one of the hospice nurses? They had been so good at making sure Cee and I were taking care of ourselves while they cared for my father.

I fished in the top drawer of the desk, looking for the book of passwords he kept there. I wanted to go through some files on his laptop that had my name on it but were password protected. The curiosity killed me. There were also folders named "Catherine," "Mason," and "Elijah" that I would not open. I'd download them onto thumb drives and give them to the corresponding person.

I looked through this book of passwords and other important information, like bank account numbers, but found nothing that unlocked the folder. What the hell could he possibly have on here that needed that much protection?

My phone dinged with a text from Silas indicating that he was here. I went to the front door to let him in. "I really thought you were going to sneak me in a back door or something," he said when I greeted him.

"This place has been Grand Central Station for the last couple of weeks. No one is paying any attention at this point." I took his jacket and put it in the closet next to mine. I led him to a room my father referred to as the 'receiving room' but probably would've been a living room in a normal, modern family. "Have a seat. Can I offer you something to drink? I'm going to go grab my tea."

"Just a glass of water. And you don't have to be so formal, it's just me. You aren't Eleanor tonight."

I took a deep breath and retraced my steps to the office to grab my tea and then to the kitchen to grab Silas some water. I added a bit of hot water to my mug and brought both beverages to the receiving room. I set both drinks down on the table without coasters and smiled at the small act of rebellion. Surely that table had never had a glass sit directly upon it. I sat next to Silas on the couch.

"Should I ask why you are smiling at a table, or is that just some weird custom?"

"That table has never held a drink without a coaster. My father would've lost his mind. I was enjoying the freedom. It's stupid, but it feels powerful somehow. I've actually been walking around without shoes for a while as well. My bare feet have literally never touched any floor in this house outside of my bedroom and bathroom."

"How is that even possible?"

"He didn't allow us to leave our rooms unless we got dressed and ready for the day. Never know who may show up, and apparently the Roberts family is always ready. Getting dressed included hair being done, makeup when we were old enough, and shoes. Thus, once I left my room, I always had shoes on. My bare feet have never touched this floor."

Silas looked down at my feet. "They still haven't."

"I suppose not, but this is close." I wiggled my toes.

"If we're breaking obscure rules, we're walking around this place barefoot." He started taking off his shoes. "Lose the tights. Time to freeze your toes on this floor." I slid my tights down my legs while he pulled off his socks. "Where to, Duchess?"

"Literally everywhere. Every floor." I giggled like a child.

"Awesome, a house tour." He slipped my hand in his, and we began walking around the house. I led him up the stairs first. "Please tell me you are breaking a 'no boys in your room rule' next."

"So that wasn't a rule. He allowed boys in my room. Mason, specifically."

"That's fucking weird, Len."

I opened the door to show him my childhood bedroom, now a guest room. It had changed little.

"So, I see they redecorated when you moved out."

I minimally decorated the room with just a vase of flowers on the dresser. There were no photos or art anywhere to be seen. "Actually, no. The only things different in this room are my clothes and other necessities not being here, and that lamp by the bed."

"I should've known posters of boy bands would have been forbidden."

"For me, yes. Follow me to Catherine's room." I walked to the next door down the hall and opened it. There was a large One Direction poster above the bed, clothes long forgotten on the floor, and pictures of Cee and her friends tacked up randomly. "Like almost everything, Cee had different rules. There were no boys in her room, well, allowed in her room. I'm certain Eli slept in here often, and indulging in pop culture was fine. But once she left this room, she had to act like a lady. Dad hasn't let anyone in this room since the day he kicked her out. Apparently, that included the housekeeper." I ran my finger through some dust on the dresser.

"Again, fucking weird, Len."

"It gets weirder. Behold! My mother's room." I opened the door across the hall. It was set up much like mine and probably also hadn't been touched since my mother left the day after Cee was kicked out.

"Your parents didn't share a room?" he asked in disbelief.

"No way, man. I vaguely recall them sharing a room when I was very young, but, at some point, my mother moved into a different room. They blamed preferring different sleeping conditions, but clearly that wasn't all that was going on." We turned a corner, and I opened my father's door. It was a typical man's generic bedroom. "And here's dear ol' Dad's room, though he had been staying downstairs the last few months because he couldn't do the stairs anymore."

We walked back downstairs and into the kitchen, and then on to the office, and then to the guest room my father used as his bedroom for the last few months he was alive. The hospital bed remained in the middle of the room, but everything else had mostly been cleaned up. "That's about it."

"And now your bare feet have touched every room. Any chance you fit into Cee's sweatpants? Because walking around this house in loungewear is probably fairly empowering as well. Also, we're gonna need to mess this hair up a bit." He stuck his hand into my hair and swished it around. I stopped cold. My internal body temperature rose rapidly, and my body thrummed with instant need. I stepped closer and leaned my head into his hand.

Silas's other hand wrapped around my waist as we stared into each other's eyes. My heart pounded rapidly in my chest. *This is such a bad idea. Have I not learned my lesson?* I reached up to rub my hands over his scruff. *Apparently not.* "Kiss me, Silas," I whispered. He pulled my head to his and lightly brushed his lips against mine.

"This is a dangerous game, Lenny," he whispered against my lips.

"If you don't want to do this, I will step back right now. Just let me know," I offered, assuming he meant he needed to protect himself.

"I've wanted to do this since August. But I promised to remember you are married."

"I don't care about that. It's cool you are trying to be respectful and all, but please be disrespectful."

"As always, my beautiful duchess, your wish is my command," he said as he pulled our bodies flush. I could feel his erection and my core throbbed in anticipation. His lips came down on mine with much more ferocity as he fisted the hand in my hair. With each touch, he replaced the stressful tension in my body with the tension of arousal and need. My hands ran down his chest and my fingers found the bottom of his shirt.

He pulled my head back and trailed open-mouthed kisses down my neck to the top of my dress then upward under my ear. I shivered. He reached behind me and pulled the zipper of my dress down, trailed a finger up and down the newly revealed skin and placed a kiss back on my lips, looking directly into my eyes for permission to continue.

I lifted the hem of his shirt to reveal his chest. He reached behind and pulled it over his head then slid the arms of my dress down, causing it to fall to my feet. I unbuttoned his jeans and pushed them down; he shook his legs until they came off.

Hands were everywhere after that. Mouths kissing chests, necks and lips as we stood just outside my father's office in nothing but underwear. I palmed his cock through his boxer briefs before sliding my hand inside and taking it into my hand. Silas hissed. "These need to go," I breathed, tugging them down.

He jutted his chin in my direction. "Those too," he said of my bra and underwear. We both stripped the clothes off and returned to kissing, one of his hands kneading a breast and the other back in my hair. I ran my hand up and down his length. "The desk," he ordered, and we moved toward the desk without losing contact. "We are going to be really fucking disrespectful with this desk. I have been thinking about fucking you on this desk since you mentioned it the other day." *Holy shit, yes.* I felt the hair rise along my arms and nape. Everything about what he had just said, and *how* he said it, had me filled with lust.

I gently tossed the laptop to the chair; Silas pushed the papers to the floor and then picked me up and sat me on the desk, spreading my legs to stand between them. He leaned over and took my nipple into his mouth and I held his head there with a moan. Using his body weight to guide my back to the desk he trailed kisses down my torso before dropping to his knees, wasting no time licking my center.

"Oh, God," I panted, trying to grab at something with my hands, but all that was under me was the solid desk.

Silas inserted a finger while he flicked his tongue over my clit. I could feel an orgasm quickly building. "Silas, I need you to fuck me." I panted.

"Not until you come on this desk," he said, adding a finger and sucking on my clit. I saw stars behind my eyes as I trembled through my orgasm. He continued his assault until it ebbed. "Stand up," he ordered.

I wasn't exactly sure my legs would hold me at that point as they were still shaking and felt like jello, but I made the effort because I still needed to feel him inside me. Turning me, he pushed my chest to the desk, grabbed my hips and aligned his cock with my entrance. He gave my ass a slap and then slammed his cock in, holding still when he was all the way in. I let out a cry, and he groaned. "You. Are. Fucking. Perfection." He slid out and back in slowly a few times, savoring the moment.

"Harder, Silas," I begged. He eagerly complied, slamming into me repeatedly, causing a second orgasm to build. "Please don't stop."

"I hate that I can't say no to you." His fingers dug into my hips harder as his speed and force increased, channeling his anger into his thrusts. There would be bruises from his fingers and I welcomed the idea that I'd have a physical reminder of him on my body, at least for a few days. I could feel tears falling down my cheeks, my emotions betraying me.

"Come for me, Len," he rasped and my walls started squeezing around his length. "Just like that." He tensed behind me, his movements jerking as he came along with me.

He turned me and pulled me to his chest tight. Sobs racked through me. He pulled away to look me in the eye. "Shit. I'm sorry. Are you okay?" He pulled further away to look me over.

"Physically, I'm fine." Emotionally, however, I was a mess. I had never been such a hot fucking mess.

"Come on. Let's get you into bed."

Twenty

"That was definitely against the rules," I commented as I led him to the kitchen for water, trying to avoid the fact I had just lost my shit while getting railed in my dead father's office. I brought him to my old bedroom. We crawled under the blankets and snuggled close, our legs tangled together, my head tucked under his chin.

"You okay?" he asked again, kissing the top of my head.

I took a deep breath. "I promise." *Liar.*

"It's late. You should get some sleep."

"I don't want to right now. I just want to lay here with you for a while. I'm not ready to say goodbye yet. Just tell me things, random things, things about what you've been doing. Anything. I just need to live in this moment with you before the real world starts hassling me."

"Matchbox Twenty reference. A classic." He then proceeded to just hold me and share band gossip, much of which he had heard from Sergio. He told me about Gia and her kids. He must have talked for an hour, with only a few comments from me.

"I've been so fucking mad at you, Len," he whispered.

"You should be. You deserve so much better than I've ever been

able to give you. Why did you come, Si?"

"I told you before, I'm a fucking masochist. And I can't stay away. I *hate* that I can't stay away. I can't stop thinking about you." He rubbed a hand up and down my arm slowly. Then, after a long silence, he asked, "What happens now, Len?"

I took a deep breath and unsuccessfully tried to hold back tears. He held me for a few minutes more before untangling himself from me and going on a hunt for our clothes. The bubble had burst, and the magic was gone. *Seven more months is too long.*

He returned wearing his boxers and holding the rest of his clothes. "I invaded Cee's room and grabbed you these." He handed me a tee shirt and leggings. "I figured you wouldn't want to put the dress back on, but I brought it just in case." He put the clothes beside me on the bed and pulled his shirt on, followed by his pants. "So, I'm gonna go, because I don't want to have this conversation right now." He kissed my cheek. "I still love you, Len."

He walked out of the bedroom and shut the door. Instantly, I felt empty. The tears poured down my cheeks as I heard him open and close the front door. I slipped Cee's tee shirt over my head and cried myself to sleep.

I woke up to my phone ringing around six. "Hey," I answered when I saw Mason's name and picture on the screen.

"I just want to make sure the coast is clear. There will be people coming to pick up the hospital bed this morning and, I don't know, a bunch of other people in and out. I'll be there in twenty. I have coffee and clothes."

"Yeah, I'm alone. I'm going to hop in the shower. Just come on up."

While I had been asleep, Silas sent a song, "Hold Me Tight or Don't" by Fall Out Boy. I didn't respond. All I wanted to do was hold him tight, but I needed to untangle the mess I was in before I could make him any promises.

A few minutes later, Mason walked into the bathroom with a clean dress, tights, and undergarments. He placed them on the counter and left without a word. I finished showering and dressed before emerging from the bathroom to meet Mason in my room. He was sitting at the desk, with two cups of coffee, a paper bag with what must have been breakfast, and his laptop.

"Thanks," I said, picking up the coffee.

"There are some shoes by the bed, but I couldn't find the nude boots. I assumed they were here, but I don't see them."

"I left them in the closet downstairs."

Mason looked up from what he was doing. "Huh, I hadn't even considered no shoes in this house. Weird."

"You bet your sweet ass! I walked barefoot into every room in this house, too. Because fuck that dude and his rules."

"I see we've hit anger on the grief scale."

"Remember when we were thirteen, and he caught us smoking? All I want to do is light up right here in my room as a *fuck you*. I don't even like smoking, but I just have this deep-seated need to fuck shit up right now."

Mason laughed. "I remember. He lost his shit. You just stood there until he finished screaming and said 'okay, sir' and walked away. It was one of those times your relationship with your parents struck me as truly fucked up. Especially because he never once mentioned it was horrible for your health. He just went on and on about the possibility of someone seeing it and ruining your reputation. That was the day you told me he didn't care about you other than how you could benefit him and his plans."

"I legitimately thought you were going to punch him in the face."

"Instead, I just made sure you knew someone loved you, and that someone would be me. You know, until you went to college, and I was a complete asshole for years."

I looked away from him and stared at the floor, refusing to

once again wonder how things would be different if I hadn't chosen a college far away and he didn't choose the military. Before that happened, I knew where I stood with Mason, and that he'd always be there for me. We were closer back then than we were now, and the messed up part was that now, we were married. "That was his fault, too. He all but made sure we split up for a while. He manipulated us like puppets."

"Yes, but he can't do that anymore, Ellie. We can do whatever we want without having to answer to him. I will always love you, but not the way Silas does. I thought I did, but there's something missing here, and it's whatever you two have." He reached out to touch me but pulled away before making contact. " I'm sorry I let my ambitions fuck that up for you."

"It wasn't just you. Or my dad. I had ambitions, too. I had the power to walk away, and I chose this. I thought it was what I wanted. I thought once he was out of sight, I'd move on like always. But I can't. I fucked up, Mason. And I don't know how to fix it." I felt sick with the realization.

He closed the distance between us and took me into a hug. "Yeah. We both did," he sighed.

> **Silas:** *Please answer the phone, Len. I don't want to text this.*
> **Me:** I need an hour. I'll call you when I get in the car. I'm out with a bunch of politicians.
> **Silas:** *I'm in Boston. I can meet you somewhere.*

I agreed to meet him in the parking garage Mason and I used when we stayed in the apartment in Cambridge. I sat in my car nervously waiting for Silas to show up, half wishing he wouldn't, so we didn't have to have this conversation. I had some major decisions and moves to make, and it was going to take time. I didn't want to ask him to wait for me anymore.

He pulled into Mason's spot, and I joined him in his car. "If I never see another coat dress, it will be too soon," he said flatly as I sat down.

"I actually don't hate these things." I looked down at my coat.

He continued to stare at the coat with disdain. "It represents all the things I can't have."

"It's just clothes, Silas."

"Lenny, I need you to say it." I looked up at him. He looked ready to crack. He knew what I was going to say. "What happens now?"

"Silas," I sighed.

"He's dead," he cut in. "I'm sorry to be so blunt, but it's true, and I don't see a reason for you to stay married to Mason."

"It's complicated, Silas." A tear slid down my cheek that I wiped away with my gloved hand.

"Bullshit, Len. Do you love him? Is that what this is about?"

"No, Silas, not the way you are thinking. We've been friends our whole lives. We've been through some crazy shit, but there isn't anything more than that there. I made a commitment. It wouldn't be good for any of us if Mason and I split up right now."

"What about me? Do you love me, Len?"

I felt sick to my stomach. There wasn't a good answer here. "Silas," I whispered, the tears multiplying down my cheeks.

"Eleanor," he replied, albeit spitefully.

"I need time."

"Time for what!? You've had time. For fuck's sake, I've given you more than time. I've played by your rules for almost a year now."

"I know. But I can't undo a marriage in a day. I don't expect you to wait around for me. You're right, I've asked you for too much already. But I literally can't make this disappear." I wanted to tell him to just drive, take me away from here, and I knew he'd do it without hesitation. Which was why I decided I had to leave immediately before I lost my head. "I have to go, Silas," I said and got out of the car, walking quickly to the stairwell so I couldn't look back. It was cowardly, but necessary. I couldn't let my emotional state ruin anything. I wasn't in a place to make any decisions.

As I walked up the stairs, he sent a text:

> **Silas:** *Love the Way You Lie, Eminem.*
> **Silas:** *Bye, Len.*

I ran into the apartment, throwing my keys and bag on the counter and kicking off my shoes as I beelined for the bedroom, tears streaming down my face. I sat down on the couch, sobbing into my hands. A few minutes later, Mason walked in and quietly sat beside me, putting a hand on my back. "Hey, you okay?"

"No."

He sighed. "I'm going to file for divorce tomorrow. I don't care what it looks like, Ellie, this is ridiculous."

"Don't you dare. It doesn't matter anymore, Mason. I just need a minute and I'll be fine. Just don't divorce me right now. Honestly, that will only make everything worse and I'm at the end of my rope. There's a way to do this with minimal destruction. I just don't know what that is right this minute."

"Yeah, okay," he sighed again, unconvinced.

Twenty-One

"What if we just throw a bomb at the whole thing?"

"Mason, what on earth do you mean by 'throw a bomb'? That is terrifying and could mean anything." We were sitting on the couch eating dinner in our D.C. apartment. I had on sweatpants and a hoodie, and Mason wore jeans and a tee shirt. It would have been most unusual in the days before my father died. After a lifetime of my father insisting I be dressed and ready if not in bed sleeping, the habit was fading. I hadn't lived with him for years, but for some reason it wasn't until he died that I realized it just wasn't that important. We just started to ignore the door in the unlikely event someone showed up after 8 p.m. *Why the hell didn't I do that before?* Mostly, people didn't show up unannounced. The phone calls and texts were plentiful, but we could answer those wearing whatever the hell we wanted.

"Our marriage. What if we just threw a bomb at it now and watched it explode? Could be a good time." A corner of his mouth tipped up in amusement.

"Why, though?"

"Because you are miserable. Because we shouldn't have done it in the first place. Because your father is dead and mine doesn't give a fuck what you do, as long as I remain in office. I already won the election, and you have solidified yourself as the kick ass campaign strategist you are. You don't need me anymore."

"I'm not miserable, and I *work for your father on his campaign*," I said with a bit of a whine in my voice. It was a lie. I was completely miserable.

"He won't fire you. Especially if it's my fault."

"You'll ruin your career. That's insane."

"Eh, I have three years before I have to worry about voters. And I happen to know a kick ass strategist who can help me out." He gave me a cocky grin.

"There has to be a better way. What on earth could you have in mind that would cause divorce before our first anniversary?"

"Elle, you are miserable. You're in love with someone who isn't me."

"I'm not in love with anyone," I grumbled into my plate. "I just don't know how to artfully undo the mess that is our marriage."

"That's bullshit. I'm thinking it's time the press knows about Wyatt."

"How is my sister's kid going to end our marriage?"

Mason stared at me for a solid minute, trying to figure out what to say. "Eleanor, tell me you know. You're her sister, you *must* know."

It was obvious at this moment what he meant, and had been staring me in the face for years, but I needed him to say it. "I must know what, Mason?"

"That I'm his father."

I ignored the fact that I was supposed to be angry that my husband was the father of my nephew. I was more concerned about dragging Wyatt and Cee through the ringer just to get me out of a marriage. And, yeah, I was probably shocked, but years of handling sticky situations for high profile people had my brain immediately considering the consequences of his suggestion instead of allowing my emotions to drive the conversation.

"I hardly think admitting to being the father of my sister's child is a good idea. We've kept him well hidden. I don't want to fuck up anyone else's life."

He sighed. "The press knows that Wyatt exists. As soon as Cee came out of the woodwork for the wedding and your dad's funeral, they found out about him. They've been trying to guess who the father is for weeks. She agrees that it's better if we control the story."

Rage hit all at once. With every word that passed between us the situation was sinking in and I was pissed. *They were discussing this behind my back? As if it didn't impact me at all?* "Control the *story*, Mason? What the fuck? Can I at least hear the real story before we release some fake shit so you can get rid of me?"

"Whoa, whoa. I'm not trying to get rid of you. Let's put down the plate before it becomes a weapon." He motioned to the plate in my hand. I put it on the table beside the couch. "I'm sorry. I really assumed she told you years ago. It was one stupid night. We were both mad at you, for different reasons. We had a few drinks. The next day we both knew it was a really stupid thing to do, but figured it was the end of it. Until she found out she was pregnant."

I sat on the couch, stunned. My husband and my sister had this secret. This walking, talking secret, and neither thought to tell me. *No, they deliberately kept it from me. How the hell did I never connect the dots on my own?* "So this *whole* time, you've been, what, ignoring your kid? I thought you were better than that shit, Mason."

"Of course not. Why would you think that?"

"Because he's almost four, you are my husband, and she is my sister, and *somehow* it was never obvious you had a child this whole time."

"Elle, we kept it quiet for the sake of everyone involved, but that doesn't mean I left her high and dry. I wouldn't do that. And to be perfectly honest, I hate that my own kid has no idea I'm more than just his uncle." I could see that the last part really was a sore spot for him as he said it. His elbows rested on his knees, his head in his hands. He took a deep breath before continuing. "I've missed every milestone. You aren't the only one who has sacrificed here, Elle. We all have. And I think we are all sick of it."

"Un-fucking-believable. So you want to drag my sister through the press?"

"It was her idea. I didn't tell her we had planned to get divorced, but we were talking about how miserable you are, and she chastised me for even marrying you to begin with. I told her that there was no way you'd just walk away, but then she said you would if this whole thing went public."

"I'm not fucking miserable. I'm livid that I'm just hearing about you being someone's father. That you fucked my baby sister. Can we talk about how fucked up that is?"

"Clearly the reason it is a buried family secret, Elle. I'm not proud of that. It was reckless and stupid, but it happened and I can't just take it back. But we can leverage it to give you your life back."

"I'm not willing to ruin a kid's life over it. He'll be the bastard son of his aunt's husband."

"It's a win for all of us. I get to see my son without hiding. He gets to see me and I won't have to be 'Uncle Mason'. Catherine doesn't have to hide Wyatt or herself from the world, and you get to walk away from a shitty situation with a very valid reason that no one will hold against you."

I was silent for a while, letting the whole situation sink in. I hadn't processed the idea of using it for divorce, instead I was trying to figure out how this was going to change Wyatt's life for both better and worse.

"Say something."

"I'm his auntie stepmom." It was all I could say. "Our family dynamic just got more complicated than I ever expected."

"Eleanor, listen to me. If you don't divorce me, I'm divorcing you. Either way, this is how it is going to happen."

"So when you asked 'what if' I, once again, don't really have a choice?"

He threw his hands into the air. "You don't have a choice about Wyatt." He took a breath and lowered his voice. "You have a choice about timing and a seat at the table to discuss how it all gets handled. If you can come up with something better, a way that we can fix all the messes with minimal destruction, I'm all for it. But for fuck's sake, take the opportunity and walk away. You have someone who is in love with you, and I know you feel something for him too, even if it isn't being in love because you don't think you know how. I don't want to be the reason you can't have that." He raked a hand through his hair.

"I would never tell you *not* to be there for my nephew and I know it is your choice how to handle that situation.. But we can turn it on its head. He can stay with us because he's my nephew as far as anyone outside of our family knows. There are other ways for you to be in his life without ruining your career."

"You want him to feel like a dirty secret growing up? Because Catherine and I really don't want that for him. We went along with your father's demands, but he's gone and Wyatt is getting older. We didn't expect it to actually *be* a secret this long. We figured somehow it would come out."

I shook my head, but I understood. "You're right. Wyatt deserves better than that. Sorry. I'm just still trying to catch up. You've had four years and I've had fifteen minutes," I reminded him, calmly.

"I honestly thought that Wyatt is the reason you've been pushing away so much the last few years. When we were younger, I always pictured this going so differently." He sighed and flopped back against the pillow.

"How so?"

"For one, I'd hoped we'd have a *real* relationship. I know our first attempt at coupledom was not ideal. It had huge expectations attached. I didn't take the pressure well when we were that young. You went off to college to get away. We needed to find the space to learn about ourselves before getting to this part of our lives when we'd be married. Somehow, I always assumed that it would just be…real. There'd be a mutual attraction. Maybe we waited too long, or maybe not long enough, but it doesn't change the fact that it's not working. There's someone out there that is so much better for you than I am."

"You thought you could get me to love you," I realized out loud.

He looked away. "You make it sound like I was trying to trick you into it. That wasn't it. I just thought this would work out differently. I'm probably a little disappointed, but I recognize that's not just a 'you' issue."

"Mason, if I had to be arrange married to anyone, I'm glad it's you. And I'm sorry that I can't be who you want me to be. But even though Silas may be in love with me, I don't think I'll ever love him in a way that matters."

A sad smile crossed his face. "You are such a goofball. You already do. I know it. Catherine knows it. Hell, Eli and Wyatt know it. And Wyatt is four. The only two people who are unsure are you and Silas."

"How is it you are so certain about this if I don't know?"

"As much as I've tried to erase the memory of you and him naked on the table, that's the day I realized there was no going back for you. You were never going to be mine. I was a selfish asshole for not calling the whole thing off then. I was a selfish asshole who doubled down on the reminder that I had dibs."

"Why that day?" I furrowed my brow trying to figure out what he would've seen to make him think that.

"Well, for one, the Eleanor I know would never have fucked just anyone out in the open, let alone on a table. I've seen you with other guys. I've jealously referred to you as my wife or something similar in their presence, and you've never once corrected me. Not until that day. You couldn't shut me down fast enough. Any other time you just let them go and moved on to the next thing on your to do list."

"I never noticed." I remained quiet, just above a whisper, trying to see it from his point of view. "I'm sorry."

"Don't be sorry for something you have no control over. I blew my chance to have you years ago. I love you enough to know this isn't what you want. I want you to let me do this for you. Don't blow your chance with Silas. Maybe you aren't in love with him, but there's enough there that you should at least give it time to figure out. I've seen the way you look at him, Elle. You've *never* looked at me that way."

There were tears in his eyes. It wasn't until that moment I realized he had the emotional attachment to our relationship that I claimed didn't exist. *Mason* loved *me*. The last four years played out in my memory as I tried to make sense of how I could've been so blind to *not* see any of this. "Mason…"

"Don't, Elle. I fucked up. Whether you knew or not doesn't matter. I took our relationship for granted. That no matter what happened, I *knew* you'd be there to marry me. Somehow, I thought that would translate into you loving me the way I love you. It didn't. Let's just make this right, please?"

"Yeah," was all I could say. Truth be told, I wasn't sure if it wasn't already too late for Silas and me, but it wasn't too late for Mason to be a father, in the open, for Wyatt. That much wasn't about me, and he was right. I didn't know what this thing was I felt for Silas, but I absolutely didn't feel it for Mason.

It was a week before we were back in Boston. We had planned to meet up with Cee and Eli at their house to talk about the next steps. It still hurt me they had kept this secret from me, but I knew my father and I understood why. The last thing Cee needed when giving birth that young was the press talking about the slutty governor's daughter, which is exactly what would've happened.

That didn't mean I wasn't furious they slept together to begin with.

My mother took Wyatt out for a few hours so that we could chat, though we didn't mention the nature of the conversation. Mason and I let ourselves into Cee's house and saw Eli sitting at the table looking angry. He was obviously not happy about the reason we were convening. I couldn't say I blamed him. For the last year or two, he'd been a father figure to Wyatt. I wasn't sure how long he had known that Mason was actually Wyatt's father, but I knew he tried to convince my sister to let him say he was when she found out she was pregnant.

Cee joined us a few minutes later, and we sat in uncomfortable silence for a few minutes before Cee burst into tears saying, "I'm so sorry I lied to you, Elle. I'm a horrible sister. I slept with your…" she moved her hand up and down toward Mason, "Mason, and then hid the fact he was the father of my baby." I saw Eli put a hand on her leg and she leaned into him, sobbing.

"I'm not mad, Cee. Shocked and a little upset you felt you couldn't tell me, but I'm not mad. I'm sorry you had to hide so much more than I thought you did. Let's just talk about how you want to unravel this."

"I'm not the political mastermind here. You throw out what you think is best and I'll consider it."

All three of them looked at me.

"This isn't my story to tell, but I think we just let it happen. We will take Wyatt out and about and someone will speculate. As far as anyone is concerned, we weren't hiding anything. We just wanted Wyatt to stay out of the media as long as possible. We can devise some kind of visitation so that Mason and Wyatt can see each other regularly. It would be best to keep it out of court for now."

"But if we weren't hiding anything, wouldn't that mean you knew all along? How does that help you get divorced?" Cee asked, dabbing at her eyes with a tissue.

"It doesn't. But before you argue with me, let me explain. I don't want Wyatt to grow up and think he's the reason his father got divorced. None of this is his fault, and I don't even want people to suspect it. There are plenty of other reasons people get divorced and we will find one of those."

Mason and Cee looked between each other and me. "Well, do you have a plan for us?" he asked.

"That I do. When I was going through dad's stuff after he died, I found a bunch of files with each of our names on them. It took a couple of weeks to get into the one with my name on it. In the file, there are pictures of me with Silas. There are plenty in which you can't see his face or identify him. If those happened to fall into the wrong hands, the gossip circus will certainly take over and before you know it, Mason will have to divorce *me* because I'm not good for his senator image. We release them when I leave on the first campaign trip. Make it look like an active affair."

"You know I'm a Davis, right? That may fit right into that image."

"Not *yours*, though. This whole time we've been putting forward this notion that you are, well, less of a party person than your family. We will give the Wyatt news some time to gain acceptance and then leak a photo or two to get the ball rolling."

"I hate it," Mason said. "We agreed you wouldn't take the fall."

"I don't have a political career to protect."

"That isn't true, though. You may not be a politician, but you work directly with them and need their trust. They would remove you from the Presidential campaign for sure." His concern was genuine.

"I'll resign as soon as we leak."

He squeezed his eyes shut for a second trying to understand. "Why the hell would you do that? After everything you've worked for. What would you even do?"

I struggled to articulate the answers to his questions. "I realized that it's not what I want. I thought it was, but I hate being this

image of me. It's all it is, an image. I've spent my entire life being this person who I was told I was, but I'm now damn sure I'm not. While clearly I can play the game convincingly, I don't want to anymore. This part *is* my choice, and this is what I want. I'm asking that you accept that."

"Are you sure?"

"Positive. We will have to plan the timing out well enough so it doesn't look as staged as it is, but a few extra months of the charade won't kill me. Plus, it'll give me time to figure out what I want to be when I grow up."

"What about Silas?" Cee asked.

"He can't know. At least until we're ready to leak the photos. Then, I don't know. Until then, I need everything to fall into place without worrying about if he is going to show up or do something else that will throw this all off-track."

"He's going to be even more pissed," Cee pointed out.

"I know. But I'm asking you not to tell him anyway."

She gave me a look that said she didn't like it, but would not argue with me.

"I don't like the timeline. It's too long for your sake."

"I don't see a choice, Mason. Because this will absolutely impact your dad's presidential bid as well. He's going to be pissed. I'm not saying it isn't the right thing to do, I'm saying you may burn a bridge you can't rebuild. Talk to him before we do this. It should be early enough in the campaign to get buried, especially if you use Wyatt as an adorable grandkid. You're going to have to do a lot of refocusing away from the fact that the mother of your child is my sister, though. At least the timing works out. We weren't together then." *This is going to be a shit show.* I had little faith this would end happily for Silas and me as Mason was likely right about it being too long and Cee was right about keeping Silas in the dark. At least it freed me from pretending to be someone I wasn't.

Twenty-Two

Like a happy little family, Mason and I took Wyatt the next weekend. He came to a fundraising brunch with us on Saturday, followed by some time at the park. He slept at our apartment and we went out for breakfast the next morning. Wyatt was excited to have a dad and loudly called to Mason more than a few times over the weekend, with Mason beaming back at the little boy each time. It filled this space in my heart I didn't know I had.

Sure enough, that was all it took for there to be chatter. Calls came in to Mason's office and we basically blew them off as "not news". On Tuesday when we were at an event, someone said to Mason, "I didn't realize you had a little boy! What is his name?"

And as he had when Wyatt called him "Dad," Mason beamed. "Yes, I do. His name is Wyatt. We like to keep him out of the public eye. Let him be a kid, you know?"

This made perfect sense to the mother he was speaking with. They carried on talking about four-year-old boys— apparently, she had one as well— as if nothing out of the ordinary was happening.

And so it continued. When asked, Mason acted as though

nothing was amiss. On weeks we were in Boston we spent at least one weeknight with Wyatt and when we were in D.C. I would pick him up every other weekend to take him down to visit us.

One such weekend, after taking the train down to D.C. with Wyatt (to his absolute delight), we were hanging out as our dysfunctional little family when things shifted in an unexpected direction.

I wasn't one to keep track of the rumor mill when it came to myself. I'd learned a very long time ago that most of what they said was trash and if it was a serious enough issue, someone would bring it to my attention. I didn't expect that someone to be Silas.

> **Silas:** *Last.Beautiful.Girl.mp3*

It was cryptic to have only received a song, but I knew the Matchbox Twenty lyrics already and I knew that this was a 'fuck you'. I just didn't know what brought it on. I assumed he was done with me that day I met him and told him I needed time. We hadn't communicated since then.

> **Silas:** *I can't do this anymore.*

I didn't think we *were* still doing this, but it still stung to see it in writing.

> **Mish:** *So, I know Wyatt is not yours (shocked/not shocked that Mason is the daddy) but is the other rumor true?*
> **Me:** Back up to the first thing. Is there a rumor that I'm his mother?
> **Mish:** *I mean, yeah, it's kind of hilarious, really.*
> **Me:** Well, that's weird.
> **Mish:** *Silas is losing his shit.*

Me: About Wyatt? He doesn't believe that, right? I mean, he's met Cee and Wyatt.
Mish: *Only for half a second, but logic returned on that front when we pointed that out. It's the other thing. The one that states y'all have a second kid on the way.*

I choked. To be honest, there had been rumors of pregnancy shortly after we married. The world seems to love a "bump watch" and we weren't immune, especially given the precipitous nature of our wedding, but those had all but dissipated. "Hey, Mace?" I called into the other room. "Did you know I am," I looked at Wyatt staring up at us intently, "P-R-E-G-N-A-N-T?"

"How the hell did that happen?" He said, shocked. "Certainly wasn't me."

"It's a rumor, Mason. A completely untrue rumor, obviously. And this rumor pairs with the one that says that he," I looked down at Wyatt again, "is my S-O-N."

"Oh, shit." He paced to think. "The second one is just weird. We've been clear about who his mother is. It'll blow over. The first one will too after a while when nothing comes of it. It's not the first time the media has decided it was happening."

"Dad, we aren't allowed to say 'shit'," Wyatt reprimanded. Mason agreed and apologized to the tiny authoritarian.

My phone vibrated.

Mish: *Elle? Are you really pregnant? Because, according to Silas, that baby is his and not Mason's and he's about ready to throw down over it. He claims you hooked up back in February.*
Me: Of course I'm not pregnant. No one has to throw down. Kindly remind everyone in the group chat not to listen to media speculation.
Mish: *xo*

Jillian MacGregor

The texts started again around midnight the next night. I was in bed with a terrible migraine that had me vomiting on the way back from bringing Wyatt home. I wasn't about to look at them because the light would've caused more vomiting, so I just covered the phone with a pillow and ignored it for the night.

There were a lot of texts from Silas when I woke up Monday morning. Reading through them, it was obvious he had been drinking.

> ***Silas:*** *I should've known.*
> ***Silas:*** *Foo Fighters.*
> ***Silas:*** *I don't know why I didn't see this coming. Of course there would be an heir to the throne, right?*
> ***Silas:*** *The thought of him touching you makes me violently angry, but it shouldn't because he's your husband.*
> ***Silas:*** *I wish I could've been enough for you to choose me.*
> ***Silas:*** *I really thought when your dad died you'd leave him for me.*
> ***Silas:*** *It's been weeks and now you're having a kid together.*
> ***Silas:*** *Was I just some kind of fling before marriage? Obviously, there is something between you two.*
> ***Silas:*** *I was an idiot to think things would end differently, but fuck, you are so hot, and down to earth, and fun. Smart. You smell amazing. You taste amazing. How long do I have to feel like this? How many more times do you have to tell me we won't be together? I know you were clear about it, but somehow I fell for you, anyway. It's probably not fair that I'm so fucking angry at you.*
> ***Silas:*** *But I also just want to fuck you so much that even just texting you is enough to make me rock hard. If I was there with you right now, would you let me? I need*

> *to feel you come all over my dick. I need to feel your body writhing against mine. I want to get my hands stuck in your hair while you suck my cock. I also just want to hold you in my arms.*
> **Silas:** *I hate that he has everything I want.*

There was a few hours before he sent another text:

> **Silas:** *You_Wont_Be_Mine.mp3*
> **Silas:** *Apparently, I channel Rob Thomas and Matchbox Twenty songs when I think of you.*

Tears were hot behind my eyes, but I refused to cry. *Do I tell him? Ask him to wait for me? That's ridiculous. I can't ask him to do that anymore.* I had to let him go, and focus on this thing with Wyatt and my divorce strategy. Even if I couldn't be with Silas when it's over, I knew I couldn't stay with Mason at this point anyway. I unfairly resented him and everything our marriage cost me, even though I was just as much to blame. I wanted the career.

Fuck the career. Fuck it all.

I hit "clear messages" from next to Silas' name and tried to go on with my day like it never happened. I never responded at all, not even to tell him he was wrong about me being pregnant. Not to ask him to wait because I was working on coming back to him. I needed to let him move on from this without further dragging him into my shit. I needed to fix myself before I could expect him to hear me out.

It took several weeks to settle the Wyatt issue. The press and others asked repeatedly what it was like to be my nephew's stepmother, and each time I answered with the same performance that included a smile and a speech about how we'd had years to work out our family dynamic and that I knew that Mason and Wyatt were a package deal.

Cee was back in the spotlight with this revelation and she did her best to summon her inner politician's daughter persona. She gushed about how she was so lucky that she had someone she loved and trusted as much as her own sister to be stepmother to her son.

In the meantime, part two of the plan was getting under way. I was out on my first (and likely only, given my plans) trip out on the campaign trail. They were long days and long nights and as much as I got a thrill from getting to be involved at such a high level, I knew I was making the right choice by leaving. I wanted something different. Some*one* different.

The folder my father had on his laptop with my name was full of pictures of me with Silas the summer before. I was rageful. I had let myself be a pawn in a game. Having a bit of distance from the situation, it disgusted me that my own parents were involved in using me like a puppet. My mom stopped years ago, but damn it all if my father wasn't up to that shit right up to his death.

And I let it happen. I didn't realize how fucked up it was, even though people on the outside told me repeatedly. I don't think I would've been unhappy in the life they planned for me, though. Not if I hadn't spent time really being myself.

Not without meeting Silas.

There was an ache in my chest as I looked at the pictures of Silas I transferred to my laptop. I closed my eyes and tried to remember how it felt to be held in his arms. The thought that it may never happen again made that ache intensify. I just needed to get this over with so I could end my marriage and go live in a cave alone somewhere. I was so sick of my every move being watched.

But to get there I needed to throw myself into the fire. I wanted to burn this existence to the ground. Some of the long nights on the campaign trail included strategic pictures of me with various men that looked a lot less innocent than they were.

Uninvited

I didn't want to drag Silas into my mess if I didn't have to. Lucky for me there were several eligible bachelors who happened to be donors that were willing to take the fall if it came to it. We did our best to ensure the pictures didn't show any faces and these men would be anonymous.

It didn't take long to get these leaked. (Thank you, social media.) I resigned my position with the campaign and announced my pending divorce.

There was a press conference in which I admitted to an affair that I insisted Mason knew nothing about, though he tried to fight me on that front. He wasn't keen on me taking the bullet for our divorce, but since I was the reason that we were getting divorced, I insisted that I be the one to take the fall. He still wanted this life, and I wanted nothing to do with it. It made little sense to take him down with me.

The nice thing about this being public was it was totally acceptable for me to look as miserable as I felt. There was no agenda from here that required the mask to be pulled on in public anymore. I had effectively quit politics, at least for the time being, and honestly, the freedom I felt was so intense that I didn't think I could ever go back.

I moved in with Cee temporarily. Since I had no intention of living in Massachusetts once the court granted the divorce, I didn't need to find a place to live. I had lofty plans that included escaping to a beach somewhere alone to wallow in my misery.

Since this was a very amicable divorce, we could have the agreements notarized and filed with the probate court the day after we announced it was going to happen.

Immediately following our court date for my divorce, I retreated south to Florida. Mish invited me to stay with her at Connor's beach house to get away from the constant gossip. I was happy to get away. Just ninety days until I was officially a single woman. I was both relieved and depressed. Every time I looked around, I saw the first time Silas and I were here. The couch where I woke up in his lap reminded me of a time when we didn't have such a complicated past.

If only I had done things differently. Where would I be right now?

On my second day there, Mish and I sat out on the beach, enjoying some early evening cocktails. "So, what's the plan with Silas?" She asked, digging into her own curiosity. Luckily, I had a nice buzz going, which was the only way I could handle this conversation.

"There isn't one. He's made it clear that he is done with me. It involved an entire night of one-sided texting. I haven't heard from him in months."

Mish laughed into her drink. "Oh sweetie, that guy is so not done with you. Pissed as hell? Absolutely, but he's had his eyes on you since day one. Don't mistake his silence for indifference."

"Oh! That reminds me. Silas and I had differing stories as to when that was."

"It was the night in Boston when you got super drunk and I made Mason come get you. You kissed Kyle."

"Well, then. Guess that was true."

"When did you think it was?"

"On the plane to Florida when he randomly kissed me."

"No, no, no. You were all up in Silas's business that night in Boston. So much so that Kyle was egging him on to make a move. He refused because you were drunk, but because Kyle was also wasted, he said he'd do it. Serge and Silas bet on whether you'd smack him in the face if he went through with it. I don't remember who won, but you didn't hit him."

"According to Silas, that would be Sergio."

"So you see, my dear friend, that guy has been chasing you long before you remembered he existed. It's probably your turn to chase him. What did the texts say?"

"Besides hating me and hating Mason, he also had some pretty explicit sexual thoughts."

"What did you say?"

"Nothing. I deleted them. What was there to say? He was pissed, and he had every right to be." I finished the can of spiked seltzer.

"Look, when was the last time you saw him?"

"He came to see me when my dad died. So, February? In that string of texts, he told me he thought once my dad died I'd leave Mason for him."

"Well, shit, we all thought that."

"It wasn't that simple, Mish. We had an agreement. At least one year."

"This whole time it's only been a one year agreement? Like, since when? Always? Because you should've mentioned that."

"No, of course not. The night before the wedding, we agreed that we'd consider divorce after a year. But we started planning after my dad died instead of waiting until September because apparently I'm a miserable bitch."

"Mason said that?!"

"Not really. Well, he said I was miserable, but not that I'm a bitch. He just wanted me to move on and be happy."

"He's not half bad, that Mason."

"I've been telling you this for years. He'll make a fine husband for the right woman. And I feel bad because there's literally nothing wrong with him, but I cannot get divorced fast enough."

"Right. Because you're in love with someone else."

I ignored that comment. "You think it's because we've gone this whole marriage without sex? Maybe I haven't really given it a fair chance?"

"*You haven't had sex with Mason!?*" Mish spilled her drink into her lap.

"It's been years since I had sex with Mason. It was okay, it just lacked something."

"Tell me it wasn't an orgasm." She was gripping the armrest of her chair with both hands, staring at me with a very concerned look as if I was some kind of abused animal.

"Of course not. Okay, well, full disclosure, he was my first and no, no orgasm those first few times, but I think that's pretty standard. We were both just kind of figuring the whole thing out. But after that he was always a complete gentleman, and I always came first."

"Phew. I thought I was going to have to send you back to Massachusetts to fuck your husband. That thing you're lacking is actual intimacy. Silas isn't just a random fuck for you. Mason was, well, providing a service."

"God, you are so crass."

"You are avoiding the fact that this issue isn't because of Mason. We agreed a long time ago there's nothing wrong with him except that you lack the ideal chemistry for a married couple. It's fine if this were an 1800s Victorian society, but it's not. You deserve a relationship that gets you hot and bothered, in the good way. Getting a divorce isn't because Mason sucks, it's because you've discovered there's something more out there to strive toward."

I sighed and opened another seltzer. "Life was easier before I knew that."

"And that brings us back to Silas."

"Michelle, that ship is so far out of port you can't see it anymore."

"Fuck that, I saw Silas *very* recently."

"Okay, but I didn't. And it's too soon, anyway. Or too late. I'm not really sure, but there's a timing issue that is just always in the way."

"There's a *you* issue always in the way. It is literally on public record that you are no longer with Mason, despite a short waiting period. You are free to pursue the incredibly hot brooding man whom you've scorned."

"I was incredibly clear and upfront about my situation."

"Yes. Initially. And then you spent an entire summer being

anything *but* casual. There were mixed signals."

"Mixed signals!? I literally went out of my way to hide his existence and wedged him into my normal life, making him fully aware it would be my full-time life at the end of said summer. For fuck's sake, Mish, he told me he loved me and I made him take it back! If that didn't scream non-committal I don't know what does."

"Your words and your actions didn't really line up, Boo. Because, fuck, anyone looking at you two together could see the sparks. I shouldn't tell you this, but I think it needs to be said because I'm sick of seeing two of my friends hurt over each other when there is a simple solution. Elle, all he wants, all he's wanted this whole time, is for you to choose him. You come *so close* to doing it and then back away. You don't have any excuses anymore. Fucking choose him so you can both be happy."

"He wants things I can't give him."

"Like what, Elle? The only thing I see he wants is *you*. That man would light the world on fire for you if you asked him to. So fucking *ask.*"

"Light the world on fire?" I puffed out my cheeks. "He's quietly retreated into his corner of the world." *Not that I knew where that was. I refused to ask.*

"He fought for you. You asked him not to. He's literally giving you what you want, even though it's torn him apart. As his friend, I have to tell you he deserves better. I know you can be that for him. You just have to let go of all the bullshit and go for it."

"How? How does a person just let go like that? I don't know how. I don't know how to be the person he needs me to be. He deserves someone who can love him back. Someone who hasn't stomped all over him."

"I get you have all this emotional baggage." She waved her hands around the metaphorical weight on my back. "Cee had it, too. Your father raised you rather clinically and taught you to put up walls. If she can pull her head out of her ass to *finally* get with

Elijah, you can do it too. I know you love him," she pointed at me accusingly. "The *in* love part we can debate, but you wouldn't be this concerned about your capability of loving him if you didn't already. Worst-case scenario you have a gorgeous boyfriend who sets your panties on fire. Let the man love you with his lust."

"So what, just call him up and say 'hey, how's it going, wanna fuck'?" There was an edge of sarcasm in my voice. I lacked relationship savvy, but I knew that wasn't how that is supposed to go.

"Not so much, no. What if you just happened to run into him because you both have meddling friends?"

"What did you do, Michelle?"

"More like what I didn't do."

"What didn't you do?"

"I didn't tell you that Silas has been staying at the in-law apartment downstairs the last few months. He's still trying to help with band management from afar. I also did not tell him you were coming here, so he wouldn't flee. Y'all have been mere feet from each other for the last twenty-four hours."

I felt instantly nauseated.

"We invited him to dinner tonight. I wasn't going to tell you, but I have a feeling you need the kick in the ass and this way we can make sure you are looking super sexy."

I let out a deep sigh. "This only solves a proximity issue, Mish. What am I supposed to say?"

"You'll figure it out. And if you don't, we will find a way to a ladies' room and I'll assist you. I think his reaction to you being there is going to determine your next move."

"What if he just gets up and leaves? That's kind of our go-to move when this shit gets too real." My palms were sweaty and shaking.

"I'll send Connor after him."

I was not okay with what was about to happen. We packed up our blanket and cooler and made our way inside to shower and get ready for dinner. I had a minor panic attack when I realized

Uninvited

I'd literally only packed beach clothes and leggings. Luckily, my meddling friend had already thought that far ahead and brought in a blue summer dress. It was backless with a halter top. The waist had a red belt, and the skirt flowed freely. She tossed me a pair of red heels. We moved into her bathroom so I could borrow her makeup, since I didn't bring any in anticipation of just wallowing while I was here. I only used the basics, as we had different complexions and I rarely used any kind of foundation. I applied eyeliner, mascara, and red lipstick (that I really didn't want to wear, but Mish told me I needed); later, the only question left was my hair.

After much back and forth because of a limited timeline and my crazy thick hair, we decided it belonged up. I twisted it up and let some hair fall over the top as if it were a ponytail. Mish approved the whole ensemble, and we went to meet Connor and Silas at the restaurant.

The whole way there, I couldn't stop myself from fidgeting, something I thought my father had long before bred out of me. *Ladies do not fidget*, I could hear my father saying to four-year-old me. I couldn't stop. Sitting still wasn't happening.

When we parked in the lot, I fought the urge to full-on flee in the other direction. Clearly Mish could see the crazy reflected in my eyes because she put her hand on my shoulder and told me to chill out. *Easy for her to say*. I spied Connor's car a few spots down, which meant they were already inside, waiting. I took several deep breaths and walked toward the restaurant.

The host showed us to the table where Connor and Silas were sitting. Seeing Silas resulted in my stomach flipping more aggressively. I painted on a practiced smile and took my seat as Silas registered the shock of me being seated next to him. Connor said hello to Mish with a kiss to the cheek, and a wave to me, so I replied with a "hey." Connor and Mish looked nervously between Silas and me, waiting to see how this went down. I gave Mish a death stare, and she took the hint and started talking about the tour starting next week.

A few minutes into Mish's rambling, Silas spoke up. "So is this like an ambush, or what?" he looked each of us in the eye.

"I didn't know you were in the area, um, generally, until a couple of hours ago." I explained.

"Because if you did, you would never have come down here, right?" His words dripped with anger. The problem was, he was spot on, I would not have come to Florida if I knew he was also here. I stayed quiet. "That's what I thought. So who do we have here? Eleanor? Len? The outfit screams Len, but the icy demeanor says Eleanor. I don't even know what to call you."

Another solid question. "You can call me whatever you want, I suppose." I replied with fake confidence, but then meekly added, "I'm having something of an identity crisis lately." A server came and took our drink orders and I was never so thankful to be interrupted in all my life. The problem was I knew what I wanted him to call me; I wanted him to call me "Lenny" and pretend like everything was perfect, but I knew that wasn't fair to him. I had a significant amount of apologizing to do and I intended to do it. I just didn't want to do it with an audience.

"We call her Elle, if that helps," Mish interjected, trying to steer the conversation away from potential violence.

"Maybe you should just be you for a change. Whoever that is," Silas spat. This was not really going well, but I deserved it. Despite knowing that, I was quickly losing control over my emotions. His words hurt me to my core.

"You can call me Al," I blurted. Everyone blurts random Paul Simon lyrics, right?

"Does this make me Betty?" he asked, his guard a little down.

"I think it's only fair." I replied. The server brought drinks, which I immediately sipped, and we ordered food. I took another deep breath and a drink of the gin and tonic in my hand, hoping for the best.

We had consumed a good amount of spiked seltzer on the

beach without eating anything, so a few large sips of the gin and tonic relaxed me to the point I was no longer struggling to stop fidgeting. Mish resumed talking about nothing for a few minutes, which helped ease the tension at the table.

We were on a second round of drinks when the food came. Before eating, I stood to excuse myself to "wash my hands" and Mish followed. She ducked into a stall while I washed my hands. The woman beside me, who was wearing a restaurant uniform, said, "Don't get too attached to Silas, he's hung up on some chick. Trust me, I've tried."

I thanked her for the advice and Mish came out of the stall with a shit-eating "I told you so" grin on her face. The server left and Mish burst into giggles. "Girl, that is not going well."

"There are a lot of words that need to be said and here isn't the place to do so. Also, he's quite hostile."

"Give it time; he will come around. At least he didn't turn and run out, right? Just try to keep to neutral topics and maybe show some thigh." She winked. She led me out of the restroom and returned to the table to eat.

Silas and I didn't make direct conversation at all during the meal, but, after he finished eating, he placed a hand on my thigh causing butterflies to take flight in my stomach. I tried to keep any reaction from my face as the conversation continued around the table and his hand roamed higher up my leg and under my skirt.

I was instantly soaked. The change in his behavior confused me. I also wasn't complaining. Everywhere his hand brushed felt instantly tingly in a way that made it very hard to sit still. He trailed a finger over the lace of my panties and I thought I was going to combust. Once again, I excused myself to the restroom. Silas did the same, and Mish took that as a sign to stay behind.

Silas and I separated into the respective restrooms. All I really needed was cold water on my face and neck to calm down, so I grabbed some paper towels and ran them under the cool water. I put the wet paper towels against the back of my neck and took a few deep breaths.

After a minute of bringing my heart rate back to normal, I exited the restroom where I saw Silas leaning against the wall waiting for me. "What about Amy?" he said.

"Who is Amy?"

"You. I'll call you Amy. You have that whole fair skin, green eyes, and a look like you could have been happy in a different life."

"And there was that time I took the amphetamines," I said, noting the name of the Everclear song he was referencing.

He took my hand and led me outside. We walked around the corner of the building and out of the bright lights. "Silas, I—"

"Nope. We aren't talking. That's not why I brought you out here." He stepped forward and backed me into the wall. Our faces were nearly touching, but not quite. His close proximity allowed me to see into his eyes despite the darkness that surrounded us. "Then why are we out here, Silas?" I asked quietly, hoping the answer had something to do with his lips basically anywhere on my body.

His hand was back on my thigh and under my dress. My head fell back into the wall and I trembled at the contact. He pushed aside the fabric of my panties and slid two fingers inside. My knees shook almost instantly, my whole body buzzed. He used his thumb to rub slow circles over my clit. I was breathing heavily, but trying to remain quiet so that no one would know what was happening.

"We are out here because I know you hate to touch things in public bathrooms, and I plan to fuck you so hard you need something to hold on to," his voice rasped in my ear. He removed his fingers and began unbuttoning his pants. "Turn around," he ordered.

I complied silently.

"I fucking hate that after all the shit you put me through I still want this so bad." I heard the wrapper of a condom. "I'm so fucking mad at you, and yet, if I don't fuck you soon I will lose my goddamn mind." He rubbed a hand across my bare back. "Lose the underwear," he said and again, I complied. No sooner had I stepped out of them, he pushed my legs apart with his leg. He moved his hand to lift the back of my dress to gain access. "This ass. Jesus."

Then he shoved his cock in me to the hilt. I gasped, and he let out a groan. He pulled my hair to the side and kissed my neck before biting me there, marking his territory. "I want to hate you so fucking much." The admission that he didn't hate me had me instantly on the edge. He pounded into me from behind with a mixture of fury and lust. I braced my arms against the wall to keep my head from hitting it as he slammed into me. I could feel the bricks causing friction burns on my arms, but I really didn't care. My whole body savored every touch of his.

He reached a hand up to palm my breast, and another wave of tingles washed over me. I could feel myself contracting around his dick. "Silas," I panted.

"Fucking Eleanor," he cursed and then gave in to his release.

We stood there, me still facing the wall and him behind me, for a few minutes as we caught our breath. He brushed my skirt down into place and picked up my underwear, putting them in his pocket. He turned me around to examine my arms. "You okay?" he asked despite the anger still in his eyes.

"Yeah. I'm fine. You?"

"Nope. Not at all," he replied, and he started walking back to the restaurant. Angry Silas was giving me whiplash.

Mish and I got in the car to head home, and she could barely contain her questions. "So, did y'all fuck in the bathroom or what?"

"Not the bathroom. Public bathrooms skeeve me out. We went outside. He angry-fucked me, put my damn underwear in his pocket and ignored me the rest of the night."

"He has frustration. And angry fucking can be super hot."

"I'm not complaining about the sex. It's the hot and cold that's making me crazy."

"You just need a chance to talk it out. This is totally the right path. Let him come to you. Fight when he wants to fight and fuck when he wants to fuck. Eventually, it will all work out."

"It's a good thing you never got into psychiatry, Mish. That's terrible advice, but I'm totally going to take it."

We parted ways when we got back to the house. Mish and Connor retreated to their room, Silas went downstairs, I presumed, and I went into the guest room to change into my wallowing clothes.

I pulled the pins out of my hair and threw it up into a messy bun. I carefully washed out the abrasions from the brick wall to prevent any infection and then brushed my teeth for bed. I crawled into the bed with my tablet, ready to binge watch *New Girl* until I fell asleep.

Halfway into an episode, I got a text.

> **Silas:** *Why do I keep letting you fuck up my life?*
> **Me:** Maybe you are at an All Time Low.
> **Silas:** *Are your arms okay?*
> **Me:** My arms are fine. We need to talk. Dinner wasn't the time, and I don't want to do it over the phone.

I practically held my breath waiting for him to reply.

> **Silas:** *I don't know that I'm ready to hear what you have to say, and I've said everything I have to say already. I need time.*

Ugh. He hit me with the same thing I said to him after my dad died.

> **Me:** That's fair. Goodnight, Silas.
> ***Silas:*** *Goodnight, Lenny.*

Twenty-Three

The emotional toll of the evening gained control of my senses and I ended up crying myself to sleep. I woke to a light knock on my door. "Come in," I said, expecting Mish, but Silas opened the door instead, holding two coffees.

"I brought you coffee. It looks like you may need it. Rough night?" He shut the door behind himself and set both coffees on the nightstand beside the bed. He took my arms in his hands and turned them over to assess any damage. "Shit. I'm sorry. I was pissed, but I didn't mean to actually injure you. That was uncalled for."

"It's fine, Silas. I mean, my arms, they are fine. Emotionally, I'm a fucking mess. Please, sit. I'm hoping the coffee and the visit mean you are ready to talk."

He sat beside me on the bed, handing a cup of coffee to me and grabbing the other for himself once settled. "Do I want to hear what you have to say, or does this conversation end with one of us running out of the room?"

"I don't know where we stand. But I have to let you know that I'm sorry. I'm so sorry that things happened the way they did. I wish things had been simpler. There is nothing I'd like more

than to figure out how to make us good again, but I'm terrified that it's too late."

"It probably should be, but I'm here, so clearly there's room for discussion. But I can't fight for you anymore, Len. I lose every fucking time and it's killing me. I just keep coming back to be broken down."

The tears flowed again. "I'm so sorry," I repeated, trying to get a hold on the waterworks. "I strung you along. I'm ashamed of my behavior, but you snuck up on me. I didn't intend to hurt you. It just got so complicated so quickly."

He placed the cup back on the table and turned to wipe the tears off my cheeks. "Please, don't cry." He sighed.

"I only seem to cry about you," I sniffled. "I need to know how to make this right, Silas. I need you in my life, but also know that it's probably the last thing you want. I don't deserve you."

He pulled me onto his lap and held my head to his chest. "It probably makes me the world's biggest idiot, but you haven't lost me, Len. I know you aren't ready for me to say this, and in no way do I expect you to return the sentiment, but I love you. I've been in love with you since the day you dropped everything to be by my side when Kyle died. I've spent all this time wishing I could stop and I can't."

I stuck out finger guns. Silas chuckled. "Prince isn't here, but Connor may be able to fill in," he referenced an episode of *New Girl*.

"I'm sorry I'm so bad at this."

He sighed. "I've been so mad at you. I'm still fucking mad. When your dad announced his illness, I thought for sure when he died it would all be over. But he died and despite that, there you were, married to Mason. Then it came out he is Wyatt's dad, I called that by the way, and I don't care what you said to the media, I *know* you didn't know. And still, you stayed. Then, fuck, Len, *then* you were out with all these other guys. That's when you decided marriage wasn't for you. It felt like a giant 'fuck you' so I assumed you were over me. That I was just a quick fuck or whatever. Why the fuck didn't you call?"

"I owe you some context. I didn't know my father was going to die until after I was married. I don't know if that would've stopped me from doing it. It was like I was on a path he put me on whether he was here to push me or not. I believed it was necessary. Seeing you after his funeral…I don't know, it just clicked. You are what I want. But I didn't want to drag you into my mess anymore. I needed to make all of that go away. No, I didn't know about Mason, though I should have. And those pictures were staged. I needed to give him a good reason to move forward without me in the eyes of the public. I hate that you think that was real." I sobbed into his shirt for a few minutes and he just held me, running his hands up and down my back soothingly. The homesick feeling I had for months dissipated and I melted into his strong arms. "Feelings aren't a thing I'm well-versed in expressing. Or identifying, to some extent. Before you, the last time I cried was when I was little. I'm scared, Silas. I've been scared. There's a whole side of me I didn't even know existed before you. And I couldn't take the risk of letting you down again if that isn't really me, either. I wished I could tear myself into two people so that I could be with you, the person who you knew me to be, and still keep the promises that I had made before you were ever in the picture. I needed time to make sure I knew myself better before I dragged you into another mess of my own making."

We were silent for a few minutes while he digested my confession. "So, did you find yourself?" He asked cautiously.

"As of yesterday, I didn't think so, but then I saw you at dinner and I knew. I felt it. That comfort in my skin even though I was terrified of being rejected by you. I was okay with that, because I deserve it, but I realized this whole time I only felt truly authentic was when I was Len. I thought Eleanor was the real me, but it turns out she was the mask, a mask I put on for the masses, a role

I was playing. With you, Connor, and Mish, and, you know, the whole group, I was just…me. I didn't pretend to like or dislike anything because it was what my father and Mason expected of me. Hell, I *never* did what they expected of me, I did whatever the fuck I wanted. And it was glorious, if a little reckless and a lot selfish."

Silas pulled me away from his chest so he could look at me. Our faces were once again so close, but still, somehow, not touching. "I'm so sorry, Silas," I said, and he closed the distance between our lips to kiss me.

I felt the kiss with my whole body. It was then that I fully relaxed, truly hopeful that this was going to work out. He gently cradled my face while his lips and tongue crashed into mine fiercely. More tears made their way down my cheeks with sheer happiness that this was really happening.

There was a quick knock, and the door opened. "Hey, Elle — oh. Sorry. I didn't realize. Um. I'm gonna go," Mish said quickly upon seeing us.

"So, that's gonna be a thing," I said, making a move to get up.

"Len? Can we just pretend we're good for a while?" Silas asked, grabbing my hand.

I smiled. "I'd love that. I'm waiting for you to be ready." I let go of his hand and grabbed my empty coffee mug to meet Mish out in the kitchen.

She looked up over her mug at me with her eyes wide and excited. "Did he sleep in there last night, young lady?" she asked hopefully.

"No. He brought me coffee this morning."

"And then pulled you into his lap to make out with you. Have you two even said words to each other or just been all over each other instead?"

"We spoke briefly this morning. I don't think we're on solid ground yet, but closer today than I was yesterday."

"Ah, see? You love when I meddle."

I rolled my eyes at her as Silas joined us in the kitchen. He stepped up close behind me and set his mug on the counter, putting his hands on my waist, eliciting a moment of déjà vu from our first weekend in this house. "I wouldn't say *I* love it, but thanks for not minding your own business," Silas said, kissing my cheek. "More, please," he said of the coffee.

I poured us both refills and after he kissed my cheek again to thank me, we both made our way to join Mish at the table. "So, Elle and I have some plans this morning," Mish informed both of us.

"Oh," said Silas. "Well then, I'll have to wait my turn in line to visit with *Elle*."

Connor came in and noted Silas at the table. "Nice work, dude," he commented.

We sat drinking coffee and talking about the plans for the day that I didn't realize I had. Mish and I apparently had an urgent shopping trip that had to happen this morning. We were hitting the beach after that and Mish was sure to let the guys know they could join us. Silas asked me to dinner. He was very clear that he was not inviting Mish. She beamed in response.

Mish and I hopped in the car about an hour later. "So, what is it exactly that we needed urgently?" I asked.

"*GIRL*. Spill."

"Like, if we don't come back with *something* this whole facade unravels."

"Who the fuck cares, *SPILL*."

"There's nothing to spill. You waltzed into my room before anything happened."

"You were on his lap making out. Last night he angry fucked you, in public, and this morning he's in your bed groping you. How are you not sure where things stand?"

"Oh, that one is easy: because sex is inevitable with Silas. I have no power to resist him, no matter how much my very logical mind tells me it's a horrible idea with terrible consequences. Our clothes just magically come off when we get near each other. I'm not complaining, the sex is always amazing. Everything else is confusing."

"That man is not confused."

"No, that's the confusing part for me, Mish. How is he so sure he loves me? How the fuck does one know? Because it can't just be amazing sex. If that were the case there wouldn't be a word for lust. The lust is very, very real."

"I think you just know. It's like this feeling, I don't know how to describe it exactly, but it's kind of like how you'd jump in front of a train to save Wyatt without a second thought. Plus the lust."

"How did you know you were in love with Connor?"

"At some point, I just realized that despite the complications of being with him, he was the best part of my day. When he's not there, even if I'm home, I feel lost."

"I've felt homesick for months. This morning that feeling finally went away."

"That's love, sweetie." She smiled at me from the driver's seat. "Come on, we'll celebrate your emotional growth with some lattes and retail therapy."

After a morning of seeking the perfect outfit for what felt like a first date, Mish and I returned to the house and switched into beach mode, donning bikinis and, for me and my pale skin, SPF 50. We grabbed the beach blanket, loaded a cooler with both bottles of water and alcoholic beverages, and some sunglasses and went out the back door and down to the beach.

It wasn't long before Connor and Silas joined us, looking fine as hell in their swim shorts. While Connor pulled Mish up by her arms to take her down to the water, Silas sat down next to where I was reading smut on my phone. "Word porn?" he teased.

I looked up from my phone, setting it aside. "Naturally. That's what one reads at the beach."

"Were you reading it before you knew I was also here?" He smirked suggestively.

"I *am* at the beach, Silas."

He ran his fingers up my arm and whispered close to my ear, "Well, how fortunate for you I'm here and I can help take care of that lady boner you're going to get. Or, at the very least, watch you do it for yourself."

My body flushed with need. "Well, maybe if our date goes well, we can arrange something like that."

"Aw, c'mon, Len. I know you like it hard and fast. I have even known you to enjoy a fuck in public. We can definitely take care of this before *and* after dinner."

Shit. My bikini bottoms were damp with the need to take these actions right here, right now, but I resisted. "That is true, but sometimes the best things come to those who wait, Silas."

"I'll wait forever," he said. I realized while I was speaking of waiting for the sex, he was talking about waiting for me, generally.

My stomach flipped. I leaned up and gave him a quick kiss. "I promise, it won't be forever. Soon." This time I was speaking of both the sex and an actual relationship with Silas.

Twenty-Four

While out with Mish earlier, I had picked up a pair of open-toed strappy sandals and a scandalously short, strapless dress to wear to dinner with Silas. The top of the dress was elastic shirring that would be very easy access for our inevitable need to get naked quickly; the rest was white with big yellow hibiscuses. I stared at my reflection in the floor-length mirror in Mish's room. "How does one sit in something this short?" I asked, having never owned a dress that barely covered my ass. The only reason I did now was because Mish insisted it was "the one."

"You look hot. Years of duchess-wear has your mind fucked. Even Kate Middleton wore dresses this short before marrying into the royal family. You've exited that life. Sexy is your new style, I promise."

I wondered how long it would take me to shake the fear of being seen in public this exposed. "But seriously, what if a breeze takes the bottom away and I'm flashing people a la Marilyn Monroe? I don't even have dress weights!"

"Jesus on a trampoline. You aren't working. You aren't going out with politicians. Hell, you aren't even going out."

"I'm not?" I asked, confused.

"No. Your hottie is downstairs cooking you dinner because, and I'm quoting 'the real dinner is you'."

"He *said that* to you?"

"Well, he said it to Connor, and Connor told me because *we* are going out tonight so we don't have to be witnesses to anything that happens. Visually or auditorily."

"Yeah, I'll go ahead and apologize now because I can't guarantee that won't be an issue after you get home." I took one final look in the mirror and, satisfied my bare ass wouldn't be hitting any public seats since we'd just be downstairs, I went out to the living room to wait like a nervous teenager for her first date.

Silas came up within a few minutes, right on time, wearing a pair of jeans that highlighted his ass in the best way. I stood to meet him. "You look amazing." His eyes roamed my body appreciatively. "And although it's a bit cave dweller of me, I'm really glad we'll be staying in tonight because I'd like to keep those legs to myself. Damn. Not even tights?"

"Thank you. I'm wearing Mish." Silas smirked. He put his arms around my waist and gave me a quick kiss.

"Come on, before I burn dinner." He took me by the hand and led me to the door to go to the in-law apartment downstairs.

"I have to say, I'm shocked we're having dinner in. You always seemed a bit, um, unhappy, that we couldn't be in public together. I assumed you would take advantage of the opportunity," I mentioned as we walked down the stairs.

"There will be plenty of opportunities in the future, Len." He opened the door to the apartment. "I figured we have a lot to talk about and it was better done privately."

"Here I was assuming you just wanted to have your way with me." I accepted a proffered glass and took a sip, "Ah, good ole Captain and Dr. Pepper." It reminded me of the night we spent in the studio drinking the same and eating candy.

"I think we've established that I can have my way with you

anywhere I want." He gave me a smoldering look that promised he planned to do so.

"And I with you. Are we having Swedish Fish for dinner?" I knew this not to be true, as I could smell the stuffed chicken in the air.

"You are going to need something far more substantial for the evening I have planned. There was a possibility we could have had it for dessert, but after seeing you in that dress, I'm pretty sure I'll be having you for dessert." He pulled me close and placed a few kisses up the side of my neck, giving a little bite of my earlobe.

"I'm pretty sure I'm the one who is supposed to be wooing you, not the other way around." I gave his ass a squeeze with both hands.

"I'm never going to stop wooing you," he whispered into my ear, causing goosebumps to erupt on my arms.

"I love you, Silas," I breathed, surprising both of us. He stilled and after a beat backed away and went to the oven to pull out dinner. My heart raced from the impromptu confession and his reaction.

"So, dinner is ready, shall we eat?" he said, trying to work through the awkward moment we found ourselves in.

"Sure," I replied, moving over to the table while taking a very large gulp of my drink.

After a few minutes of prolonged silence while we busied ourselves with eating, Silas asked, "So, what's next for Eleanor?"

I blanched at the use of my more formal name. "Well, Eleanor is waiting for her divorce to be final so she can disappear into obscurity. Me, on the other hand, I'm not sure what is next. I have to find some work so I don't feel like the trust fund kid that I am. I need to do something real."

"So, Eleanor is free of any future commitments?"

I hated this line of questioning, but it was absolutely necessary to resolve this aspect of our past in order to move forward. I really yearned to move forward with Silas. "Other than the aforementioned divorce, all of my personalities are free of any kind of commitment to anyone else. The only commitment I have is the one I have to correct the horrible mistake I made in not choosing to ditch the old commitments and run away with you. I fully expect that to take a really long time, and potentially we never resolve it. I can't take it back. I wish I could. I wish I had been better at doing what was right for me instead of sticking to the plans other people made for me. I can't do that, though. I can only change my priorities for the future."

He sat silently for a few more minutes, taking a few bites of his chicken while he contemplated what I said. "You aren't the only one at fault here, Lenny. You were very clear from day one what you could give and what you couldn't. Despite that, I didn't accept that answer or didn't believe that it was what you really were going to do. I thought I could change your mind. I'm sorry for that. I think I made you feel unnecessarily at fault for the fact my feelings didn't align with your reality."

"My reality was fucking weird," I said, finally agreeing with his assessment of so many aspects of my life to this point. "Luckily, it isn't my reality anymore."

"You know, I've waited a literal year for you to have a different reality and now that you do, I feel like the whole thing is going to drop out of the center and we will be right back where we started."

"I don't blame you. There are a lot of remnants of that life that I'm working through. Like, if we were out of the house and I was in this dress, I'd be very uncomfortable with the length of this hem. I fight the urge to check in with Mason or his assistant several times a day because it's what I did for so long. But I don't want that life back."

A few more minutes passed and, although dinner was delicious, I was mostly pushing it around the plate.

"How do I know this is real, Len?" He stared into my eyes from across the table.

"What?"

"I've seen you. You are very good at being the person you need to be in the moment to accomplish whatever objective is on the table. How do I know if that's what's happening right now or not?"

I felt defensive and my tone reflected it. "I have *never* lied to you, Silas."

"Let me rephrase, because I agree, you've never lied to me. How do I know *you* know this is real? Your parents wired you to be what people need in the moment. Everyone else's agenda comes first. I need to know that you aren't doing this out of some kind of obligation you feel to me." He ran his hand through his hair and it rested on the back of his neck as he spoke frantically.

He made a fair point. "I guess we don't. What I know is that I feel the most relaxed and comfortable when you are there. I crave the sound of your voice because it sounds like home. For the last year no matter what I did, you were in my head. It's the only thing that's felt real to me in a long time. Being Eleanor, old Eleanor, was exhausting. I was following a strict set of guidelines. With you, there aren't these rules. For the last month I've been free of that old life and I've still been miserable. The second I saw you last night, I felt less fragmented. A bit more steady. I'm not sure how else to make you comfortable with this, but I'm willing to stick around and wait."

He stood and picked up his plate, then mine, and brought them over to the sink. "I want to believe it, and that's why it's so hard for me to do."

"I understand. It's too much too soon. Or too little, too late. All I can do is tell you how I feel and hope that at some point you believe I mean it." I walked over to him at the counter and took his hand. He pulled me close and kissed me, catching me off guard. He rubbed a hand over my ass and the other caressed my face as his tongue slid into my mouth to meet mine.

I felt my whole body flush. I knew I should stop before we got carried away. The lines always get crossed when we get this close and we do not settle the serious shit. But damn, did it feel good to have him kiss me like this. Like he couldn't control himself. His hand on my ass bunched up the fabric so that he was touching my skin. I inhaled sharply, welcoming the contact. I slid my hands under his shirt and up the muscles of his back. The hand on my face moved down to brush the swell of my breasts. I moved to unbutton his pants, freeing his hard cock from the confines of both the pants and his boxer briefs. I stroked him up and down a few times before he kicked the clothes off all the way. "Sit back down, Silas." I pointed at the chair.

Silas sat in the chair as requested. I straddled his lap and slid down onto his cock slowly, my head falling back with the sensation. He pulled the top of my dress down to expose my breasts and palmed both as I rose and slowly slid back down his shaft. His hips jutted up, and I rocked my hips to get every angle. He pulled my mouth to his for a fiery kiss before grabbing my hips and increasing the pace of me crashing down onto his cock. "Silas, yes."

His thumb found my clit, and he circled it a few times as my orgasm built to a frenzy. "Oh god, yes," I moaned.

"That's not God, sweetie, that's me making you feel that good."

I moaned again as he put more pressure on my clit.

"Come for me, Len."

I chased the high and felt Silas doing the same below me.

"So fucking good."

I came with a cry, and he followed shortly after, groaning. As we recovered, he trailed kisses along my collarbone. "You're going to fucking kill me one of these days," he said as I tried to stand. My legs were fairly useless after the strenuous workout followed by such an intense release, so when he held me down I was no match. "Stay there another minute." I obliged and laid my head on his shoulder.

After a few more minutes, I had the leg strength to get up and clean myself up in the bathroom. Silas took a turn after me and met me back in the living room wearing just his jeans.

"I appreciate your commitment to the easy access outfit," he toyed with my dress. "Absolutely no undergarments is fucking hot as hell."

"The fewer steps required to fucking you, the better for me." I smiled. He sat down on the end of the couch and pulled me into his lap. I snuggled in close, taking in his scent. "Though I really like this as well."

He inhaled deeply, tightening his arms around me. "Me, too." We sat there like that for a few minutes before he reached for the remote and turned on *New Girl* on Netflix. He selected my favorite episode and I kissed his cheek.

When that episode was over, he got up and retrieved a bag of Swedish Fish from the kitchen and repositioned us on the couch so that I was sitting beside him with my legs draped over his. Though it wasn't remotely late, I guess I drifted off for a bit because I awoke to Silas carrying me to his bed. After placing me under the blankets, he removed his jeans and joined me, pulling me close, my head in the crook of his arm. He ran his fingers through my hair and I sighed, content. "I love when you do that."

"I know," he replied.

I looked up at him. "I love *you,* Silas."

"I love you, too, Lenny." My heart soared in my chest.

"I know."

My cell phone started ringing, but Silas pressed his lips against my own so I was not inclined to see who was calling. The call went to voicemail as he moved his hand under my shirt. A minute later there was a knock at the door. Silas sighed with frustration. "I guess we have visitors."

We threw on some clothes and he went to the door and opened it to see Mish and Connor. "Hey. Sorry to interrupt. Cee is trying to reach you. "

I looked at my phone to see she had texted a few times and was the missed call. Immediately, I was concerned for Wyatt. "Is it Wyatt?"

"No. Wyatt is fine. But Elijah was in a serious car accident," Mish said with a worried look on her face.

I hit Cee's name on my cell phone immediately.

"Elle. Elle, it's bad," she answered.

"It's okay, Cee. I'm on my way. While I get to an airport, tell me what happened." Silas held me close.

"I… I'm not sure exactly. All I know is that I got a call saying he's been in a car accident. I'm in the waiting room at UMass. No one has told me anything."

"Is anyone with you?"

"No. Mom has Wyatt, but I just rushed here as soon as I could. You were the only one I thought of to call."

"I'll be there as soon as possible. Text me if you hear anything. I'll have Mason come sit with you until I get there, but I have to call him and get to an airport. Just hold tight."

"Thanks, Elle."

At the mention of Mason, Silas backed away from me. As soon as I ended the call with Cee, I hit Mason's number on my phone. "Elle. I did not expect to hear from you."

"Mason, I need you to go to the UMass emergency department. Catherine is there. Elijah was in a serious accident. "

"Shit."

"She's there alone and I just need her to have someone with her until I can get there, but I'm in Florida."

"Yeah, of course. Let me know when you get a flight home. I'm headed to the hospital now. I'll be there in about forty minutes."

"Thank you so much, Mason. I know this isn't ideal."

I turned to face Silas. "I need to go. I'm so sorry, I know this is horrible timing, but—"

"Of course, I get it. He's family."

"Will you come with me?"

"Mason is there. You'll be fine." He turned and walked into his room. Connor followed. I realized in that moment that Silas thought I still thought of Mason as my husband.

I looked to Mish. "What do I do? I need to go, but now he's mad about Mason. I don't want to leave like this." Tears pricked the back of my eyes. Too much was happening all at once.

"You go in that room and tell him you need him." She pointed toward Silas's room.

When I went into the room, Connor was saying something to Silas in a hushed tone. I cleared my voice to announce my presence. "Silas. I'm sorry if my calling Mason upset you. Please know that I wanted Mason there for *Cee,* not for me. She's alone in an emergency room. He's her son's father. They've become good friends the last few months. She needs someone. He's not there for me, he's there for her." A tear fell down my cheek. *I really need to stop fucking crying all the time.*

He stared into my eyes for a minute while I heard Mish calling an airline to arrange a flight behind me. "This will not work if you are always running back to him, Len. I can't share you anymore. I never wanted to."

"I'm not asking you to share. I'm yours. Everyone knows I'm yours, Silas. I have to go and I don't want to fight with you about it. I'm begging you to please just come with me. We can talk all you want about Mason on the flight there, but I need to get to my sister. I'll kick him out as soon as we get there, whatever you want, I just need you there with me. Please."

He sighed, then nodded.

Twenty-Five

Connor and Mish took Silas and me to the airport. Mish, the goddess that she is, got us on a charter from Florida to Boston almost immediately. The only thing I had on me was my purse as we didn't have the time to pack anything.

The ride to the airport was tense, but relatively quick. We made our way onto the plane and into our seats; Silas chuckled to himself as he buckled in.

"What's so funny?" I asked.

"Do you always arrive at the airport when the flight is basically ready to leave?"

I smiled, remembering our first flight together over a year ago. "I'm not sure it counts if it's a chartered flight and it literally waits for me, but yes. I'm always rushing to get on a damn plane, it seems."

> **Me:** taking off in a minute. Mason is on his way too. Love you.
> ***Cee:*** *He's here. See you soon.*

Turning to Silas, I said, "So, we should talk about this Mason thing now. We have hours to argue and literally cannot walk away from each other."

"I agree. Because this is…*Mason* is a hard pill to swallow. For whatever stupid reason, I let it go before, but I'm not doing it anymore."

"I need you to know that there's nothing there. No ties. I burned nearly every bridge to that life. I don't expect you to accept that immediately."

"I would be lying if I said I did. He's been this thing in the way the whole time."

"I can't say I will never see him again. He's Wyatt's dad. We've been friends *literally* our entire lives. But I know, and he knows, that I need space. A lot of space."

"I'd like to punch him in the throat when I see him so he may want to think of that space as being bigger." He looked away from me, hands tightening in fists. "How do I know he won't decide he needs you in a month, or a year?"

"I would only ever be there as a friend and he knows that. He knows I love you and that I'm not letting anything impede being with you ever again."

"You told him you love me? That doesn't sound like you."

"No, I didn't. He, along with countless other people, pointed out how they knew I love you."

He turned back to face me. "How do *you* know, Len? After a year of telling me that it isn't possible, that love doesn't exist, how is it you've suddenly changed your mind?"

"Fair question, but it wasn't sudden, Silas. I think I've known that I love you since the day before I got married. But I shoved all that down, because that's just who I was. And yeah, it took me entirely too long to let that sink in. I needed to be sure, Silas. *Especially* considering what I did to you. Before I considered walking back into your life, I needed to make sure I knew this was a real thing because the thought of breaking your heart again guts me." The tears slipped down my cheeks. *Fuck, why does this man make me cry?* "I don't deserve you. I don't deserve your forgiveness or a second chance. But I'm asking for one anyway because I don't want to live another day without you. I've already lost too many."

"Are you done?" he asked, taking my face in his hands. He used his thumbs to wipe under my eyes and I nodded. "I don't want to live another day without you either, which is why I'm letting all of that shit go. I'm trying, anyway. I know better than to assume we'll never see Mason. I just need to know that I come first this time."

"I think there are at least a dozen people that will come for me if I do anything to fuck this up. That includes Mason."

He nodded and pulled me into his chest. I inhaled his scent, allowing it to wash over me.

This may just be okay.

We arrived at the hospital and found Cee and Mason in a private waiting room. I rushed to Cee and pulled her into my arms. I saw Mason stand out of the corner of my eye.

"I'm gonna go. I'll pick up Wyatt and take him for however long you need. Just call." He shifted awkwardly on his feet.

Cee was crying into my neck and I looked over to Mason. "Thanks. I'll have her update you."

"What the hell happened?" Mish grabbed Mason's arm.

Mason gave a nervous look toward Silas. "He's in surgery now. Some internal injuries from the seatbelt or something. Broken leg and arm. Some asshat was driving on the wrong side of the highway. A few other cars were also hit. One dead, six people here with various injuries. They said the surgery would be several hours depending on how bad it was when they got in there. She hasn't eaten or even had a drink in the last three hours."

Cee peeled herself from me and hugged Mason. "Thank you so much for being here. Do you have to go?"

"I think that's best. Elle and Mish are here. You're in good hands." He kissed the top of her head and made his way to the exit. He stopped and turned back. "Silas?" The tension was so thick I could hardly breathe. Silas turned to Mason. "She was always yours. I'm sorry it took so long for me to see that." Silas just nodded. Mason turned around and walked out.

Cee smacked my chest. "Breathe, you're scaring me." I inhaled deeply.

"Why don't we get you something to eat and drink. Sounds like we won't hear anything for a while still," I suggested.

"I'm not hungry." She sat back down in the chair. I took the one to her left and Mish the one on her right.

"Connor will go get you a bottle of water. You at least need to hydrate," Mish offered. "It's high time he assists you rather than you assisting him."

Cee cracked a smile. Connor and Silas went off to find water. "So that was awkward, eh?" She changed the subject.

"More than just a little. An hour ago, Silas was saying he was going to punch Mason in the throat. Wasn't really sure how that was all going to go down."

"Can you imagine the headline? 'The Boyfriend of Senator Davis's Ex-wife Punches Senator in Hospital Waiting Room'," she mused.

"I'm sure they will point out how quickly I've moved on." I rolled my eyes.

We were quiet a moment. "I can't live without him." She started shaking.

"Let's not think like that, okay?"

We sat for about an hour before a doctor came out looking for us. "Family of Elijah Jenkins?"

"Me! Here." Cee popped up out of the seat. The rest of us crowded around her anxiously. She grabbed my hand and squeezed tightly.

"So, in addition to the broken leg and arm, Elijah had some internal injuries. We were able to stop the internal bleeding. A CAT scan shows some minor trauma to the brain, but we don't think it will be an issue. We will monitor him closely for the next twenty-four hours, but I'd expect him to wake up in that time."

"But he's going to be okay?" Cee asked, hopefully.

"We don't expect the injuries sustained in the accident to have long-term effects."

"When can I see him?"

The doctor explained they were getting him set up in a room and as soon as that was settled he could have two visitors at a time. Cee made it clear she wasn't leaving until Elijah did and I wasn't inclined to leave her here alone, at least not until she could see Eli. We sent Mish and Connor back to their place to sleep. I tried to convince Silas to go as well, but he refused.

Silas: *Did you find that very vague?*
Me: Yes.

He leaned over and kissed my cheek. It was another hour before a nurse came to grab Cee to show her to Eli's room. She pulled me by the hand to join her, leaving Silas sitting by himself. We walked into the room; they had hooked Eli up to all kinds of wires. His body was covered in cuts and bruises, and his left arm and leg in temporary casts. Cee burst into tears again in the doorway.

"Come on. You heard the nurse, it looks worse than it is." I urged her toward the bedside.

"You should go home and get some sleep. I'm just going to sit here and make sure this idiot knows he isn't allowed to leave me."

I nodded and made my way back to grab Silas. We took an Uber to Cee's place since it was closer than Mish and Connor's and I didn't want to be too far away. It was nearing dawn as we arrived at the house and I noticed Mason's car in the driveway. *Shit.* I turned to Silas. "Sorry, I didn't think about where Mason would be with Wyatt. My mom must have brought him here to go to bed."

"It's fine. Let's just go to bed," he sighed in resignation.

I unlocked the door, and we quietly went inside. I could see Mason passed out on the couch, and I led Silas to the room I had been staying in. We stripped out of our clothes and crawled into the bed. He wrapped his arms around me, my back to his chest. I tried to relax into the warmth of his body, my hands holding his arms in place so that he couldn't let go. *Why did I ever let go?*

That last thought pulled me over the edge. I refused to cry again. Things were going to be fine. I took some deep breaths to stave off the tears. Silas tightened his hold on me and whispered in my ear, "Shh. Everything is going to be fine. I've got you."

"I love you, Silas."

Silas and I woke up a few hours later to Wyatt crashing his cars into the door. "My friend Wyatt is here," Silas pointed out.

"Um. Yes. That child has too much energy." We rolled out of bed and threw on some clothes. Opening the door, I caught a toy car to the foot. "Wyatt. You ran me over!"

"Eleanor," he sighed, "you're late."

"Eleanor?" Silas raised his eyebrows.

"It's his most recent phase. Everyone calls me Eleanor so 'Auntie' has gone out the window. Kid thinks he's grown."

"Oh, shit." Mason came down the hall. "I didn't realize you were here; I would've taken him out."

"Dad. We don't say 'shit'." Wyatt gave a sly smile, knowing he was saying a word he wasn't supposed to.

"Wy, can you go make Auntie some cereal?" I redirected the sassy child. Since Wyatt's favorite thing to do was "cook" in the kitchen, he sped off to make a mess. "So… we are going to grab some stuff for Cee and head out after I eat the mess Wyatt makes me."

"It's cool. Take your time. I'm going to take Wyatt back to my place later. I just need to pack up some extra stuff. How's Elijah?"

I gave a rundown of what I knew when we left the night before while the three of us stood awkwardly in the hallway, the sounds of cereal hitting the floor in the background. "That sounds promising, right?" he asked.

"So far."

"Great. Great. Listen, I'm glad to see this whole thing worked out," Mason pointed between Silas and me.

I stood paralyzed with tension.

"Me too," Silas spoke up. "But, uh, sorry not sorry about your divorce."

"She was a great business partner, but a shitty wife. Hung up on some other guy this whole time."

I looked between the two men, assuming this was their way of settling the issue. "We all good here? No one is going to get violent, right?"

"We're good, Len." Silas kissed the top of my head. He went toward the kitchen, calling out for Wyatt.

I winced a smile at Mason. "Thanks. For what you said. I know this is weird."

"Are you happy, Ellie?"

"Yeah, I am. I love that guy."

"Would you look who has finally learned to emote!" He smirked.

I went to the kitchen to find cereal covering the table. Wyatt was handing Silas a spoon and instructing him to "eat up so you can go to school." He saw me and ordered me to sit down and eat as well.

Silas reached for my hand under the table and squeezed. "Doesn't Dad have to eat, too?" He asked Wyatt.

"I fed The Senator hours ago," he replied. Silas and I laughed.

Jillian MacGregor

Mason just rubbed his hand over his face. "Buddy, I've asked you not to call me The Senator."

"But you're the senator."

"Come on, let's get ready to go to my house." Mason reached out for Wyatt's hand and led him to his bedroom to collect his random bag of things.

"Thank you," I said to Silas.

"For what?"

"Loving me enough to let the past go."

He leaned over and kissed me hard. "Just promise me I won't have to share anymore. I've waited a long time to have you to myself."

I grinned. "Promise."

Acknowledgments

Despite being the second book in the *All Over You* series, *Uninvited* was written first. It was written out of order as part of NaNoWriMo 2021 with no intention for it to ever see the light of day.

But I have very insistent friends.

Enter my beta readers. Thank you for reading the very rough versions of this book. I hope we've made Elle far less horrible than she was in version one.

The entire team at Tala Editorial: thank you for not strangling me every time I answered your questions with, "I have no idea," as well as all of your support and assistance getting this book out into the world.

For my family: thank you for not being upset that I have constantly had my face in my laptop for the last year. I'd love to say it'll be better now, but it's November and Book Three awaits.

For all of the artists on the 177 song playlist I used to write this novel, thanks. I've put the songs mentioned in the book into a Spotify playlist. You can find it on my profile, cleverly named "Jillian MacGregor."

About the Author

Jillian MacGregor is a fictional character who writes spicy romance. Her real-life alter ego works a corporate job that is nowhere near as sexy as working with a band, but it pays the bills. Jillian has a husband, two adult children, and two very spoiled rescue dogs. You can find her on TikTok as @authorjillianmacgregor.

Visit her website at www.jillianmacgregor.com

Also by
Jillian MacGregor

All Over You (free novelette available on my website!)
No Way Back
Coming in 2023: *Girl Like That* – Cee's getting her own story!

Girl Like That

Cee has been working for the Handheld Ninjas for a year. In that year, she's been dragged through the press for having her brother-in-law's baby (hey, they weren't together at the time!) and adjusting to shared custody after four years with full custody. Just when she thinks things will calm down, she gets a call saying her boyfriend has been in an accident. The thought of losing him has Cee remembering how much they have already been through together. Can they get through this, too?

Made in the USA
Middletown, DE
24 November 2022